Twisted Vines

Katherine Ginbey

Also by Katherine Ginbey

The Valkyrie Ellis Trilogy

Valkyrie's Sight

God Save The Prom Queen

Fresher

The Survivors

Copyright © 2024 by Katherine Ginbey

All rights reserved. No part of this book may be reproduced in any manner whatsoever without written permission except in the case of brief quotations embodied in critical articles and reviews. All characters and events in this publication, other than those clearly in the public domain, are fictitious, and any resemblance to real persons, living or dead, is purely coincidental.

First Printing, 2024

For Mark, the greatest father I never had to
ask for...

Twisted Vines

Katherine Ginbey

VILERIA
WELORIS
Noble Estate
ALCARLIAN
Noble Estate
The Royal Palace
NEUTRAL GROUND
ALTHANIA
The Royal Palace
Noble Estate
THE ACADEMY
PARLITAN
The Royal Palace
SICONIA
WHITLOCK ESTATE
Noble Estate
The Sacred Lake
CALENT
The Royal Palace
Noble Estate
BLENDORA
The Royal Palace
Noble Estate
JARIAN
Noble Estate
The Royal Palace
TULINTH
The Royal Palace
Noble Estate

Chapter One

I am stunning.

Summer solstice always means a beautiful dress, but this year, Cameron has outdone himself. The dress is thin and a dark blue. It flows beautifully around my legs and has a slit to its mid-thigh. The top is tight from the corset, but the most impressive part was the thin, pure gold vines that intertwined around my chest and the tops of my arms. It took away the need for a necklace, but my pointed ears have new studs in the shape of suns in the lobes.

I reach up to run my finger at the pointed tips. Mum had promised me that I could get those pierced just like her, but it had conveniently not happened yet. Too many events, too long of a healing period, etc, etc.

Natalie hadn't told me what she had planned to do with my hair or makeup, but the smoky eyes brought out the ice blue of my eyes better than ever before, and the ink-black plait was flawless. There is not a hair out of place. She has outdone herself, but when I turn around to tell her, she's gone.

I stare at myself in the mirror for another moment and nod. I'm being silly worrying. It's not my first solstice ball since I came of age, not even the first ball of the year. But I'm hyperaware with every small breath that this summer is being widely and jokingly referred to as 'fae mating season'; anyone interested now didn't have to check with my father first, and my secret human boyfriend was going to be a waiter.

I could try and hide out with Donaugh, but there was only so much time I wanted to spend with my brother at these things. He'd be flanked by Corvus and Maverick like always, which would be a nice buffer, but he would still try and limit my drinking. Convincing him I had an unrequited crush on Mav had been enough of a challenge two years ago while sober, but keeping up with that lie for a whole night with Dean in the same room and unlimited booze seemed borderline impossible.

I should have told him I was into Corvus. It wouldn't exactly have been a lie. I had been head over heels for the werewolf up until I was thirteen years old. Dragging back those embarrassing feelings would have been a lot easier. Wolves were generally a lot more rugged than Mermaids and that showed when Mav and Corvus were together.

Corvus's ears were almost as pointed as my own, his canines slightly larger at both the top and bottom. The first time I heard him growl, I literally whimpered; Don thought it was from fear and tore him a new one. In comparison to that, Maverick's basic human features were dull to a pre-teen girl. Of course, I wasn't blind, and when Mav's scales came out in the rain, he was gorgeous and glinting with rainbows.

I smile at myself in the mirror as I realise how quickly and drastically my tastes have changed. From pointy-eared, muscled brother's best friend to round-eared, skinny human son of a seam master. It had only taken one spring scavenger hunt four years ago, and suddenly, Corvus hadn't seemed as perfect as before.

"Ivy!" The shout was barely finished before my bedroom door was opened, and my mother, Lady Violet Whitlock, stood in the doorway. We are almost identical. The changes are slight and mostly about angles.

Her cheekbones were slightly higher, her lips slightly thinner. Her ears had piercings all the way down their length, usually decorated with silver chains and studs. Today, they were gold, just like mine. She was one hundred and eighty-nine years old, and she barely looked twenty-five.

"Oh, you look beautiful." She coos at me, taking long strides to my side. Her dress is similar to mine but with no slit and the fabric a light green. Family outfits will come in pairs this time, then. I wonder how Don's suit will incorporate the gold vines. He will almost certainly be in the same blue shade, with my father in the same green of my mother's dress.

Her hands are gentle and cold on my cheeks as she tilts my gaze upwards. She even has the same makeup on as me, smoky eyeshadow with eyeliner as sharp as a blade. "I want some photos of you and Don this evening before you both get too tipsy. We need to get another portrait done."

"Why?" I fight to keep the bitterness from my voice. "It's not like I'm leaving in September anymore."

My mother's eyes turn into slits. She sighs as she drops her hands from my face. I square my shoulders, ready for the lecture she has given me every week since we celebrated the new year. *We will get you an instructor instead. Do you really want to move all the way to Althania? You don't need to go to the Academy. I dropped out, and I'm doing fine! I only went to prove myself, you are already a noble, you don't have to do that,* blah blah blah.

My mother was the first female fae to ever be admitted to the Academy. She was in history books. People still talked about her high ability with water - something she had never shown me or even Don. Her magic in the house was basic: small displays to entertain rather than intense fighting forms.

Yet here she was, making it her mission to keep me from a place I had yearned to go to since I first made a spark. It made no sense, and I had spent every day since being told I couldn't go making my opinion on it clear.

"One day, when you have children, you'll understand." Mum's voice breaks slightly, and I'm jarred out of my proud position.

"Mama, I have to move out sometime," I whisper back.

"I know." She grumbles. "But you could at least stay in the same country. Parlitan is prettier than Althania, I promise." Her hands now squeeze my own. "You love the lakes and the forests. They don't have those there, and they don't have Maverick there either."

Ah. There we are. The reason me and Dean have played off our relationship as simply friends for the last two years. Anyone I love would be used as an excuse to keep me here, even Maverick, who was the son of a different lord all the way in Weloris. Corvus and Maverick were both second-born sons sent as wards back when I was still learning to walk. Don had connected with them instantly, and I'm assuming he ran straight to our mother, who was almost giddy as he told her that there was a chance one of them would be his actual brother.

"I'm not with Maverick." My response is quick and blunt, but I duck my head and pull my hands back to play with the golden chain around my wrist. People denying a crush get awkward. They fiddle.

"Oh?" Mum's voice is almost playful now. My heart thumps as she gestures with her hand, a thin piece of card from the side of my desk flying into it. I hadn't looked at my dance card as it was brought up with all the jewellery. The very thought of fluttering my lashes at people as they used cliché or sleazy lines to get their names added left a sour taste in my mouth.

"Then why is he the first name on your dance card?" My mother's voice is overly cheerful.

I snap my head up to look at her, finding her eyebrow raised and a pleased smirk on her lips. She thinks she's helped me and that she's handing me some kind of lifeline that will smooth over our relationship. We had been so strong and steady before. I had argued with my father often but rarely with her. I had taken her words as gospel up until six months ago. She was trying to help with a boy's problem that didn't exist to mend that metaphorical gap. The smile on my face as I take the card from her is genuine, even if the reason behind it isn't.

I look down at the card and frown. "This is already half full," I speak slowly, waiting for her to cut me off and say the wrong one was delivered, and this was actually hers. Some of the names on the list were expected - Don, my father, Maverick, and Corvus - because if Maverick got one, then Corvus got one, too. The family dances.

Malachi Parlin, an Angel who had been the first person to ask me to dance at every ball I had ever been to. That was also expected.

But underneath them, and they were all in my mother's perfect scrawl, were names that absolutely shouldn't have been there.

Channing Lennox, a werewolf who had been my mother's friend at the Academy one hundred and seventy-two years ago. He was also the first non-vampire to ever be knighted in Althania.

And the Crown Prince of Vampires and Althania, Hal Alenium, who was also my mother's friend at the Academy.

Malachi, I could handle. He stutters and overcompliments, but overall, he is harmless. We are almost friends and probably would be friends if he stayed nearby rather than on the very outskirts of our country. He and his mother fly in for every event and nothing more.

Channing and Hal, however, had been stuttering parts of my own life. They had arrived once a year, maybe a few times more if they were feeling generous, up until a few years ago. My mother sent them invitations to all her events, but they hadn't ever even bothered to RSVP. My father often muttered under his breath about how rude it was.

When they visited the estate, they were either overly friendly or incredibly distant. I knew that we were considered lucky, myself and Don especially, to have the favour of a royal. But each time Hal gifted me with something, the attention felt too much.

The grinning man handing me elaborate chocolate shapes has never matched the scowling crowned figure I see on the news. It makes me uncomfortable how he can switch between them. The fact he ghosted my family without so much as a note makes that feeling even worse, like suddenly being smothered in shade after standing directly in a sunbeam.

Channing is a part of Hal's royal circle despite being a wolf, although no one here knew officially what that meant. He had a thick, raised scar going through his eyebrow, and I had always assumed that it was from his duties. He was bulky, short, and not as handsome as the prince, but there was something about him that made the girls at the estate giggle when he used to visit. Maybe it was the same reason I had liked Corvus, whatever primal reason that was.

'I didn't realise they were here." I sigh. "Dad never said anything."

"We weren't sure, but they sent word this morning. They are excited to see you." My mother's smile doesn't falter for even a second.

I snort in an incredibly unladylike fashion but fasten the card to my chain anyway. I'm not exactly in a position to tell a royal no, and even if I were, the fact they are on the card means my mother has already told them yes.

"Thank you." My mother loops her arm through mine. "Pre-emptively. For being your incredibly charming self for those three dances."

I look over at her as she leads me from the room towards the family dining area that housed a private balcony we would pose on before being officially declared at the ball. A family tradition.

We walk down the hall, heels clicking on the white marble floors as we pass all our other portraits, which are laid down the halls in chronological order. The doors to my room open to the first of the portraits to feature me as a tiny infant in a bundle of blankets. Donaugh, who is five years older than me, holding me in his tiny infant arms.

It's one of my favourites, mostly because of my brother's lopsided grin as he looks down at baby me. It's a grin I've never seen him share with anyone else, the same grin we shared at stuffy luncheons after a snide comment or when we ran into each other in the same hiding space during game night. Our artist captures it perfectly.

Together, we push open the doors to the dining room. The glass doors leading out to the balcony are thrown open, and the other half of our family stands there in the sunlight, already sipping at the light pink sparkling wine that our region is known for. My mother drops my arm and moves to my father's side, wrapping herself around him and kissing his cheek. He grins down at her, the picture of a perfect couple. Don turns his head and shoots me that lopsided grin as he rolls his eyes. I laugh, moving to the table to grab my own glass.

He tuts at me as he watches me down it, but he's not the one who's spending the evening dancing with people centuries older than him, so he can disapprove of all he likes. I need wine.

I grab my second glass as he strolls over. His suit is an identical match to my dress in its colour, but the vines on him are embroidered rather than metal. He looks like me and my mother anyway, with dark hair and icy eyes. Dad always playfully grumbles that we are both 'Violet's heirs' rather than his. A glance back at my parents shows me I was right. The green of my father's suit is the same as my mother's dress.

"Maverick's wearing blue tonight." Don doesn't bother with a compliment or a hello. We are close enough that we rarely do. Some Fae siblings were oddly distant. I had listened to far too many girls at school gush about their brothers in intimate tones. Usually, if I was being kind enough to not be grossed out by it, I would tell myself that they had a few decades between them. I suppose to them, me and Don were the odd ones for growing up together.

"He always wears blue. It reminds him of the ocean." I grumble. "What else are you going to tell me? That Corvus will be drinking whiskey?"

Don throws his arm over my shoulder and leads me away from the table and out to the balcony. The air smells sweet, like the roses growing in the bushes below. We come to a stop against the railing, looking out over the grounds that Don would one day inherit. The large open field is lined with dense woodland, with a large water fountain all the way at the far end. The woods were filled with statues and other hidden treasures. Behind the woodland was the staff housing, an area resembling a small village as all staff had their own house and garden. Everything we could see was ours.

I frown as I realise the field has been set up for the ball as well, with decorations and ornate miniature stalls that would be full of food and drink. The woods would be lit up. I wrinkle my nose as I think about my favourite little hiding spots getting ruined by handsy couples. I never thought about it when I was younger, even when I had started to meet Dean by the warrior princess statue.

"You know, little sister, if you don't want to make the first move, I could always drop a few hints." Don drops his arm to hold onto the railing. The offer sounds genuine if a little too eager. I can't stop myself from teasing him a little about it.

"If I was interested in Corvus, would you be so happy?" I take a small sip of my wine as Don stills for a second.

"That's different." Don decides.

"Oh? Is it because wolves are generally more primal and possessive than mermaids or because you couldn't beat him in a fight?" I finally turn my head to look at him and smile at the look on his face.

"I could beat Corvus in a fight." Don insisted. "And I think we both know that you're not a possession."

"You've missed out on the primal part."

"Don't push me, Ivy."

"Over the railing? I think you're decent enough with air to slow your fall."

"God, you're annoying."

"It's a family trait. Hopefully, mine and Corvus's multiple children from our scandalously passionate love affair won't inherit it."

"Do you want me to throw up?"

"Well, if you skip the ball, then Corvus could have your dance, and we could slip away into the woods for…"

Don makes a dramatic turn on his heel, shouting "Nope!" as he heads back towards our parents. I throw my head back and laugh after him.

Chapter Two

Dean is standing by the side of the doors leading outside, holding a full tray of red wine. I keep glancing over at him, even as Prince Hal is announced and the entire room bows. After my own announcement, I managed to slip away from Don to my own circle of friends. They were always easy to spot, thanks to Harlan's bright ginger hair and Sienna's loud cackle.

Parlitan was the country of the face, but everyone was welcome, the same as all the other countries. Vileria was a country at peace; friction about borderlines was usually minimal, and countries always came to a compromise to ensure peace. There had not been a territorial war for centuries, since before the great war against demon kind. People could not just walk into a new country and start completely anew, but it made travel and changing citizenship much easier when everyone's royal councils got along. It also meant all of my friends had some interesting differences from each other. There was never a boring night when a witch was pouring the shots.

Valentina was a vampire, and Sienna was a witch. Harlan was a fae like me, but unlike me, he had been allowed to apply to the academy and found out two days ago that he had been accepted. We were all happy for him, although Valentina, who had spent half the year in Althania with her mother, was ecstatic.

"I just want to dance already," Sienna grumbles, playing with a blond curl as she stares around the room. "Or to have someone at least ask. Harlan is the only one on my dance card! It's embarrassing."

"Thanks," Harlan says dryly as he finishes up writing his name on my card.

"You know what I mean. Ivy has *royalty* on her card, and yet here we are, her best friends, with nothing."

"The man is two hundred years old and friends with my mother. It's not like he's Prince Silas or Apoll or…"

"Or Prince Atlas." Valentina practically purrs. "God, he's gorgeous. Prince of the Fae *and* the wolves."

"He's also engaged." Harlan snaps at them all.

"If he wants a witch bride, he can have me," Sienna wiggles her eyebrows at him.

Sometimes I feel bad for him. He's the only man out of the four of us, and girl talk could only interest him so much. But the idea of the only Fae hybrid in existence coming to my family's ball was intriguing.

Prince Atlas was only two years older than us, and Valentina was right - he was gorgeous. He was always on the news, his very existence a wonder, and people said he had the elegance of the fae but the brutality of a wolf right before they mentioned his heightened power level.

He had been engaged to some cousin of a princess of Calent since he was three days old. That cousin was at least four hundred years old. I always felt a little uneasy when people talked about that. My parents had promised both me and Don that they would never arrange a match for us, but we were middle-range fae nobility, not heirs to two countries.

I pretend to look completely around the room again as I take a long sip of my drink. My gaze ends up on Dean, who now, gods help him, was talking to Corvus and Maverick. Don was only a few steps away from them, talking to some angel girl. Oh, goddess.

They are friends, I remind myself. Dean is Don's personal helper and has been ever since he turned sixteen. They spend hours together, and since Corvus and Maverick spend all *their* time with Don, they spend hours with Dean as well. That's all.

I must be less subtle than I think because all three boys turn to look at me. I clear my throat and quickly turn back to Harlan, who is arguing with Sienna about whether she had a chance to dance with Channing. I lock eyes with Valentina, and we both start to laugh.

A few minutes later, my father calls the room to attention. His speech is as perfect as it is every year, welcoming to all and welcoming in the solstice. He praises my mother, and then he compliments me and Don. He doesn't mention Prince Hal or Channing at all. A quick glance over at Don shows that he noticed that as well, but then the first song starts, and my view is blocked by a beaming, blonde mermaid.

"I heard I'm your first dance." Maverick holds out his hand. "Can I say that I'm honoured?"

I take his hand and dramatically sigh. "I'm sure you could say it, but I won't believe you."

Maverick laughs as loud as a wave crashing against the shore, and I am spun onto the dance floor.

Maverick is a good dancer when you consider the fact that most mermaids barely learn to walk. They are so much more fluid in the water, meaning they tend to stick to mermaid and siren-accessible clubs. But Maverick had been raised for the most part by my mother, so when Don learned to dance, so did Maverick and Corvus.

Maverick waits until the dancefloor fills up with other couples before smirking down at me. His eyes are such a bright blue that they are almost translucent, something a human's eyes could never be. I used them to try to convince Don of my fake feelings. Who would know the exact shade of someone's eyes if they weren't desperately in love with them?

"You're not actually in love with me, are you?" He whispers. "You're playing it well, I'll give you that."

I miss a step as I stare up at him in horror. *Donaugh, you little snake…*

"Don really believes it. Maybe you should give up that Academy dream and take up acting." Maverick gently spins us around a twisting fae couple who are out of time with the music.

"But if I give up the Academy dream, how will I get away with the murder of the Whitlock heir?" I grind out, head peering around to try and catch sight of my traitorous older brother. I didn't care if the feelings weren't real; the fact that he went and told Maverick about them left a sour taste in my mouth.

"Corvus told me." Maverick leans forward to whisper in my ear. I once again misstep as I pull back to stare at him, and Maverick smiles before giving me a gentle twirl. "He noticed how you look at our human friend over there. Why am I your cover story exactly?"

I'm pulled back close to him, and I take a second before I answer. He's either made us this close so the conversation stays private or to help me with my cover story. I smile up at him. "I know you well enough that I could play the lovesick girl angle."

"You know me better than you know Harlan."

"Don knows Harlan well enough to know I'm missing some key biological parts for him," I smirk. "Which you also know."

"I just want you to tell me I'm the cutest option." Maverick sighs. "Or at least cuter than Corvus. His ego is a little bruised, but you picked me instead."

"Don gets a little insecure around Corvus. I think it's all to do with Missy the Siren back when they were kids."

"Yeah, you really didn't like her."

"I don't like people messing with my brother." I lie quickly. I just hadn't liked Corvus giving some green-haired girl extra attention. The excuse of Don also liking her as well was just incredibly convenient.

"You're messing with your brother right now by lying."

"*I'm* the little sister. It's my birthright."

The song starts to come to a close, and I see Maverick smirking at someone behind me. I turn to look, only to be spun from his arms and to be caught in another's. I let out a tiny yelp as my brother laughs down at me.

I scowl at him as he moves us into position. "You both planned that." I accuse him.

"Aren't you clever?" Don smiles. "Look, if you'd have preferred for that Malachi boy to swoop in and grab you next, then I can hand you ov…" Don laughs again as my fingers grip his arms. "Exactly. Corvus is next, and by then, I might have a plan to push back everyone else a little."

"Don…the dance after Malachi is *Channing.* Mum is going to kill you for cutting the line anyway." I grumble even if the gesture means more to me than I can let on. Don was willing to slight the leader of a country for me for something as pointless as me not being comfortable for three minutes.

"Maybe I just keep spinning you back to Maverick all evening, and no one else gets any dance at all. Or Corvus falls into the bar, there's a crash, and suddenly, no one can find you anywhere." Don muses in a whisper as he moves us through the crowd, perfectly in time to the music.

"Don. It's two dances. At worst, I get my toes stepped on. Then I can dance with Harlan, and it's all back to normal again."

"It's never normal when they are here." Don hisses at me, and then his face smooths out as he gets his anger back on its leash. Mum always said he had terrible tantrums as a child but that he calmed when he had me to look after, to be the protective big brother. Don needed responsibility even then.

"Well, we can't exactly kick out the crown prince of Althania and his guard dog for no reason." I hiss back. "They are mum's friends. They never stay for long. Tonight is a solstice ball. I am now officially an adult, and I want to enjoy it. We look far too good to spend the evening getting angry about things we can't change."

Don's face softens, and I know that I have won. I don't doubt, however, that he would spin me to Corvus to delay it a little longer. So, when the song goes through its final notes, I drop my hands from his shoulders and quickly step back.

Don huffs his disapproval, but we share a smirk and an understanding. We will be the perfect example our parents want us to be. We will enjoy the ball, and once those special guests are gone, we will complain and be glad they won't be back soon.

I head over to Dean before anyone can stop me. I need a drink, and he has a tray of them. There was nothing more to it than that and – and Malachi, god damned, Parlin steps in front of me, holding two glasses of the fizzing wine and an awkward smile on his face.

"I figured you'd be thirsty." Malachi smiles and it's so awkward that my heart hurts. He may fly in for all the social events, but his mother had home-schooled him for his entire life. He didn't really know how to act around people, and that was something no book could tell him.

"Thanks, Mal." I breathe, plastering a thankful grin on my face as I take a glass from him. "Are you having fun?"

"Yeah. Yeah, it's great. It's always gorgeous here." Mal nods eagerly, looking around.

The decorators had done an amazing job. The hall was the same white marble and silver it always was, but glass tables with legs fashioned like tree trucks lined the opposite wall to the doors to the garden. They were full of fresh fruit and decanters of water and wine.

The glass doors to the garden were lined with multicoloured roses, vases of the same flowers lining the bar next to the doors. The bar would be gone by tomorrow morning, and the tables would be replaced and moved back into their rightful places.

"My mother really has an eye." I agree, pretending to look at the floors as I see Dean walk past with an empty tray, getting it filled with more glasses from the bar. He doesn't even glance at me. My throat tightens. We had a conversation about this only two days ago, but it still hurts. I wonder if our coin is in his pocket and if he'll give it back to me tonight.

We had stolen the idea from a book. The couple in the book were also in a secret relationship for better reasons than ours. They both had to do things that would hurt the other, and so they picked a phrase. If one of them said the first part, it meant that they were sorry. The other said the second part back once they had accepted the apology.

We tweaked it. Instead of a phrase, it was a coin, an old one that neither of us recognised and that we had found in the ground fountain. When I give him that coin, it means *I'm sorry, and I love you.* When he gives it back to me, it means *I forgive you, and I love you.* We have never used it the other way around. Dean has never done anything that would hurt me, but we know that if we do, then we will just say 'swapsies.'

I zone back in to find Mal still talking and pointing out everything he loves about the room. Mal could talk for hours, and a part of me was tempted to let him, but I had just told Don that we needed to play nice. So, instead, I gently take Mal by the arm and lead him over to Harlan.

He stops talking as soon as I touch him, but I make sure I'm not brushing against his wings. I'd made that mistake before, but I couldn't help myself from reaching out and touching the grey feathers. They had looked too soft to be real, but Mal had gone bright red and practically ran from me after our dance that year.

"Malachi! Good to see you." Harlan smiles, reaching out to hug Mal as if they were the best of friends. "We missed you at the last one."

Mal beams at that, and I drop from his arm. Sienna is a shameless flirt, and Mal isn't unattractive. But Sienna isn't here. If they aren't with Harlan, then they must be dancing.

It took me a moment to find them with all the other people spinning and twisting around each other, but there they were, dancing with two fae boys. Valentina is blushing, and I wink at her as I think she is looking over. I can't tell if she saw it.

"You're tall." A gruff voice says from next to me, and I turn. My eyes catch on the scar before focussing on Channing's face.

"It happens when you grow up." The comment is out of my mouth before I can stop it. But Channing lets out a breathy laugh before staring at me.

"I almost forgot how blunt you were." He tells me. "Or maybe I just thought that was something you'd grow out of."

I have no response. At least, not one I'm willing to say to him right now. I should probably say that I missed him. Could I maybe ask him why he had waited so long to come back? For all the things I had said to Don, I really had felt awkward that first year they didn't come back. Like we had done something wrong even though I knew mum still got calls and letters.

"No chocolate animals this year?" I turn back to the dancefloor. I keep my tone light.

"We thought you were maybe a little old for that." Channing moves so his hands are clasped behind his back. He stands tall, a half-head above me, even with my heels. I remember him being massive, but back then, everyone was taller than me.

"No one is ever too old for chocolate." I gasp playfully. "I'll be seven hundred and seventy-seven, and I will still want a life-sized chocolate stag."

"Violet didn't appreciate that one."

"That's because I didn't want her to have any."

Channing's second laugh booms across the room. I laugh with him almost automatically, even as I can feel people looking over. His laugh is overwhelming and genuine.

I remember hearing it echoing through the trees after convincing him and Prince Hal to join in on Hide and Seek. I couldn't have been more than eight years old.

"This makes two dances," Channing tells me as another song starts, and I stay by his side. "That you've stood on the sidelines for."

"Mal has the next one technically." I wave in my friend's direction. "I don't have the heart to take him away at the moment."

"And your brother's little trio is doing terrifyingly well at stopping anyone not already on your dance card getting within twenty feet of you."

"Keyword being terrifying, I suppose."

"They would have been amazing at the Academy." Channing's tone changes, and he cocks his head to look at me, a wolfish gesture that I always associate with Corvus.

"I was surprised you weren't on the applicant list for September."

My fingers twitch, and I suddenly want my wine glass back. I don't remember putting it down. Did I hand it back to Mal? Did I finish it? I try and swallow the lump in my throat. I don't want to admit that I hadn't been allowed. I didn't want to cast any blame on my parents, but Channing sounded almost disappointed. He *wanted* me there. He hadn't seen me in years, but he knew that I belonged there.

"I'll be getting a private instructor instead." I force the words out and make myself look away. I last two seconds before I turn back to look at Channing and find his gaze locked on my father. The look in his eyes reminds me who I am talking to. This isn't just a family friend who's been gone a little while.

This is Channing Lennox, the only non-Vampire to ever be on the Althanian inner council, and apparently, I made him angry at Lord Dalerian Whitlock of the Fae.

Chapter Three

"I'm sure Mal won't mind if I skip and dance with you first," I say quickly, and Channing stops glaring at my father to look over at me. Thankfully, his expression had changed from pure rage to awkward confusion. Like he hadn't expected me to offer or hadn't even expected for the dance to happen at all.

"The song's almost over," I add and hold out my hand for him to take.

It's not that how he just looked at my father doesn't scare me. It terrifies me. I have always seen my father as an impenetrable force - a people person who could also slug it out in a ring. But I know without a doubt that if Channing and my father go toe to toe, it won't be the man who raised me leaving that ring.

I also know that Channing would never hurt me. I felt that in my gut and heard the echoes of the few stories mum had told me on a loop in my head. Channing has morals. Channing is good. Channing pretends not to see you hiding in the woods so that you can win the game.

Channing is slow to take my hand. His hands are rough and worn, nicked with tiny little scars that are most likely from blades. Some of them are more raised than others. I smile at him, and he seems to be relaxed a little. I wonder how often people have flinched.

The girls I grew up with acted like a papercut was the end of the world, and even Sienna, who thought the scar on Channing's face made him interesting, had gone pale when she had seen a particularly nasty scratch on my leg after an accident with my practice daggers. That one hadn't left a scar purely from Maverick's quick medical attention. I can't imagine the girls at a royal court were any different.

The song changes, and we move onto the dancefloor. "I'll let you lead." I joke as we find a space. Well. A space has been made for us. Anyone who thought they were in the way quickly moved. The song is upbeat, a stark difference from the last few that had been slow, dramatic waltzes.

"Yeah…you're definitely Violet's daughter."
He says it so softly that I'm not sure if I was
even supposed to hear.

I ignore him, just in case, and start to dance.
The music is uplifting enough that I keep my
smile, but as Channing gives me a twirl and
then a lift into the air, I can't help but laugh
yet again. My feet hit the ground gently, and I
look up.

Channing is grinning down at me, all traces
of anger gone from his eyes. He looks happy,
and his face changes completely. His smile
flickers from his face as he realises the song
is coming to an end. I feel mine fall from my
face as well.

I suddenly wanted to ask why he stopped
visiting and what adult reason there was for it
because no one had ever explained it to me.
He had never called or sent a letter or a
birthday present. We didn't even receive a
card for the winter solstice.

I open my mouth to ask, but the questions get
all mixed up, and he is leading me away from
the dancefloor. I stay silent. My brain is such
a jumble that I don't even realise where he's
dropped me off until a pair of jade-green eyes
blink at me.

"You look like you're having fun," Dean tells me softly, slowly extending the tray towards me. His lips twitch as he tries to hold back a smile, and I want nothing more than to reach out and tangle my hands in his ridiculously soft-looking brown hair. Even from here, he smelt like apples. I take a deep breath in, and the cocky prat smirks at me.

"I'm suddenly feeling a little faint, actually," I smirk back. "I'll have one more dance, and then I may need someone to help me outside for some fresh air." I reach forward and finally take a glass from the tray. I tentatively sip it, keeping my eyes locked on his. From the outside, this would be an innocent enough conversation. At worst, I would be teasing my brother's servant.

Dean's eyes leave me, and his voice is neutral as he responds. "Well, if you need me, I'm here."

I turn my head slightly, expecting Don or maybe my mother. I wasn't expecting Crown Prince Hal to be standing there, fighting a smile and holding two glasses of...water.

"I thought you might be thirsty." Hal's voice isn't as deep as Channing's, but there's something in it that tells you he is more powerful than he looks. He isn't as bulky as Channing either- in fact, he looks like he has lost weight over the last few years. His face has slight stubble but no markings, and as he hands me the water, I see his hands are as smooth as porcelain. I suppose if I had a royal guard or mind powers, I wouldn't get the brunt of the injuries either.

Back when I was little, I apparently begged Hal to use his powers on me. He would slip into my mind, make me think I was in one of my favourite shows, or talk to me at the dinner table without my parents knowing. As a teenager, the thought of anyone having easy access to my thoughts seemed like a nightmare.

I look down at the two drinks in my hands, debating for a moment. I had already sipped the alcohol, but I knew the decanters had been enchanted, so the water would taste like anything I wanted.

I should also probably stop with the wine. I'm already not thinking as clearly as I should be, or I would have connected my last two thoughts: Hal can read my mind, and he brought me water. I had given him a door to my mind back before I could properly walk.

I take a gulp of the water. It tastes like the sour candies Valentina sends over from her hometown when she's gone. Dean juggles the tray into one hand and then gently takes the wine glass from me with the other. I thank him softly, and he bows his head before walking away to get rid of it.

"Thank you. For the water," I tell Prince Hal to avoid the awkward silence that threatens to creep in.

"You're welcome." He responds. "You looked a little flushed."

A warmth creeps up into my cheeks, and I take a few sips of the water again. I try to think of an excuse, but Hal is already giving me an out.

"Are you still okay to dance? I overheard the end there- sorry- and I could help you outside. The fresh air will do you some good." Hal offers out his arm, and I take it. He leads me outside and continues. "Don't feel embarrassed. When I was your age, I was always drinking too fast at these things. I don't think I made it to the end of one until I was twenty-four."

He was babbling. The Crown Prince of Vampires was helping me outside and babbling at me. The summer air hits us, the scent of roses swirling around my hair. Hal turns us immediately left, heading towards the wall of rose topiaries. Towards privacy. He's walking ridiculously slowly and keeps glancing at me as if he expects me to stumble. I've not drunk *that* much.

We come to a stop behind the bush shaped like a rook. He lets go of my arm and scans my face for a second. I clench my jaw and stare right back at him. He lets out a tiny, amused noise, and I scowl.

"You've grown," Hal whispers.

"You're the second person to say that to me in the last hour." I snap, "And both of you haven't bothered with me for three years."

Hal blinks at me.

"Why is that?" I continue. "I was fourteen. Anything I did, you shouldn't have punished Don for. You've been calling and writing to mum, so it can't be something to do with her." I pause and look at him, but he still just stares at me. "Do you know what it's like? For everyone to ohhh and ahhh because we have a *Crown Prince* visiting us and teaching us chess and then suddenly having to explain to them that you just don't bother with us anymore?"

"You didn't do anything," Hal tells me slowly. "Things just came up, and it became…difficult to come back here."

"For three years? My mother says she doesn't know why you didn't come back. You managed to avoid her asking for three years?" I scoff. "My mother could get the meaning of life from the goddess herself if she wanted to."

"Maybe it was easier for her not to want us back here." Hal taunted.

"You're her friends." I push.

"We were. Live a few centuries, and you'll realise that word means something different than what you think."

"I'm going to want my friends around me in two hundred years." I declare confidently.

Hal's answering smirk irritates me. If he doesn't consider himself a friend, then why come here? He still speaks to my mother, and he said it had become difficult to come here,

so they couldn't have had a disagreement.
Vileria was at peace, so it can't have been
political.

Don had made it clear to me that he didn't
like it when they visited, and he was already
an adult when they were here last. Maybe his
drink had got the best of him; a comment
made that insulted Hal or Channing or both.
That would have made the next visit
uncomfortable but not *difficult*. Don was the
heir, not the…

"Dad." I realise out loud. Hal looks startled.
"Something happened between you and him,
didn't it?"

Maybe I should drink more often. My mind is
racing through all the connections, my mouth
blurting them out before I can think it all
through. "You argued with Lord Whitlock,
but you still talk to Lady Whitlock. You stop
visiting, and I'm told I'm not allowed to go to
Althania, to the Academy."

"You'll be going." Hal interrupts me.
"Channing is talking to Violet now."

This time, I blink at him. He sounded so sure,
so confident that I would be going, that for a
second, I believed him. But I had not applied,

and the deadline had passed, and even the Crown Prince of Vampires would not be telling Lord and Lady Whitlock of the Fae where their daughter would be going in the fall. If I would be going anywhere at all.

"You think Channing is going to convince my mother in one conversation when I couldn't convince her for a whole year?" I ask slowly.

"He's known her longer." Hal's attempt at a joke is weak, but I chuckle anyway. It sounds biting to even my own ears.

"You do want to come to Althania, don't you?" Hal whispers. "You always said you did. You haven't changed your mind?"

"More than anything," I answer immediately. "I know I'm not as powerful as some of the graduates, but I can control all the elements well enough, and I can fight; I can. I've been practising with Don and the boys. I mean, Harlan's great, but I beat him all the time."

I cut myself off. I don't need to bring Harlan into this. He deserved his spot, and I was proud of him, I really was, even if the jealousy swirling around in my stomach threatened to move up and suffocate me sometimes. That jealousy twisted into guilt and shame as I saw Hal glance towards the doors, back to the ballroom. Back to Harlan.

"Harlan is great," I repeat firmly. "I've never seen anyone better with the earth than him. These roses were him." I reach out and touch the bright blue petals. "No one else in our class could ever make a solid blue rose, and he can make them in every shade of blue you could ever want. He does all the roses for mum. She won't go to anyone else."

"Ivy." Hal laughs. "I'm not going to take away Harlan's spot because you can beat him."

"Good." I nod. "Good."

"I'd be more worried if you couldn't beat him." Hal looks at me, and his smile widens into a grin. "I've been telling all the instructors that you'll blow them out of the water."

Hal suddenly becomes blurry, and my response turns into a sort of gurgle coming out of my throat. I'm not sure of what I was saying anyway. I quickly blink a few times and look back towards the main party. I blame it on the wine and the dancing, the conversation with Don and Maverick, and finding out about Dean, but as I turn back to Hal after taking a deep breath, I realise he knows exactly why I just got emotional.

Every other person in my life has spent the last year telling me I didn't need to go to the academy, I could train privately, I could stay here with Don, and I could be comfortable on the estate. I could stay near the lakes, and wouldn't it be fun to stay here?

They didn't want me to leave, or they thought that when I left, I wouldn't be able to handle it. But here stood a Crown Prince who hadn't seen me train, hadn't seen me learn to make shapes out of lake foam, believing that I would be the best.

"I've missed you. Both of you." I whisper. It's not a lie, although I wouldn't have said it ten minutes ago. I hadn't exactly been sitting waiting for him and Channing to come back. I had been confused and then annoyed. I hadn't even cared enough to be properly angry about it.

But standing here with him in the garden, being twirled by Channing on the dance floor, I start to think of all the balls and

dinners and trips to the lakes that they
missed.

I wonder if Hal would have encouraged me
when I made my first fire shape rather than
telling me the proportions were wrong like
my father did. I wonder if Channing would
have helped me with my footwork rather than
use it against me until I figured it out for
myself like Don had. I didn't care at the time.
They were making me better. I just wonder if
I would have gotten there sooner with Hal
and Channing around.

"We've missed you too." Hal's voice is thick,
and his stance is more rigid. A glimpse at the
prince I see on the TV. Our eyes lock, and he
smiles again. "I have some presents for you. I
missed a lot of your birthdays."

"Three. Three birthdays aren't a lot. You
didn't need to get me anything."

"I didn't bring them," Hal adds quickly.
"They are waiting for you in Althania."

"You really think I'll be going?" I reach out
to gently stroke the petals of a purple rose.
It's almost unnaturally smooth as all of
Harlan's roses are. He has made the bushes
an unorganised rainbow. It's beautiful and

bright, just like him. He would shine like the sun in gloomy Althania, and my heart sings as I realise that there is a chance for me to see him do it. Maybe I'm not as selfish as I thought I was.

"I promise you that you'll be going," Hal says firmly. It unlocks a core memory from somewhere in the back of my brain.

I make my voice low, a poor imitation of a man's, as I say, "A prince's promise is as sure as the sun."

I finally turn to look back at him, hand still on the flower. He's smiling so widely, fangs on proud display, that I grin. My fae canines are pointed but not as long as his; his skin is pale as moonlight. He makes my ivory skin look sunkissed.

Fae and vampires have always been the most similar of the species, and right now, I can feel that. There is an understanding between us. He'll make sure I go to the Academy, and I'll make him proud. He won't disappear again, and I won't hold those years he did against him. He has never broken a promise to me before, and I know he won't break this one.

Chapter Four

Dean's bed is the comfiest in the entire estate. I'm biased, obviously, but I have slept more soundly in his arms on this worn-out, springy mattress than in my two-foot-thick memory foam one.

It has everything to do with the human currently spooning me, even though his arm has trapped my hair against the pillow and taken more than half of the blankets. I nuzzle myself against him, and he whines before tightening his hold on me. Adorable.

The alarm ruins it. His phone blares a rock song, and he is moving away from me, leaving my back and shoulders suddenly cold. I turn with him, but he's already sitting up, phone in his hand, as he cuts off the music. I hug his pillow to me and pout up at him.

He places his phone back gently on the side table before giving me a sad smile. His hands move into my hair, gently untangling it with his fingers.

"The alarm is your fault, you know." Dean leans forward to kiss my temple. His voice is grave. If this was a normal morning, I would get up, struggle with his coffee machine, and triumphantly hand him the steaming mug to him as he gets out of the shower. Instead, Dean gets up, heads straight to the coffee machine, and I lie there for a moment, taking deep, nervous breaths.

I head to the Academy at noon. I leave Dean and my family behind in six hours. In half an hour, I'll meet Harlan by his room and pretend that we spent the whole night having one last evening with Sienna and Valentina. The girls would lie for me automatically, but Harlan filled them in on the details anyway.

Harlan lived with his parents in the cottage two doors down from Dean's. All staff and their families were given separate housing on the other side of the woods from my family.

They were much smaller, with the largest of them having four bedrooms, while the main house had thirteen, but all were well-furnished and updated. My parents make sure of it, just as they make sure to pay above the minimum wage for every member of staff as well.

The cottage that separated Dean and Harlan had been given to our Chef Nova back before even my father was born. Nova was the only non-human I had ever met who looked older than forty. Maverick had once dared Don to ask her exactly how old she was. Don had come back pale and terrified and never told us if he ever got an answer.

Nova was the kindest woman I had ever known, although she said the same about my mother. She looked harmless as well, her face lined, her body soft and wrinkled, something succubus rarely became. Her hair was pure white and curly. People stared at her whenever they saw her outside of the kitchen, and more than one rich visitor had tried to poach her after trying her salmon.

I was going to miss her and her food. Even as I reluctantly move out of Dean's bed, heading towards the shower, I think about stopping to see her and beg her to make it for me as an early lunch.

I know she's seen me sneaking out of here before. She's the only person who lives in this part of the 'staff village' that needs to be up before dawn. The old woman had simply wiggled her fingers at me in a wave and smiled into her coffee cup. She thought she was funny making sausages for dinner that night.

The cold water jolts me awake, and I sigh contently as I tilt my head up into the stream. I almost wanted to stay in it, but Dean was out there, and I needed to cram in as much time with him as possible.

I wash my hair quickly, hop out and start to brush my teeth. I bite into my toothbrush to keep it firmly in my mouth as I reach for a towel, a great big fluffy grey one embroidered with my family crest. I'm halfway through wrapping it around myself when I catch sight of Dean in the mirror.

He's dressed for a day off, with grey joggers and a dark green t-shirt. I'm tempted to say screw Harlan and drag him back to the bedroom. I could tell my dad I overslept, and no one could wake me…

Dean locks eyes with me through the mirror, and he smirks. I finish wrapping the towel around myself and finish off brushing my teeth as if I hadn't seen him there. He pouts at me and walks forward to wrap his arms around my waist. He rests his chin on my shoulder.

"You're gonna get wet," I tell him thickly before rinsing.

"I also need to shower, you know. Corvus invited me around for drinks after you leave, and I don't really want to explain why I smell like you."

"Are you telling me I stink?"

"I'm saying your fae noses have a habit of picking up all sorts of things, and I'm not going to risk it. Not when Don will be in a mood."

"You're not gonna be in a mood?" I whisper, turning my head ever so slightly. I end up kissing his eyebrow.

"I'm going to be inconsolable." Dean plants a kiss on my pulse point, and I whine. "But I also know that I'll be seeing you a lot sooner than you'll be seeing him."

"You're going to have to get used to portal travel," I mumble, twisting in his arms to loop my arms around his neck and plant a hard kiss on his mouth. "Is it terrible that I can't wait for next Saturday? When I meet you at Althania station, can we do this in public?"

"I don't think you can walk around naked even in Althania." Dean presses a kiss on the tip of my nose.

"I'm in a towel." I tut, and my eyes widened as Dean's smile turned wicked. "No!" I cackle and fight to keep the towel knotted. We are both laughing as I slap his hands away and move towards the door. "I have to meet Harlan!"

"Harlan will understand!" Dean laughs as he catches me, picking me up and carrying me back into the bedroom. I silently thank the goddess that Dean's sections of the house have been soundproofed.

Cameron had asked for the work to be done on his workspace when they moved here, and my father, in his infinite wisdom, had offered to pay for Dean's bedroom and ensuite to get done as well. Teenage boys needed privacy, and it was right next to the workroom where Cameron would work late into the night. Whatever the actual reason had been, I doubted my father would have done it if he had realised exactly how helpful it would be to me personally.

Dean throws me onto the bed. Despite what he just said, he left me a coffee and a slice of toast on the side table. A change of clothes from my stash here has been left at the end of the bed. Our coin has been placed on top.

"Thank you," I whisper up at him as he props himself up on his elbows so he doesn't directly lay on top of me. His only response is a kiss.

"It must be nice waking up to a gorgeous human and then knowing you're going to spend the next three years with me." Harlan nudges my shoulder with his own as we walk through the trees. The walk from the staff village to mine takes twenty minutes at our slowest pace, and we both try to soak in this last morning's stroll.

"Oh, Harlan." I sigh dramatically. "We both know that if you would only have glanced at me, I would have been yours forever." I drape my arm over his shoulders as we pass the statue of the satyr right on the edge of the tree line.

"You're such a cow!" Harlan laughs, looping his arm around my waist.

I moo at him, and my laugh turns into a
cackle as he gives me a shove away from
him. Suddenly, we are both bolting towards
my home, chasing each other and leaping out
of the way of water balls and swipes of air.
Neither of us uses fire. It is an established
rule that has been around for over a decade.

Harlan puts on a burst of speed as we get
closer to the door, but like I told Hal two
months ago, Harlan has never beaten me, and
he won't today. I let out a whoop of victory
as my hand smashes against the side of the
wall, Harlan's hand hitting next to mine a
whole four seconds later. Harlan dramatically
throws his hands up into the air as I break
into a victory dance.

"Very dignified!" A voice yells, echoing
around the hall, just inside the doors. A quick
peek shows my brother, Corvus and
Maverick in their workout gear and holding
their practice swords. Well, Corvus is
wearing half his workout gear. His shirt has
been thrown to the side, and his abs are
smeared with blue and yellow paint streaks.
A quick glance shows Don's sword tipped
with blue. Ah. Don really was in a mood if he
was playing this game so early in the day. I

stick my middle finger up at Don, and he pokes his tongue out at me.

"No, no, let her dance." Maverick laughs. "I'm enjoying it."

Don reaches over to whack him around the head just as Corvus hits out at his knees. All three boys end up on the floor wrestling. I roll my eyes and turn to give Harlan a smirk, but my friend's eyes are hyper focused on my brother's arse.

"Gross." I tease him, shoving him towards the stairs. We quickly pad up the stairs, avoiding the discarded fake weapons that the boys have left scattered everywhere. They must have been up for hours already. Harlan leads the way to my room, and I trail behind him, taking this time to try and appreciate the halls I had grown up in.

I had tried to soak in as much of it as I could over the past few weeks. I had joined Don for his evening runs and read with my mother in the library. My father had been particularly affectionate ever since he told me I was allowed to go. He had joined me in horse riding, taken me shopping in the capital and had been present at every single dinner since. If someone tried to tell him he needed to do something else, some lordly duty, he made it wait.

He didn't tell me what Channing had said to sway them, but he had made me promise to message them daily, and if I had any issues, then I was to go to Channing before anyone else. I had a feeling that Channing had been made to promise all sorts of things in order to get them to budge. He was getting an extra big gift this winter solstice.

By the time I get to my room, Harlan is lounging in the armchair by my balcony, his suitcase that he had packed and dropped off the day before open at his feet. Wait. That was *my* suitcase.

"You little snoop!" I scowl as I strut over.

"I wanted to see how many gowns you'd packed!" Harlan defended. "We both know you'd have lied if I asked." Harlan pulls out a short black dress, and the top part is a leather corset. "Your dad definitely didn't buy you this one."

I snatch it back from him with a sigh. "That case was nicely folded, you know."

"Not by you, it wasn't." Harlan smirks, "and that case, just like mine, has been enchanted.

It's practically bottomless. Unfolded dresses are hardly going to take up precious space."

"You just want to know if I'm taking anything you could borrow. Where *has* my Love Feathers tour hoodie gone exactly?" I tease, gently folding the dress and placing it back into the suitcase.

Harlan taps his finger on his chin as if debating if that was true and where, exactly, he may have left my comfiest jumper after borrowing it last autumn.

I laugh and settle myself on his lap. "Of course, if there is anything, you can have it whenever you like."

Harlan immediately looks down at the suitcase at our feet and grins. "Think we could fit your brother in there?"

"Fit me where?" Don asks as he walks into my room without so much as a knock. Noisy footsteps and whispers from the hall tell me that the other two aren't far behind. Don throws himself down on the corner of my four posters.

"Don't sit on that! You haven't even showered." I wrinkle my nose at him.

"You're not gonna be sleeping in it anymore." Corvus reminds me as he and Maverick strut into the room. He's still shirtless, and the sweat has smeared the paint all over him. He catches me looking and raises his eyebrows.

"If you get paint on my bed, I'll coat the walls in your blood," I tell him as I feel a creeping heat on the back of my neck.

Maverick laughs, throwing himself on the floor by Don's feet. Corvus smirks, but he remains standing in the doorway.

"Breakfast is in half an hour," Don tells me, looking down at the suitcase. I reach out with my foot and shut it. His eyes flick up to look at me, but he knows it's best not to ask. He doesn't want to bicker today. I don't want to either, which is why I made sure he didn't see the leather dress.

"It took all three of you to come and tell us that?" Harlan teases them, "Aren't we lucky?"

"Considering you're the one man I would let be alone with my sister in her bedroom, you should count yourself as such." Don purrs at him. I flick my fingers, and a water ball hits him in the face.

"Don't tease my Harlan." I pout. My brother knows about Harlan's crush or affection or whatever the best word for it was. Harlan had boyfriends over the past few years, so it wasn't like he had pinned all his hopes and dreams on Donaugh. That didn't mean Don didn't like to play into it.

Don spluttered and wiped at his face with a scowl as Maverick laughed again. He cuts himself off and then looks up at Don with a pout. "I wouldn't be allowed to be alone in a bedroom with Ivy?" He sighs and looks over at me. "I told you the broom closet was our best opti…OWW!"

Don had kicked out his leg and hit Maverick in the rib. "Rule number two!"

"I was KIDDING." Maverick scowls as he rubs at his wound.

"Obviously, he was kidding… We all know Ivy prefers the woods." Corvus slowly grins before bolting from the room as Don lunges toward him. Maverick is cackling as we hear a crash from the corridor.

"Donaugh that BETTER NOT HAVE BEEN A VASE." My mother's voice booms around the house, helped along by magic. The three of us in the room burst into another roar of laughter.

"Maverick and Corvus." Harlan beams at me, "Haven't you been a busy little heiress?"

"They are nothing on you, gorgeous." I winked, patting his cheek twice. "Nothing on you."

"I'm still here, so, ya know, that's hurtful." Mav looks at us with a twinkle in his eye. He pushes himself to his feet and offers me his hand. "Wanna go give Don a heart attack over some pancakes?"

"There's nothing else I could imagine doing on my last breakfast here." I reach out to take his hand. He decides as soon as I'm close that it's not enough, and I squeal as he throws me over his shoulder.

Chapter Five

Portal travel always makes my stomach queasy. It doesn't matter if I close my eyes or keep them open if I've starved myself beforehand or gorged myself on bacon pancakes like I had this morning. There would always be a gut-wrenching stomach flip as I stepped into the hazy purple doorway and out into wherever it was I was going.

I had never seen Althania in person. I had obsessively watched any footage I could find on the Academy as a child, although that was limited to pre-approved showcases and graduate interviews. The Academy never let anything else leak.

I had written reports on the battles fought there and how it bordered Alcarlian, the wolf country. It had held the last of the wars and some of the bloodiest battles that Vileria had witnessed. A treaty had finally drawn up the final territory lines 197 years ago. Both sides lost territories. The memorials were heartbreaking, even in the photos. I couldn't wait to see them, to drag Dean to them on the weekends.

Our family portal is located in its own room, in the very centre of the house. The permanent portal runes are etched into the stone. The portal had been arranged to open at exactly noon and would remain open for ten minutes.

It was currently 11:53 am. I know because I had spent breakfast watching every clock I could - the one on the wall, the one on my brother's wrist and the one on my phone. The large clock built into the wall above the portal was no different.

"You have my number," Corvus whispers as he gives me the first hug goodbye. "Let us know how much ass you're kicking, okay?"

I laugh into his ear and pull back with a nod. Maverick hugs me next, so tight that I can't breathe for a second. "Don't let anyone break that pretty face, Iv." Maverick winks, tapping the tip of my nose before sliding back into place.

Harlan and his parents are having their goodbyes to the side, and the two boys head over to say goodbye to him, leaving me with only my blood relatives. A sweet gesture, although I love them just as much as I love Don.

My mother pulls me closer to her as if the small step away from the portal would make me change my mind and have me racing back to my room. She smells like the flower she is named after, a special perfume my father had made for her as a gift for their first anniversary. I take a deep breath of it.

"You go straight to Channing if anything happens. If anyone makes a comment or you hurt yourself or you want to come home." My mother says into my shoulder, her voice breaking a little at the end. My heart sinks a little bit in my chest, but I cannot change my mind. I won't. Like I told her before, I would move out eventually, and I wanted this more than I wanted her happy, even if it made me selfish.

"I know, mum." I hug her back, catching my father's eye and smiling as I run my hand gently over her back. His eyes are glassy, but he's smiling, smiling as if he understands. Like he's proud. My mum pulls away and gently cups my face in her hands to look at me.

"You are so beautiful. Don't forget that, even when you're all bruised and tired and muddy and…"

"You're not putting me off, ya know." I smile.

"Worth a shot." She chuckles, and my smile widens.

She moves back in between Don and my dad. The two Whitlock men look at each other for a split second before I'm wrapped in my father's arms. His hug is even tighter than Maverick's and he is tall enough that he needs to lean down to rest his chin on my head. His goodbye was shorter than my mother's.

"Show them what a Whitlock can do."

"And how amazing we look while doing it." I finish off our unofficial family mantra. Our family motto may be 'Loyalty above all', but it didn't quite roll off the tongue as well as narcissism did. My father's chest rumbles as he laughs, and I give him an extra squeeze as he tries to pull away. He stays there until we hear a soft whoosh from behind us.

I turn. The purple doorway has become translucent, and through it, I can see

Channing and a blonde woman. Their hands are behind their backs, and they are dressed casually in all black. I lock eyes with Channing and get a small smile. I spin back and run to hug Don. I know in the back of my head that I have ten minutes before the portal closes. But something in me panicked as I needed to tell Don goodbye.

"I'm gonna miss you," I say as my arms wrap around him. I hear my own voice crack a little, and I clear my throat as I carry on. "I don't know how to live without you breathing down my neck."

"Well, you know where to find me, and I hear Althania has some wicked clubs. Think I can sleep on your floor every weekend?" Don chuckles as he holds me.

"I don't think anyone could stop you." I laugh and pull back. "I remember crying when I heard you were looking at colleges. I didn't want you to ever leave me." Don's face starts to swim, and I blink the tears away. "Now I'm the one leaving you."

"You were five. You didn't know what college was, and I'm never leaving you. You're gonna get so sick of me, you're gonna want to get a new number." Don's face turns serious for a second as he adds. "But I'll get ahold of whatever you change it to."

I laugh and lean in to kiss his cheek. "See you later, big brother."

Don doesn't answer. He opens his mouth to, but then stops and quickly wipes at his eyes before gently pushing me towards the portal. Harlan is waiting for me there, suitcase in one hand and the other stretched towards me. I move to his side and pick up my own case.

Don finds his voice as I take Harlan's hand. "Look after her rose boy."

Harlan smirks at me before we both turn to the portal. The blonde woman is scowling, but Channing is still smiling.

"We took our first steps together." Harlan reminds me. "Seems only fitting that we take this one together too."

I grin and start to count down. "One…two…three…"

Harlan and I are in complete unison as we finally head to the Academy.

Chapter Six

I'm not sure if I'm supposed to hug Channing. It feels like the right thing to do. After he convinced my parents to let me come here, Channing sent me multiple letters with information I would need, some of which I suspected hadn't been given to other students.

He recommended what to pack and sent me brochures for events coming up in the city that he thought I might like. He was the one who told me Academy students weren't restricted to the campus or dorms, something Harlan had been unsure of.

If I was supposed to hug him, the moment has passed as the grumpy blonde shoves two folders at us. Harlan drops my hand as we grab them. I put down my suitcase so I could flip through it.

"You can look through it at orientation. We need to set up the next portal." The blonde doesn't deign to introduce herself. Channing frowns at her.

"Welcome to the Academy," Channing tells us. "Leave your bags here. They'll get taken to your rooms for you. I'll take you to the others."

Harlan moves to put his suitcase out of the way of the once again purple doorway. He reaches to take mine as well. Channing starts walking towards the doorway, and I scramble after him, taking a second to look around the room.

Their permanent portal was also in a stone room, although it was significantly larger and emptier. No vase of flowers for decoration or chairs to wait in. The walls were completely bare rather than full of the paintings of landscapes that my father had decorated ours with.

Channing holds the door open for us, Harlan being quick on my heels. The door is thick, solid oak. Once we are out in the hall, I see that all the doors. Their room numbers are elegantly carved into them. A quick glance behind me shows Channing closing the one simply labelled *Portal.*

"Ignore Celeste," Channing tells us once we start moving down the hall. "She's a little…Orientation takes a lot out of her."

"That name sounds familiar." I blurt out, thinking back to the few stories my mother had shared with me about her time here.

"I doubt it," Channing tells me quickly. "Celeste and Violet never got along."

I glance over at Harlan, who shrugs in response. I'm not an idiot. I know that no one can ever be universally loved. But I had never heard anyone say a bad word about my mother, not really. The closest had been some grumbling from another Fae lord that we paid our servants too much. I had never taken that as genuine criticism. Of course, no one was going to insult the host of a ball while in earshot of her children.

"Is that why she was so…" Harlan trails off as if he realises insulting a potential instructor was a bad move. Or maybe he just isn't as comfortable around Channing as I am.

Harlan had been my friend since my first breath. He was only two months older than I was, so he had been around when Channing or Hal had visited. We often shared the chocolate they brought. But he was also a low-born fae, and this was someone who outranked both of us after being granted a position that no other member of his species ever had.

Channing's lip twitches into a smile as he drawls. "Yeah. Probably. She's been in a particularly bad mood ever since she was told Ivy would be attending this year." He looks over at me. "So it's going to be particularly fun when you show up and knock everyone on their ass."

"You're really setting me up on a pedestal there." I joke nervously. After my acceptance, I had been doing extra training. I didn't want to let Hal down. A Prince's promise was as sure as the sun, and I planned on showing everyone he had talked to about me that he was right.

"You're Violet's daughter," Channing says softly as if that is the only answer I should need. I don't have the heart to tell him that it doesn't explain his faith in me.

My mother used her magic in small doses, never anything spectacular, and she monitored our training, but she had never sparred with me directly. She demonstrated proper form and called out to us to change something if we were wrong.

She is no longer the person she was a century and a half ago. She talks about a water wielder who had caused gossip circles to combust as she ran into the arms of a fae lord far above her station. Our silence prompts Channing to keep talking.

"You're the second group to turn up. The group from the station arrived late. The speeches start at one, and then you guys have some free time to get settled in your rooms." Channing takes us down a sharp left.

"How many were in the group?" I ask. A whole hour between portals?! They must have had an extension which probably hadn't helped Celeste's mood. I assumed she was a witch since I hadn't seen any pointed ears, wings or fangs. Extending a portal takes a ton of energy, even for a witch who is powerful enough to be an instructor here.

Channing looks back at us as he continues to walk and slowly grins. "Nineteen. Someone had the brilliant idea of getting all the people without their own portals to the Althania station for one large portal here this morning. Never seemed to occur to them that it would take a while to get all those individual portals approved. There was a bit of an overlap."

Harlan and I laugh, although it's a little too loud. I have never had to rely on public portals, and Harlan has always just had to ask and been given permission to use ours. Neither of us wanted to admit to that privilege, though.

Our private portals were different and didn't need to be approved. I don't even know how long it would take to approve one if I needed it. Even at the portal stations, the few times I had been to one, I simply waved my hand over the rune and stepped through whenever I wanted.

Channing takes two more turns, and we face a set of large double doors labelled *Meeting Hall*.

The lettering on this door had been carved into the oak and then filled in with some kind of shimmering solid metal. If I had to guess, it was infused with magic, something that is rare nowadays.

To infuse metal with magic, it took blood and a lot of it. Each weapon made of the stuff usually had a bloody history behind it. My family's sword was infused with Fae magic, and it had stayed on the mantel above our main fireplace for longer than even my grandfather remembered. My father had told me and Don the story once, and only once, before telling us not to talk about it again. He didn't like to remember that our ancestor had slaughtered his twin sons simply because "he could always make more."

My stomach flips as Channing opens the door, and his finger brushes just beneath the metal. If I was right, and I couldn't think of anything else that would make metal shimmer like that, then someone had been seriously hurt - at best - to make this lettering.

Harlan let out a low whistle as we catch sight of what is behind those doors. The thoughts of torture, murder and dead babies leave my mind quicker than they had come. The Academy's meeting hall was larger than I thought it would be and far too gorgeous to not be intimidating.

The walls were lined with stained glass showcasing the academy's crest and members of each species. We walk in wordlessly, my eyes focusing on the stained glass portraits rather than the twenty other people in the room.

There is a dark-haired angel swinging a sword, a red-haired mermaid holding a dagger while she lounges on a rock. Each one was clearly based on a real person. The features were too specific not to be. I come to a halt halfway across the room, at the one meant to signify the fae.

It's my mother.

Chapter Seven

She is facing forward, her glass eyes a perfect match for the real thing. Her hands are splayed at either side, symbols of the elements floating around her. She was wearing a tight, deep blue tunic. Whoever created it went to great lengths with slivers of gold glass to showcase the runes that ran along the sleeves. She had matching trousers.

She was smiling, although it wasn't a smile I had ever seen on the real her. It was almost like a challenge, daring whoever was looking up at her to come and fight her. It was perfect other than that. Gorgeous. I wonder if she knows it's here, if she had to pose for it, or if someone had created it from a memory. Maybe that's why the smile was wrong.

I'm so focused on catching all the details, staring up at the glass that could have been me if it was only slightly more abstract, that Harlan has to nudge me when people come up behind us. I glance over.

Three people, one a vampire. Her mouth is purposely open enough to show us the glint of her fangs. She is paper pale, a contrast to her dark eyes and makeup, but her lipstick is bright red. Very cliché of her. The two boys at her side are less cliche.

The blonde is short and thick. I don't think my hand would be able to wrap around his arm, and I doubted both my hands would wrap fully around his neck. He looks practically human, but his bow-legged walk and slightly salty scent tell me he's a mermaid. In the back of my mind, I make a note to text Maverick that he's still the prettiest one I've met so far. He loves a stroke to his ego.

The third of them is the most eye-catching, thanks to his purple hair and bright yellow eyes. An oracle. I had never met one before, although I had seen them on TV. Every royal council had one, and usually, they were a part of press conferences. From what I know, they get overwhelmed by senses of good or bad but can be trained to physically see the future as well. That must be why he's here. I smile brilliantly at them.

"You're Ivy Whitlock." The girl pronounces my name with a hard 'k' at the end. She whips her high ponytail and holds out her hand for me to take. "I'm Proxima. Proxima Rymer."

"Hi." I reach out and take her hand, giving it a gentle shake before pulling back. She glances down at my hand, then at Harlan, and then looks back up at the stained glass.

"You look just like her." She states. I ignore her and make a point of looping my arm through Harlan's.

"This is Harlan." I look over at the other two. "What are your names?"

The oracle grins as Proxima snaps her head to look at me. "I'm Knox. Nice to meet you."

"Atticus." The mermaid grumbles.

"Hi Knox. Hi Atticus." I smile at both of them. Harlan mimics me before pressing his lips together to stop his own smile as Proxima clears her throat.

"You don't think you look like her?" She presses, pointing up to my mother's portrait in case I'm confused by what she meant. "You were staring at her long enough."

Oh. Okay. Classic first day, mean girl. My smile doesn't falter as I cock my head up to look at the glass and shrug. "I suppose so. Mothers and daughters generally do look alike, though." I swivel my head to look at Harlan as I continue. "It's gorgeous though, isn't it, Harlan? Looks just like her."

"Uncanny." Harlan agrees. "Even on the piercings."

"The piercings are perfect." I nod vigorously.

"And her eyes are the exact same shade as yours."

"A perfect match." I agree.

"You should ask her who she posed for. Get your whole house redone. I would love a life-sized portrait of Don facing the garden."

"You're a genius." I pull my phone out of my pocket and make a point of leaning back to get the best angle for a photo. Once I have one, I look over at Proxima, who is staring at us like we have just burst into song. She opens her mouth to speak but is cut off as Knox laughs into his hand, fake coughing as she turns to scowl at him.

"Sorry." I smile brilliantly at them all. My eyes lock on Proxima. "Me and Harlan are basically the same person. The same sense of humour. He's just much prettier than me, so I love and loath him."

I hope the message is clear - mess with Harlan, and you mess with me. She knew my name and made a point of coming over. I recognise her last name as well. She's a noble, and for the last five minutes, she was the type to only care about status.

Atticus hadn't given me his last name, but I'm willing to bet he was noble or powerful enough to get a noble's attention. They look far too comfortable with each other to have only met today. Knox was an Oracle, so he would be quite an asset to her. He didn't look anywhere near as comfortable with Proxima as Atticus did, though. Maybe they met during the mess-up with the portals.

"Aw, Iv." Harlan coos, throwing his arm over my shoulder. "I loathe you, too."

Proxima looks between the two of us, and her eyes widen ever so slightly as if she's just realised something. I would bet all the gold in my case that she thinks we are screwing. Her smile certainly gets warmer as she tells Harlan. "You two are so funny. I'm so glad you're on our table. My dad says the welcome speech is going to be done by…well. You guys will see."

I finally turn to look at the rest of the room. It's full of round tables with five chairs at each. In front of each chair is an empty silver plate, a glass goblet, and a name tag. From Proxima's tone, she wants us to ask about the welcome speech. She wants us to beg and gasp when she tells us. I'm happy to wait.

Knox smiles at us and starts slowly heading over to the tables. Forcing myself not to look back at my mother's window, I follow him. Proxima quickly hurries to the front of the group with Atticus seemingly happy to dawdle along behind us. Harlan smirks.

We are at the table front and centre. The top half of the hall has no stage or barrier. The largest stained-glass window takes up almost the entire wall. It takes me a second to absorb it all. It is a perfect map of Vileria.

All the countries are shown in their royal colours. Red for the vampires of Althania, yellow for the wolves of Alcarlian, green for the fae of Parlitan, etc, etc. The blue for the mermaids and sirens surrounds Vileria. Realistically, their territories are not as vast. Half of the ocean was unliveable, too far away from the mainland to be feasible. But I suppose it looks better than having it as simple glass.

I slide myself into my allotted chair, the one that stares straight forward at the glass. The best view in the house. Harlan is on my left, and Knox is on my right. Harlan scowls for a split second as he sees Proxima on his other side. I hide my smile behind the folder Celeste gave us.

"There's nothing in there that your mother won't have told you." Proxima leans forward to tell me quickly. I'm suddenly glad I hid my face. Only Knox sees me roll my eyes before I respond.

"I like to be thorough," I respond with forced boredom. "It's been a century and a half. I hope it's gotten more modern."

Proxima gets that startled look on her face again, but she has no argument. She looks almost defeated, and my heart sinks a little in my chest. She's trying too hard, sure, but this is a brand-new school for all of us. She might genuinely just want a friend, and she latched on to the people she might have similarities with. If I hadn't had Harlan, I might have done the same.

"Team Building Exercises." I read out from the table of contents at the front. I quickly skim past the map of the grounds, the timetables, and various other pages until I get to it. I shoot Proxima a smile. "I'm a sucker for a movie night."

Proxima smiles back at me, and the tension eases a little. Harlan leans back in his seat, slowly looking around at the other tables. The other students have already formed their own cliques and are mingling around tables or scribbling in each other's files. I assume room or phone numbers, but I'm not going to be giving those out to people straight away.

Others start trickling through the door. I spy an angel with bright gold wings that perfectly match his hair and what is undoubtedly a shapeshifter, walking around with a wolf's tail. I couldn't say I would want to make that my first impression if I had the choice, but she was walking with confidence and straight over to a girl wearing a large crystal around her neck, most likely a witch. She didn't so much as glance at anyone else.

The rest of the group scatter before I can look for tell-tale signs of what they are, but I count at least seven of them. They were probably the final portal. The Academy take thirty students each year, no more and no less. I lean over to look at Harlan's watch, a thick thing with a worn leather strap that looks heavy on his wrist. His father gave it to him after his acceptance to the Academy, and I haven't seen him without it since. The speeches started in ten minutes.

"I've gotten three texts about you already," Harlan tells me softly. "When I think about your brother texting me, it's not about if you like your room or not."

I roll my eyes and check my phone. "I have nothing."

"Overprotective sibling?" Knox asks.

"Overprotective hot sibling." Harlan laughs.

"So you two aren't..." Atticus pipes up. His voice is higher than I expected. He gestures between me and Harlan with a lazy wag of his finger.

"I'm as queer as a nine-faced coin." Harlan purrs at him with a wink.

"I thought I would have heard if you were courting someone," Proxima says quickly. "Noble gossip spreads so quickly. Well, I'm sure you know that. I hear your mother throws the best balls in Parlitan. That's why-well. You know who goes." Proxima winks at me like we share a secret.

"Well, Hal doesn't always come," I say quickly, and I'm surprised to hear slightly bitterly. Proxima gapes at me.

"You call The Crown Prince Of Althania…Hal?" Her voice is definitely bitter. "Not even *Prince* Hal?"

Even the people at the table next to ours glance over them. It strikes me like lightning, the thought that I have done something I can't take back. Hal had never let me bow or curtsy for him. I tried to after seeing Harlan do it when we were kids, but he had told me not to and quickly followed it up with a 'and it's not your highness either. It's…Hal.' Maybe that's why Don said it was never normal when he visited. Not even the most basic royal treatments were followed when he was on our estate.

I'm saved from answering, but not from the glances, as Harlan's watch ticks over to exactly one, and the doors open and in walks Channing, Celeste, Hal and a snow leopard.

Chapter Eight

I focus on the snow leopard. Channing and Celeste pause once inside and let their superiors pass. The snow leopard leads the four to the front of the room. For it to be leading Hal, she could only be one person. The headmistress of the Academy, Lela Brookes.

I'm proven right a moment later, once the four have settled into their positions. Channing, behind and to the left of Hal. Celeste, behind and to the right of the leopard, who suddenly turned into a terrifying middle-aged woman.

Her pure white hair was in a tight bun, showcasing a slightly wrinkled face full of sharp angles. Her dark eyes scan over each of us. The room is deadly silent. I don't dare look away when her eyes lock on mine, not even to glance at Hal.

The Crown Prince of Althania couldn't be an instructor at the Academy. It would take up too much time. Channing was only a mentor rather than an instructor because of the same reasons, and who would Hal even…Oh goddess… Please no. The thought swims around my head as Headmistress Brookes finally moves her gaze over to Harlan.

My gaze moves over to Hal, who is already looking at me. He smiles.

Knock Knock, A voice in my head whispers. Hal's voice. I release a breath.

Who's there? I think back.

I…didn't plan a joke. Hal admits. *Like your table?*

Some of them are a little…intense. My eyes flicker over to Proxima, and Hal chuckles telepathically.

She was very excited to meet you.

She was very excited for you to arrive. Kept hinting someone special was doing to the speech. I hesitate for a second as Headmistress Brookes booms a welcome. But she can't read my thoughts, and so I quickly say

*IjustcalledyouHalandeveryonelookedatmelike
Iwasinsane.*

My attention turns completely back to the
Headmistress.

"The rules of the academy are simple and are
printed into your orientation packs. There is
to be no fighting without a member of staff or
mentor present. Abuse of any kind towards
the Academy's staff will not be tolerated.
Weekly mentor meetings are never optional.
If you are sick, your mentor will still expect
you. No transformative magic is to be used
on anyone else while on campus. If any of
these rules are broken, the student involved
will be immediately expelled."

Every word is clear. I doubt anyone in the
room has a single question, although the
headmistress opens up the floor to any. The
shapeshifter that had come in moments
before proves me wrong as she immediately
raises her hands and asks about the training
centres. Channing had already told me all
about those. The next question comes from
the angel next to her, asking about dorm
rules.

You can call me whatever you like. Hal
whispers into my mind again. *And I'm not*

doing any speech. Lela thought it best for the other students that they see her as the main figure.

Isn't she?

Of course, she is. But the Academy is something I hold very dear to me. There's hesitation as if he is weighing his words and then changes his mind about what to say next. *I offered to be your mentor. So did Channing.*

Oh. My heart seizes up in my chest as I realise I was right. Hal wants to be my mentor. He's going to be around at least once a week.

You get to choose. Hal tells me quickly. *If someone has more than one offer, they can always choose. I understand if you pick Channing.*

I guess I didn't realise people offered to be mentors. I thought they were just assigned. Channing never said.

Channing didn't think I should offer. Hal's voice was somehow bitter and amused. *He worried about how it would look when you tried to make friends.*

There's a stained glass window of my mother on the wall. I think that ship's already sailed.

Hal's laugh is real then, out loud and cutting off Headmistress Brookes as she goes through the expectations of students when they go into the city. He presses his lips together and clears his throat, holding up a hand in apology. The headmistress doesn't look amused. Channing even less so.

I'm gonna need you to formally accept me as a mentor if Lela doesn't kill me at the end of this. Telling her you told me mentally that Channing's worries are invalid won't slide.

You want it in writing?

Or you tell Uncle Channing that you can handle it all just fine. The bitterness is gone from his voice now, changed to the same sad tone my dad uses whenever he brings up memories from when I was small.

I haven't heard Channing referred to as 'uncle' in a long time. Maybe Hal can sense that as he swirls around in my brain. Maybe he can see the memories as I can, running on my lanky little legs into my father's arms, squealing that 'Uncle Channing couldn't find me!'

He used to call me little cub, I remember. My eyes catch on Channing, and I smile at him. He winks back at me, but he's still frowning. *Is it offensive to make a joke about you being in his doghouse?*

You've had a werewolf living with you for over a decade. Hal is interrupted as the room bursts into applause. I quickly join in, my face turning red as I realise I have no idea why. Another table is brought out to the front of the room, followed by waiters with food.

Corvus never gets offended by anything, I think, although my mind feels strangely empty now as if a connection had been broken. I look over and find Channing and Hal in a whispered conversation, Celeste and Headmistress Brookes to the side of them, silent. They are watching the students instead.

My view is interrupted as a plate is placed in front of me. I smile, thank the fae that put it there and then laugh slightly. I look over at Harlan's plate, and he is smiling too. My plate is overflowing with salt and pepper squid on chilli rice, one of my absolute favourites. Harlan has a whole meat feast pizza.

"I don't remember telling them my top ten meals." Harlan jokes as he happily picks up his cutlery.

Atticus's eyes lock onto the pizza. "That looks good." He says gruffly. His plate is full of steak and potatoes. The mermaid frowns as he sees Harlan start cutting the pizza up into little pieces. I grin at my plate.

What on earth are you eating? It's bright red! Hal's voice is back. I choke on my mouthful. He quickly adds a *Sorry. Bad timing.*

Salt and pepper squid on chilli rice. Not as good as Nova's, obviously, but it looks a lot better than Proxima's raw meatballs.

They aren't raw just...blue.

A quick glance over at the top table shows Hal is eating a very pink-looking burger.

Vamp thing. Rigggghhhhttt. I smirk as I sip at my...I take another sip. My water tastes like the coffee Dean made me this morning, with his special vanilla syrups imported from Siconia. He had made a dirty joke about the succubus making drinks you wanted to constantly suck down. I realise I haven't thought about him since I left this house. The squid seems less appealing.

I told your mother she should have taken in a vampire instead of a mermaid.

And live a life without Maverick? I'd rather not live at all. The thought is genuine and instant, more of an instinct than an actual response to Hal. Speaking telepathically was…strange. I wasn't sure what Hal could and couldn't see.

I had never met anyone else with the gift - that I knew of, and it wasn't like he sat down and gave me a play-by-play of all his secrets. I wasn't sure if he could see how deeply my feelings for the boys went or if he had people like that in his life so he would even really understand.

You looked close. Not as close as you did with the human boy. Hal waited for me to finish my bite this time.

I chew slowly and try to zone back into the conversation at the table. It sounds like Proxima and Atticus are talking to us about things to do in the city, and I throw my mind back to the list Channing sent me.

Did I hit a nerve? I thought it was obvious.
Hal whispers to me. *I'm sorry.*

*Mum never figured it out. I told her I was
desperately into Maverick.*

Hence, the dance.

*No. We dance every year. Corvus usually
takes the first one.* Speaking like this, I'm not
thinking about what I should or shouldn't
say, if he would even care. The responses are
just flowing out of me.

Why? Hal sounded curious, and the response
came with barely a second gap. He did care.

*Don was teasing me that no one had asked
me to the ball. I was fifteen and hormonal.
When he said the only boys that would dance
with me were him and Harlan, I almost cried.
Corvus saw. When the ball started, Corvus
left his date and came straight over to me. He
did the same thing every time he saw me
alone that night.*

That night had meant the world to me, even if
my crush on Corvus had dwindled by then.
Corvus was twenty now, but thanks to me
being a fae, he was only half a head taller
than me. I didn't look like a small child being
led around as a favour as Sienna had once

joked I would. He hadn't teased me or lectured me like Don would always do when we danced. He just smiled and led me around. The only thing he said to me was that I looked pretty.

Don makes fun of you? Hal's voice changes. *You two always look-*

Hal cuts off abruptly, and when I look over at his table to see why, I notice that everyone at my table is now looking at me. It can't have been for long. Harlan was more than comfortable enough with me to kick my shin or something if it had been.

"Sorry," I say quickly to them. "Just thinking."

I hear Knox let out an amused breath through his nose and glance at him. Psychics can't hear telepathic conversations, can they?

"Harlan was just saying how you're from the fae family that Maverick Kanlore lives with. I know his brothers." Atticus tells me. "Brutal fighters."

"Maverick's amazing in a fight." I agree quickly. I wouldn't have used the word brutal. He was strong, but he played fair. "Training with him was amazing."

Knox makes the noise again. This time, I finally glance up at Hal and find him in another deep conversation with Channing. Both pause and look over at our table. I'm not the only one to notice. Proxima immediately sits up straighter.

"You also have the second-born Dalloway, right?" Atticus continues. "I heard he was at the same place as Maverick."

"Corvus lives with us." I tell him slowly. "They both decided to stay with us when they turned seventeen."

Maverick mentioned his family only in passing comments, same as Corvus. Neither of them were heirs, so there was less pressure to go back to their lands. They didn't go back on major holidays, but they would take the occasional random break. They would never be gone for more than a week. Don had told me never to mention it, and I hadn't. Corvus and Maverick were happy with us. That's what I care about.

"Must be one hell of an estate," Knox speaks up, lolling his head to look at Harlan.

Harlan nods at him. "Gorgeous."

"Thanks to Harlan. He makes our rose bushes stunning." I beam at him. Harlan's ears turn pink at the praise.

"That is the most privileged thing I've ever heard," Knox tells me bluntly. His arms are crossed, and he's scowling.

"If mentioning rose bushes on an estate you asked about is the most privileged thing you've ever heard, I'm guessing you don't get out much," I tell him coolly. Knox smirks back at me.

"You aren't frightened of insulting me, little fae? Of all the things I might know? Things I might have seen about your future?" Knox's tone is taunting, but his eyes flash with something else. I stare straight into them as I respond.

"I can honestly say that thought never crossed my mind. But now it has? No. I'm not."

"You don't want to get on my good side? Get some warning about all those tragedies?"

All those tragedies. That was very specific phrasing. It didn't mean he was telling the truth. He was trying to get a reaction, and I'm petty enough to not give him the one he wants. I will not grovel, even to a psychic.

"So I can stress about them beforehand? I can't think of anything worse." I lean back in my chair, resting my elbows on the back. Don always sat like this after he thought he won an argument between us. It always shut me up, even if I had a response.

Knox slowly grins at me. I have won the approval I didn't want. The thought makes me feel warm inside. This is now an official friendship in my eyes. I grin back.

"Is that how your powers work?" Harlan asks him bluntly, but it's not unkind. It's curious. Harlan saw an opening, and he grabbed a hold of it. "You actually *see* things? Like visions? I thought it was all about senses."

"No." Knox turns his gaze to Harlan. "At least…that's very rare for me. It *is* just all senses and feelings. I had a feeling I was going to meet someone important today. The Crown Prince of Althania is here. I had a feeling that I would get into the academy if I applied, and here I am." Knox gestures with both his hands to his body.

"Well, isn't that useful in a fight," Atticus grumbled. I'm not sure if it's because he's jealous since it actually did sound useful, or if maybe he was so focused on being a 'brutal' fighter that he didn't realise that, and he was just trying to be insulting. Proxima seemed to be ignoring us all, focusing solely on the table at the front.

"We have to be going to our rooms soon. Everyone's almost done." Proxima whines to herself. "I want to decorate and unpack before the mixer."

Harlan and I share a look. Channing had made the mixer sound more casual than a ball, but Proxima was noble. She would have been at more than a few balls here in Althania. Were we under-packed? Impossible. I had made sure to have a type of dress for *everything*. I think.

"The mixer isn't until seven, Prox." Atticus tells her kindly. "You have time."

"We are going to have it in the *Palace* this year, Atticus. I have to look perfect."

"What?" I blurt out and snap my head to look at her. "How do you know that?"

"My dad is on the Althanian royal council." Proxima purrs. "The Crown Prince and…Sir Channing are taking a hands-on approach with the academy this year." Proxima has to force out Channing's title.

Apparently, Channing being knighted still isn't widely accepted even though it happened decades before any of us were born. I even forget that he is a knight until someone else mentions it, and no one back home ever does. But then, as I am going to be painfully reminded throughout the year, we are far too familiar with them. I turn to look at the stained window version of my mother.

Why is it here? I have a sinking feeling in my stomach that it's not the only thing she hasn't told me about. My mother has clearly downplayed her time here.

Was it to deter me? To keep me back in Parlitan with the rest of my family? Did she hate it here? Did she really hate the idea of *me* here so much that she tucked away a whole part of her life? What could possibly have happened here, where she was clearly idolised, that made her not want to tell me and Don?

I turn my head to the front table. Channing is staring directly at me as the Headmistress tells us about the rest of our day.

Chapter Nine

The walk to the part of the academy that holds all the rooms takes just over ten minutes. Thankfully, these doors aren't branded with the same metal as the meeting room. Instead, my name is displayed on a bronze plaque, along with the words 'first year.'

My things have already been unpacked. It's the first thing I notice when I walk into my new room. A family photo in a silver frame is on my oak bedside table. The whole room is full of oak actually; four poster beds, wardrobe and cabinets. The bedding is a rich red, the same as the thick curtains. A rectangular black gift box has been placed on the end of the bed, but I'll open that later. It's probably something generic, like a coffee mug or stationary with the academy crest. Maybe even a pin.

I gently tug them open and find that the windows take up a majority of the wall. The view is breathtaking…and fake. The view is the exact same as my one at home. I move to check out the stones that make up the rest of the wall. There we go.

There are tiny runes etched into them with clean lines. I don't recognise them exactly, but I know how this kind of spell works. I begged my father to have it installed for my birthday when I was younger. I got a new horse instead.

I gently ran my thumb down the runes. If I don't think of a place, then it will revert back into a real window. The real view isn't as generically beautiful as the rolling fields and woods back home, but I fell in love with it instantly.

It's the outdoor training grounds. Even from here, and my room must be at least five storeys up, I can see the perfect white circle of chalk drawn on a large concrete square in the corner. There's a group practising wrestling in it now. I wince as a bulky angel's body slams what looks like a fae into the ground. That must hurt.

The rest of the space has lanes for running, large hay targets for either magic or arrows and large pieces of gym equipment. I spot someone in the free space next to the wrestling, lifting weights in the weak sunlight.

Althania really is gloomier than home. The clouds are thick and grey, seemingly unending. They look ready to drop an ocean's worth of rain down on everyone at any moment, but no one seems to care. I suppose if you're training to fight demons and go dimension jumping, rain is hardly an issue. I usually make a thin layer of air hover over me to stop the rain from hitting me anyway.

Finding my things takes no time at all. My makeup, toothbrush and other hygiene things are all in the bathroom directly attached to my room, the door to which is right next to the bed. The claw-footed tub in the centre is massive, and the small bookcase next to it is filled with all sorts of fancy-looking soaps, fizzers and lotions in a range of colours. I let out a low whistle as I crouch in front of it. I notice that a lot of them boast about soothing muscles and helping to heal bruised skin. They plan on going hard on us if they have to supply things like that. I grin at the thought.

I decided on the dress with the leather corset top that Harlan had pulled out of my case earlier. I want to make an impression, so I spend more time than usual on my makeup. As it sets, I curl my hair. For training and class, I will need to have it up. Tonight, it will be completely down.

Even with that extra work, I have some time to kill. Harlan is in the room to my right and Knox in the room to my left. Somehow, Harlan decided I would meet them both outside our doors at a quarter to seven. They were both going to escort me. How they decided that, I have no idea since Proxima spent the whole walk talking my ear off about her family's estate. It sounded lovely, although I had the horrifying thought that I might have agreed to go to their winter solstice ball. My mother would kill me. Kill her, actually, and anyone who tried to stop me from going back. Her balls were her passion, second only to her family.

I waste another five minutes spinning around in front of the floor-length mirror in the corner. The dress would be too short for a respectable ball, but for a school mixer, it would be okay. It was just above my knees, and the bottom part flowed nicely. It was soft and silky to the touch, its colour a perfect black that matched the tight leather.

I settle myself on the end of the bed with a gentle huff. I reach over and grab the gift that was left for me. Maybe I can waste the remaining seven minutes finding a place for whatever propaganda is inside. I could always wear a t-shirt to train in.

I tug roughly at the ribbon. The lid to the box is surprisingly heavy. I open it slowly, suddenly realising that there might be something delicate inside if they made sure to put it in such a lovely box. They have also covered the contents with deep red silk. How very dramatic of them. It must be one hell of a mug. I pull carefully at the silk and let out a breath.

It is not a mug but two beautiful glass and steel daggers. The hilts are domed and inside the thin glass are different elements. The first dagger is full of water with tiny air bubbles settled at the top. The other makes me smile. The hilt is a terrarium. The very bottom is packed with tiny multicoloured rocks. The middle layer is thick brown dirt. The top layer is packed full of preserved tiny flowers.

I pick them both up, one in each hand. They are a perfect weight and a perfect fit in my palm. I give the water dagger a delicate spin around my fingers. Perfect indeed. I can easily see myself slicing and dicing through the training arenas with these. The gift feels strangely intimate, though. My strongest element has always been air, which is always all around me, and I had spent years making sure fire would never harm me. These were my two weakest elements out of the four.

I settle the daggers onto the bedspread next to me and root around in the box. There would be something else in there, a sticker of the school's crest or a small welcome card. Ah. The edge of thick stationery paper slices at my fingertip. I bring the cut to my lips and gently suck away the singular drop of blood. My other hand fumbles to find the card again and flip it over so I can read the swirling handwriting on the other side.

Happy birthday.

Presents two and three are on the way.

Sincerely,

Hal

My comments about missed birthdays have clearly hit a nerve with the crown prince. I should tell him that it was unnecessary and that I never expected any gifts from him. I should tell him I was only kidding, even about the chocolate. That would be the appropriate thing to do. I doubted that he would take these daggers back because of it.

"Ivy!" Harlan's voice booms through the door, followed by three quick pounds on the door.

"My goddess, Harlan," I call as I strut towards the door. I rip it open and tut at the pair I find there. Knox looks striking in a dark purple suit. It makes his hair look even brighter than before, and his eyes are somehow more cat-like. I half expect to find them slitted.

"How do you look prettier than me?" I demand of my best friend. His suit was an eye-catching forest green that, when paired with his auburn hair, made him look almost ethereal. His face has been shaved of all its stubble. I narrow my eyes slightly as I try to see if he has put mascara on.

"Lovely working-class genetics." Harlan purrs. He makes an impatient gesture that we have to go. I roll my eyes as I slowly close the door and fight back a grin as it takes me almost five seconds just to tap the lock rune located just under the handle.

As soon as I was done, Harlan threw his arm over my shoulder and practically dragged me down the corridors. Knox keeps pace with us, hands carelessly shoved into his trouser pockets and eyes scanning over the hall.

The tapestries that line the walls display parts of the school's history. Almost all of them involved a depiction of The Goddess or the pale blonde woman known as 'the founder.' Her real name had been lost to the ages. No amount of searching could get me any information on her. She was the woman who founded this Academy back during the great war. She could be a fae, or a vamp, or a witch. In all drawings, she was something different. No one could confirm who or what she really was.

I could not think of a worse fate. This woman had created the most prestigious Academy to ever exist, and now, not one of us knew her name. It had been written in books long lost or destroyed, and her title was used instead of her given name. The life span of the average species on this planet was 800 years old. That she was lost to time…

"Have you decided on your mentor yet, Whitlock?" Knox's voice cuts through my internal history lesson. I blink as if that's going to suddenly give me an answer to the question I had subconsciously been avoiding since lunch.

"Not yet. It's a big decision." I say slowly. "What are your options?"

"Ryder Terrance," Knox says as if it were obvious. It should have been. Ryder was the personal psychic to Althania Royalty. If Hal was offering to be a mentor, then it made sense for him to offer up Ryder as well.

"You'll pick Channing." Harlan scoffs at me as we turn a corner. The corridor widens, and a few other students, drenched in gym gear, pass us in the opposite direction. The group chortles once they are at the other end. I suddenly can't wait to be a second year, watching all the new students scramble around in fancy clothing, to turn to Harlan and say *remember when we were like that?*

"Oh, will I now?" I raise my eyebrows at him.

"It's what your mother would want you to do." Harlan points out.

"Oh. So you are just trying to goad me towards Hal now, hmm?"

"Not very subtly." Know drawls.

"Not very subtly." I agree.

"But did it work?" Harlan asks.

I open my mouth but hesitate in my answer. Channing would make a good mentor. He would make me phenomenal. The offer of mentorship from him was an honour. But Harlan was right.

He would have been my parent's choice. The mother approved the choice. The choice that Don would have made. *Go to Channing.* I loved my family, but a part of me yearned to make a different one.

"I'm going to pick Hal." I whisper as we get to the entrance hall. Knox nods once, which I think is approval. That's reassuring, at least. The flush of calm that runs over me causes my chin to tilt slightly higher in the air. I can see why all the royals have a psychic. Such a small decision being approved by one has set me at ease, and I am not in charge of a country.

"Ivy!" A high-pitched yell echoes around the stones. The three of us turn and find Proxima in a ruffled rouge dress, the matching lipstick making her look as if she had just finished drinking a colleague. "You look *so* pretty."

"Proxima. I love your dress!" I lie because it's always the polite thing to do at these things. The rest of the room finishes glancing around and turns their attention back to the large double doors or their own conversations.

"Thank you." Proxima gave a playful twirl showing that there was a large black bow on her back. I hold back a grimace. It suited her, but it was very cliché. Atticus shuffles after her, wearing a light blue suit. It was nothing spectacular, but he still looked nice.

"You look good too, Atticus." I smile. Atticus scratches the back of his head but smiles back awkwardly.

"Are you excited? This will be your first time in the castle, right?" Proxima speaks slowly, calmly, as if not to spook me. That calmness from before is quickly washed away with a flash of heat. I'm not sure if it's from embarrassment or anger. She was right. I had never stepped foot in Esker Castle, named due to its famous secret tunnels that are rumoured to flow through the entire mountain range. I had asked to once, back when I was in my adventurer phase. I wanted to pack a bag and live in the tunnels for a summer. I had been told I was too young for such a task. I had ended up never coming to Althania at all.

"Uh-huh." I nod.

"It's so gorgeous." Proxima continues. I have a feeling she didn't hear my answer. "It has an events hall that is full of mirrors! Such an amazing design idea. I adore it in there and in there, and I'm sure that you'll be shown it eventually, there is a secret exit to a side chamber where they host exclusive dinner parties."

Proxima loops her arm through mine and walks me towards the doors, effectively dragging me from Harlan's hold. I look back at him with wide eyes. He and Knox are trying not to laugh. I narrow my eyes at them.

Proxima quickly tugs me to the left, and an angel's feather barely misses my nose. I jolt back, facing forward. She dragged us both right into the centre of the other 25 students waiting for the mixer. Our progress has slowed, but she keeps moving forward with elbows pointed outward to help create room.

"You want to get into the front compartment. It has the best view. Atticus will make sure the other two can join us." Proxima whispers into my ear, shooting me a wink as she pulls back. My heart melts at how hard she is trying.

"How do you know all this stuff? You're a first-year, just like me." I whisper back, a sad attempt at trying for friendship. She latches onto it as if it were a lifeline.

"My father trained here. The happiest time of his life. He told me everything." Proxima says it so casually that I wonder if she knows how wrong that sounds. My father always described the happiest time of his life as his wedding ceremony to my mother, or the days me and Don were born. School never came into it. It was never even added onto the tail end of the conversation.

"That must have been nice." I say after a second.

"Your mother really never told you anything about her time here?" Proxima's tone is probing, trying to figure out if I am lying and, if I am, why.

"We talked about other things." I shrug. "Like how quickly Don would figure out I had switched his conditioner. If I could get a dog. Ball planning and ya know…that kind of stuff."

"Nothing about The Academy? Even when the prince visited you?"

I shake my head. The doors open as if waiting for my gesture, and I am saved from another conversation about Prince Hal. They will be coming in thick and fast soon enough. I want to take the normal moments, the simply Whitlock moments, and extend them for as long as I can.

Proxima lets out a sound that is almost a squeal and once again pulls us forward. The night air hits me, and I shudder. It's colder than it is at home, and a different, sharper smell wraps around us. There is no gentle floral rose scent or freshly cut grass. This place smells like iron. I take a deep breath of it and grin.

Proxima has somehow made it so we are leading the rest of the class. Well. She is. I'm just along for the ride here. I crane my neck back to look for Harlan. I see his ginger hair moving swiftly through the crowd towards us. Good.

Proxima is gentle as she twists me to the left and towards what looks like a small, well-kept shed. It's jet black with sleek metal doors that slowly slide open as we approach. They reveal a well-lit chamber leading down at a slight slope. I raise my eyebrows but keep my questions to myself. Proxima answers them anyway.

"The academy's private station is charmed to open only for students and staff. You can't get off the train here when the doors open if you aren't supposed to." Proxima takes a large step over the threshold with a giggle. I hear a scoff from behind us and turn my head to scowl. The angel that made that sound looks away quickly.

I look back at Proxima and playfully hop over the threshold as well, relinking our arms. I speed up slightly and shoot her a cocky side-eye grin. She grins back at me. I don't know if she means to speed up as much as she does, but suddenly, we are both racing each other down the slope. I hear our laughter mingling and echoing behind us towards the rest of the group.

A few seconds later, when Proxima has almost beaten me to the glass doors at the bottom, I hear two more sets of running footsteps. I don't turn to check who it is. The glass doors open too slowly for both of us to fit, so Proxima officially takes the win if these doors are at the finish line, and since they lead right onto the platform, it is. She slows down quickly as she approaches a bench.

Arms wrap around me from behind. I squeal as I am spun around in a circle. Harlan's aftershave almost chokes me. It's a new one, more masculine and earthy than his usual floral one. It reminds me more of…

I turn in his hold as a disbelieving laugh bursts from my throat. Proxima's explanation whips through my brain, but she has to be lying or mistaken because Dean was not a student and yet Dean is here. I am staring into his gorgeous green eyes. I am being held in his arms.

"Heya, gorgeous." He whispers. "Have enough time to miss me?"

"I had more than 5 seconds without you, so definitely." I quip back. In the back of my mind, I know that the platform is filling up around us. I know that Harlan is somewhere in the crowd. I know this moment can't last, and it will only get worse when I genuinely go a day without him. But I don't focus on that. I stay focused on him.

"Hmph." Dean makes an amused noise as he gently reaches up and twists a strand of my hair around his finger. His lips are twisted into a soft smile. It warms me to my very soul. How could I have ever agreed to leave him behind? To leave this feeling behind? He needed to stay. He needed to stay here with me.

Something clicks in my brain. Dean would be staying here. Dean would be staying here because Hal knew how I felt about him, and I was owed a present. He had done everything but gift wrap him for me.

A small part of me was offended on Dean's behalf. He was a person. He was not something that could be gifted to me. It felt so dangerously close to the slave trade that was shut down only a few decades ago. But the larger part of me knew that this was a symbolic gesture, that Dean would have come willingly, that it would have been a hassle for the prince to organise. This was not done with the *humans are lower* mindset.

This was done because of affection, because of love.

Our bubble is broken as a sleek metal train comes to a smooth stop at the platform. The doors open without a sound. They are the only reason I know the train's approach was equally silent, and I wasn't just lost in my boyfriend's eyes like a silly schoolgirl. Which, I remember with a grin as we step into the compartment, is exactly what I am.

Chapter Ten

Proxima cannot keep her eyes off Dean. I would usually be jealous (Goddess knows that Dean is the only reason I don't get on with Melinda, the maid back home), but she was studying him like a painting rather than something she wanted to jump on. Her eyes are slightly squinted, and her head moving ever so slightly back and forth.

Knox is paying more attention to Harlan as my friend goes into an exaggerated tale of how we met our newest ones. Atticus could not have cared less about Dean joining us. He was staring down the compartment, taking in the other students. Dean doesn't mind. He pulls me into his side, lounging back into the plush bench as if it was made for him.

"Does Don know you are here?" Harlan asks once he had finished his thrilling description of what his bathroom looks like.

Dean gives a helpless shrug. "I was through a portal to Althania five minutes after Ivy left mine this morning."

"You were?" I whisper. My mouth is so close to his ear that anything louder would have been unnecessary. "How long have you and Hal been planning this exactly?" I have a thousand more questions, but that one flies off my tongue.

"Channing." Dean corrects me. "Channing was the one that talked to me about it and sorted out an apartment for me in the city. It's a little further away from you than I'm used to being, but I'm sure I can cope with the twenty-minute commute."

"Only staff and students are allowed on the grounds outside of visitation days." Proxima points out. Her brow furrowed in confusion. I'd known her only for a few hours and already realised that Proxima was a fan of clarification. There would be no grey areas with her.

"I'm going to be staff," Dean tells her gently. "I'll be mostly in the training centres or doing admin stuff. It's a pay cut from the Whitlock estate." Dean gives me a playful squeeze.

"But they are paying all of my rent and bills, plus staff eat free just like you guys."

"What a deal." Atticus drawls sarcastically.

"Spot the spoilt rich kid." Knox sneers before me or Harlan get the chance. "Let me guess, Atticus. You always got what you wanted for winter solstice, and you're going to inherit at least a thousand acres when your daddy dies."

Atticus's cheeks slowly turn pink. His jaw was subtly moving as if he were gnawing on his tongue to avoid talking back. His eyes flick over to Proxima. Interesting.

"Well, it's nice that the academy looks after its staff as well as its students," Proxima says politically.

Thankfully, the train comes to a smooth stop only a second later. The station outside the windows looks almost identical to the academies. The lights are bright white, and the stones are light grey. It's as welcoming as a train station could be. The other students on the carriage (who I had no doubt were paying attention to our little group) slowly filtered out to the platform and then up the stairwell on the right.

Dean and I are the last off the train. I keep a tight hold of his hand even though I know it's almost completely unnecessary. He will not disappear if I stop touching him. This will not slowly disappear like a dream if I even slightly loosen my grip.

Harlan and Knox stay only an arm's width ahead of us. Atticus and Proxima have shot way ahead. I notice that Atticus has his arms hovering around her waist as if he is unsure if he is allowed to touch her but doesn't want anyone else to either. It almost makes me smile.

"This tunnel leads us straight into the castle," Dean whispers in my ear as we are roughly halfway up the slope.

"And how do you know that?" I smile back.

"Me and your uncle Channing are besties now." Dean declares proudly. "Told me all about how to get here. I also have a special map. I think he thinks I'm stupid."

"Don't call him that. It's not funny." I mutter. "It feels…" borderline cruel. Inaccurate. Something that may have been true in an alternate reality if there was a word for that.

"Okay. Just Channing it is." Dean agrees softly.

"I think his official title is Sir Channing."

Dean's head tilts back as he laughs. The sound echoes behind us. I slow my steps to try and revel in it. He never laughed like this when we were around other people. He couldn't. But tonight…tonight, he wasn't working. Tonight, he was in a nice suit. He was my date, and he would be treated as such.

If there was dancing, then we would dance together. When we are thirsty, they can drink together. We would leave at the same time and say goodbye to the same people. It sends a small thrill down my spine that we can do such normal things together now. There's a small part of me that is disgusted at how quickly I had become a lovestruck girl. The larger part of me quickly squashes it. I was lovestruck because I was in love and loved in return. There was nothing shameful or disgusting about that.

Crown Prince Hal of Althania should be disgusted with how much he had obviously spent on this party. It was supposed to be a simple academy mixer and yet two diamond chandeliers hung above us once we stepped through the tunnel. I assume there had been some revamping (no wordplay intended) so that the students would only be allowed in this specific hall.

Whether it was a hidden portal as we stepped through the doorframe or spectacular decorators that had transformed the space, it was impressive. Golden tables were littered around the back part of the hall, with ample space between them and piles of food and drink on top. The overall colour scheme of the decorations is black and red, which doesn't surprise me. They were the royal colours of Althania. The banners that hung from the dark wooden beams were beautiful and showed the academy's crest all in metal. I had a feeling that metal was also pure gold.

"Miss Acker! How good to have you back! The boys have missed you so much." An elderly angel, her wings almost as bent as her back with half of her grey feathers so thin they were almost see-through. Her smile lights up her heavily lined face. It breaks my heart to correct her.

"I'm sorry. I'm Ivy. Ivy Whitlock." I smile back at her, soft and polite. The angel searches my face as if she doesn't believe me.

Something around the top half of my face tells her I'm not who she thinks I am.

"Oh. I'm sorry, dear. You just look so much like Violet. Such a unique girl that one." The angel's smile turns sad. The world seems to slow down for a second. Acker was my mother's maiden name, but it was a common one among lower-born fae. Violet Acker was too on the nose.

"Violet Acker is my mother. She's now lady Whitlock of the fae." I tell the angel softly. Most people are happy at the information, happy that she had married up and gotten herself a happier slice of life. The happy, easy life that she deserved. But the angel's face dropped as if I had thrown a fireball at her.

"Oh no." The angel shook her head. "No, that's not right. Not my Violet. She wouldn't settle for that little fae lad."

My Violet. Little fae lad. There is a lot to unwrap there. For one, my father is well over six feet tall, and according to my grandmother, he had always been tall for his age. My mother had also never mentioned an angel when she briefly told us about her time in Althania. She would not have been close

enough to one to be lovelily claimed in such a
way.

"April." The voice that interrupts is gentle
and loving. It goes completely against
Channing's gruff exterior and yet fills me
with comfort. He has used that tone before.
He used it with me when I scraped my knees
falling in the woodlands back home. The
angel turns, and her smile somehow widens.
She reaches up to cup the werewolf's face.

"There you are, my boy. I was looking for
you." The angel tuts.

"I was just with the prince, April. I'm sorry I
kept you waiting." Channing's smile matches
the angel's, but it doesn't reach his eyes.
Those dark eyes are swirling with a
completely different emotion. I feel my heart
slowly rise to my throat and start to choke
me.

The angel is so old that her mind can no
longer hold it all in. I had never seen it
happen to someone, not personally. I hope,
like I know my parents do, that when the time
comes, I would rather die than be stuck inside
my own mind.

"Well, as long as you are here now." The angel pats his face twice before turning back to me. "Violet here is still too thin. You all train too much but eat too little at that academy." April pinches my arm and shakes her head in disapproval. I feel Dean shift on my other side.

"Come on now." April starts to wave towards a table. "Same rules as always. No dancing until I see you eat at least two sandwiches." She presses her hand against my back and tries to shove me along. It's a weak attempt. I loop my arm through hers and try to mimic my mother. It shouldn't be hard. I have been around her every day of my seventeen years.

"Of course, April." I agree as I help her along. People move out of our way, but I don't look at anyone's face. I don't care if they are students or teachers. All I care about is getting April to a table and setting her down on one of the chairs. They are a little high, and I would have to help her up, but it would be better than her standing all night.

"Doesn't our prince look handsome, hmm?" April's eyes are on the front of the room as she shuffles next to me. I nod without looking. She doesn't appreciate it and scoffs before gesturing at him. My lips twitch into a smile as we reach the table. I pull out the chair and gesture for her hand, but Channing and Dean have already flanked her. April rolls her eyes but allows them to help.

I finally look over at Hal and agree with April. Hal looks more princely than I have ever seen him, and all of my memories involve him in fancy clothes.

He is finally wearing a crown, a thick band of gold embedded with star-shaped rubies. His tunic is jet black and embroidered with blood-red thread. I can't quite make out the pattern of it, but I imagine it has something to do with Althanian history. It might be the family motto, although I forgot what his was. He is surveying the room so slowly that I briefly wonder if he is trying to read everyone's thoughts.

"See?" April says smugly.

"Yes, April." I smile, forgetting for a moment that I am pretending to be my mother. I reach for the decanter of wine in the centre of the table and pour it generously into four goblets. I hand two of them to Channing and Dean. Dean takes a large gulp of his immediately.

"Thank you." Channing breathes. He doesn't so much as sip from it.

"You're welcome," I tell him as I hand the other glass to April. The angel picks up the goblet with both hands and grins like a child.

"There you are!" A voice yells from behind us. Dean takes another gulp as Proxima, Atticus, Knox and Harlan join us.

"We turned around, and you were gone!" Harlan threw his arm over my shoulder. The wine glass shifts in my hand, and drops spill over my fingers. I scowl and start to suck the dark red droplets from my skin. Harlan plucks the goblet from my fingers instead and takes a sip. I roll my eyes.

"Channing, Channing, who are these people?" April's voice shakes as she reaches over for Channing's hand. Channing quickly takes it and, despite being a highly decorated warrior and royal advisor, freezes in his response.

"These are my friends from the academy, April," I say slowly, reaching out to take her other hand with a smile. "They can be a little loud, but they are nice. I promise."

"Not too nice, I hope, or you will end up eating them alive." April's eyes twinkle as she grips my hand tightly. I grin wickedly back at her. April looks pointedly between my face and the sandwiches on the platter in front of me. I chuckle and release her hand so I can make a show of biting into one. April nods her approval.

"Sir Channing." Proxima bows her head at the werewolf. The other three that came with her quickly followed suit. Channing smiles at them all before focusing back on April. A flash of something runs across Proxima's face. As the song changes, I see the opportunity to make everyone a little more comfortable.

"You guys should go dance. I'll stay here." I tell them all.

"You don't want to dance at a royal ball?" Harlan raises his eyebrows at me.

"It's an academy mixer, and I have only had one sandwich." I shrug in a what-can-you-do gesture. Harlan's brow furrows in confusion, but Knox places his hand on his arm and gently leads him away. Proxima and Atticus take each other's hand to join in on the waltz.

My eyes flit over to Dean with an apologetic smile. He still has the coin, or I would slip it over to him. I find him looking at me with such softness only my Dean could convey it properly. He understood why I was sacrificing our dancing to stay with April. He didn't need me to verbalise it.

It was two and a half songs before Hal joined us. Dean had settled himself in the seat next to me and was charming April in between picking at the fruit selection. Channing stayed by April's side and left his hand on the table for her to pat or grab if she needed to. Every time she called me Violet, he would shoot me a sad smile.

"Hello, April." Hal appears in the space between Dean and the angel. April cranes her neck to look up at the prince and beams.

"Your Highness," April says adoringly. "Have you eaten? I've made sure Violet has. Channing claims he had dinner before he arrived." April shoots Channing an unimpressed look.

"You know my diet, April." Channing shrugs helplessly.

"Yes, yes, yes." April waves him off. "All that meat is very filling, I'm sure. Just remember how embarrassing it will be for Violet if, mid-dance, her partner feints. If you won't eat for me, then eat for her."

"I've eaten April. I promise, and I am sure that Channing is being honest and has eaten as well." Hal tells her slowly. Dean slides himself off the chair, and Hal takes it with a grateful smile in his direction.

April shoots me a look as if to ask if I really believed either of them. It reminds me so much of the one my mother gives my father when the boys are clearly lying. Nervous laughter bursts from my throat. April is so similar to her, but I'm not sure if it is based on basic mothering instincts or if my mother had somehow integrated some of April into her during her years here.

She had clearly lied to me and Don about those years. The betrayal leaves a bitter taste in my mouth. April had been important to Channing and Hal and to my mother. Channing and Hal were clearly more important than we were allowed to believe. My mother had been more important than I had been allowed to believe.

Hal's attention turns to me, and the smile falls from my face. Hal and Channing would know why she wanted to lie to me. Out of the two, Hal would be the weakest link there. My mother wanted me to go to Channing when I had an issue, so it made sense that their cover story would be the most airtight. Hal had tried the hardest to speak to me these past few months, sending multiple letters and care packages. He wanted me to go back to calling him 'Uncle Hal' and had reassured me I would get to live in Althania. I could stroke his ego and get all of my answers before the end of the night if I was clever enough.

"Unc-Hal." I pretend to catch the phrase so as not to confuse April. I look up at Hal through my lashes and find him fighting back a smile. "Would you like to dance? I've had my two sandwiches."

"I would be honoured," Hal tells me softly, taking long strides to my side of the table and offering his hand. I take it and shoot Dean a reassuring smile.

"You are next," I promise. "Unless Channing wants a spin."

"I can be third," Channing tells me. April looks between all of us, hiding her smile behind her hands. Her eyes catch on me, then Hal, and she gasps. Hal starts to lead me away, but not before I hear her whisper to Channing. "Little cub?"

Chapter Eleven

"I am sorry if April upset you," Hal tells me as soon as we are out of earshot. He gently spins me into his hold. People have made a space for us. Some are outright staring.

"Not at all." I shake my head as we begin to move. Hal is an exceptional dancer. I suppose he would have to be with the overwhelming number of mixers, feasts and balls that he has attended in his long life. "She's sweet. I just…I never knew about her. My mother never mentioned her."

A bubble of anger threatens to burst in my stomach. That sweet Angel over there who was so worried about 'Violet' eating sandwiches and being embarrassed while dancing had never once been mentioned in the Whitlock household. Violet had never bothered to so much as mutter her name.

"April adored Violet," Hal says softly after gently twirling me. "When we were preparing for the Vilerian games, your mother and Channing both lived here in the castle. It was best for our training and our strategies. April worked in the castle and now lives here as my guest. I can't - I won't put her in one of those homes. I won't leave her alone like that."

It surprises me how little pushing that took. It crosses my mind that Hal might be lonely. Lonely men have loose mouths. He had no children or spouse. He didn't even have the rumours of an engagement around him. All he had was Channing, the soldier, and Alice, the angel, who only remembers things from almost two centuries ago.

"My mother never mentioned her. Not once." I can't hold back the rage in my voice, although I instantly regret it.

"No. No, I doubt she mentions any of us. Violet loved it while she was here, but after she left…It became too hard for her. In her letters, she always asked after Alice. She sent her letters directly before Alice's condition got too bad. She does care, Ivy. I promise." Hal cuts right to the thing that terrifies me, right to the realisation that my mother could easily put parts of her life into a box and shove them into the back of a mental closet without a second glance.

"Alice called me little cub just now. I know Channing used to call me that back when I was little." I pause so he can dip me. He answers the question I didn't have a chance to ask.

"Violet sent us pictures of her life. Pictures of you and your brother. I think Alice even has them on display in her room." The song comes to an end. Hal's grip on my hands slackens, but I do not let go.

"One more?" I ask with a coy smile. Hal chuckles but gets back into position. He starts to lead me around the room in slow circles. People move as if we have a bubble around us. No one comes too close.

"You really think she loved it here?" I whisper. "She left so quickly. She didn't even finish the games."

"She picked your father." Hal's answer is too clean and too instant. It's practised. "He needed to go back to Parlitan, and she followed him. She hated to do it, but it was what was best for her. She put her love for him above her love for fighting."

"You make it sound so noble. She was going to be a part of the Vilerian guard. She would have ensured peace across the world and protected its leaders." I am aware that I sound like a recruitment pamphlet for the cause.

The Vilerian guards are the most elite warriors in existence. They protect the royal families and, in turn, ensure their designated country stays safe, fed, and healthy. They have the power to overturn a royal decision, too, if enough of their legion vote. A thought crosses my mind, and I can't stop myself from blurting it out.

"She could have been a part of your guard. If she had stayed, then she could have been at your side for centuries. Yours and Channing's." My mother had given up a chance to stay here and followed a boy halfway across the world.

"And instead, you could be." Hal looks me in the eye as he says it. I feel my lips turn up into a sly grin.

"You would pick me for the Althanian legion?" I raise my eyebrows. We have stopped dancing properly now, simply swaying back and forth.

"Unless you would rather go somewhere else?" Hal raises his eyebrows back at me.

"It's a big decision. It's…"

"Every moment of the rest of your life."
Hal's smile twitches. "Luckily, you have
three years to make it."

The second song comes to an end, but this
time, I have no chance to keep a hold of Hal's
hands. Hal leads me over to a waiting Dean
and then bows to me respectfully and deeply.
It's such a mockery of how this should be
that I laugh and continue laughing even as
people around me gasp and mutter about my
rudeness. Hal looks up at me from his still
bowed position, and the Crown Prince of
Althania's laugh echoes with mine around the
hall.

Chapter Twelve

Classes the next day are particularly rough. I'm not sure which is more to blame: the hangover from all the wine I drank at the mixer or the awkward silence between me and my classmates after I ignored them the whole evening. I'm not particularly angry about either choice.

I came out of that mixer on my human boyfriend's arm, drunk and giddy because I had finally started to understand my mother's choice 172 years ago.

Harlan was my saving grace in *elemental theory*. He fielded basic questions from the tutor, so I didn't have to speak around my severely dry mouth. Yes, I knew that all creatures except humans had a connection to the elements. Yes, I knew that Vampires had a stronger connection to the Earth due to the iron in it. Yes, I knew that witches had the second strongest connection to the elements and the fae had the greatest. There was no need for me to say that out loud for an hour straight.

Lawful ethics and social responsibilities were next, and I said a silent prayer to the goddess that I was born a noble because the introduction to the course was full of basic things I had learnt before I had hit double digits. *Historical Strategy* had simply outlined the rest of the course. Then, finally, it was lunch.

I throw myself down on an empty chair, groaning at the clashing sound my lunch tray makes as it hits the metal tabletop. Harlen laughs and then winces at how loud his voice sounds, even to his own ears. He is in a better position than I am, but he is not as unaffected as he wants me to think.

"We may have messed up," I tell him. My voice is gravelly, and I take a long slurp of my juice.

"Shut up and eat. We have combat training all afternoon." Harlen moans. I prod my fork into my pasta and then squint suspiciously at one of the prawns. I'm not sure if I should eat or hold out until dinner. My stomach rumbles, but the idea of chewing anything makes me almost gag. Eating is the best cure for a hangover…

I take a tentative bite. The chef here is good, but the noodles are still too greasy, and I have to force myself to swallow them. Harlan mirrors me, taking small bites of his panini. We don't talk again until the rest of the group arrives. Proxima has an almost raw steak. The blood glistens under the fluorescent lights. I have to look away as the prawns squirm in my stomach.

Atticus shoots a disgusted glance at my seafood before digging into his burger with vigour.

Knox ignores all of us as he twirls his own noodles around his fork. There is no sarcastic comment about us having the same meal. He doesn't even say hello. He sat with us out of pure convenience- we wouldn't force him to speak to us.

I decided after forcing down another bite that I would be nicknaming him something feline-based. If he wanted to act as petty as a housecat, then I would refer to him as one.

The hall around us grew louder as various years all settled in. It's easy to tell us the first years are apart from the rest. We are noisier, shuffling around and trying to find our place around the more seasoned students. We walked around in groups, pairs at a minimum, whereas final years were strutting around all by themselves.

One particular strutting figure catches my eye. Channing twists and turns around the students, but he is making a beeline towards us. I pause mid-bite and then wash down the mouthful with the last of my juice. This can't be good.

After I had drunkenly scampered back to Dean's apartment in the city centre after the mixer, I logged onto the school system and officially declared Hal as my mentor. Channing had no reason to be on Academy grounds.

Proxima straightens as soon as she catches sight of him. My stomach churns, but it has nothing to do with my hangover. Had Channing offered to be her mentor, too? I didn't think I would get jealous of Channing, of all people. I had expected to be jealous of Harlen and all the new friends he would undoubtedly make. I expected to be jealous of Valentina and her years of experience in Althania. She would know all the best places to go, and Harlen would find people he wanted to hang out with instead of me. Channing…

Channing would have made me a better fighter. That is a fact. He would have taught me new techniques. He would have made me physically stronger.

Hal would make me the better Vilerian guard. He would help me with my magic and my mentality. I could always do weight training and go on runs later. I would just need to be good enough to pass the physical exams. It was the written and oral exams that people failed. They came off as too eager or too biased and were not allowed to continue. Psychology would not be my downfall. A mind-reading prince was the perfect teacher for that.

"Sir Channing." Proxima ducks her head so low she almost headbutts her steak. Interesting. What exactly did I miss- or forget- from the ball last night?

"Proxima." Channing politely smiles. He then looks at me. My brain starts to play a grainy slice of memory from last night to try and prod me along.

I was dancing in Dean's arms and then being handed over to Channing. Channing had asked me if I could keep a secret and then let sip that the academy would host the Vilerian games this year, something it hadn't done since my mother was a student. I asked how long I would have to keep the secret, meaning how long I would have this edge. Channing had laughed and told me it would be announced at midnight. The rest of the memory refuses to play, buffering in the back of my mind. It hasn't helped me realise why he is here. Would it be his job to oversee that sort of thing?

"Channing." I greet him with a soft smile. Harlan and Knox mimic me, whereas Atticus just grunts around his mouthful. Channing smiles at them before turning his full attention to me.

"The prince cannot make it to your training course this afternoon. He has sent me to monitor you instead, if that's alright." Channing's voice is soft, but it is clearly not an actual question. It has to be alright, or I would be the only first-year in that class without a mentor.

It wouldn't be noticeable at first- most students would share a mentor with a few others. But when it came to the end of the first part of the session, and the mentors came over to start to correct us and point out our weak spots, I would have no one if I turned Channing away. It feels so much like a child waiting for their parent only to get the nanny instead.

"Of course. That's better for me, actually." I tell him as I gently spin my fork around on my plate. "Little cub has some serious claws, ya know," The sad attempt at a joke is not wasted. Channing lets out a chuckle.

He looks younger when he laughs. It might be the slight second of shock that crosses his face as he does it or the way his eyes crinkle. He is almost two hundred years old but physically is the same as my mother, frozen around twenty-five. The laugh transforms him back to his late teens.

Still, he looks out of place sitting here next to us. He almost has a barrier around him of his own making. It wasn't the sheer power that radiated off of him, although I had no doubts he could beat everyone in this hall blindfolded and at the same time.

Channing purposefully made himself look dissatisfied with the world to the point where he looked angry at his own sheer existence. It was angsty but effective. If the werewolf hadn't once put my hair in pigtails for me, I'm sure I would be as skittish around him as Atticus was. The mermaid keeps glancing out of the corner of his eye at him, waiting for him to leave.

Proxima shoots me a confused look, but I ignore it. I can explain what a nickname is to her later.

"Make sure to eat," Channing tells us unnecessarily. I make a point of taking an extra-large bite of my pasta as he gets up to leave. Once Channing's retreating back has slipped out of the hall's doors, I turn my attention back to the table and find Knox holding back a laugh.

"What?" I demand.

His response is a cackle.

"What?" I repeat. This time, I turn to look at Harlan to see if he knows what I've done, which is so side-splitting and hilarious. Harlan's hungry eyes are latched onto Knox's mouth, watching as it splits into a toothy grin. Oh, goddess.

Chapter Thirteen

I found out what Knox found so hilarious earlier as a prick of an Angel called Ryle knocks me on my ass for the third time in fifteen minutes. I assume that's what it was, anyway. Knox said he doesn't see 'exact' visions, but he could be lying. He could also have just enjoyed 'seeing' a rich girl get knocked around a little.

Ryle doesn't have the decency to help me up to my feet after the kick to my abdomen that winded me. I scowl up at him as I push myself up into a crouch. My breath is coming out in wheezes, and I can taste the sharp tang of blood filling my mouth.

"Time!" Channing calls from his stance on the outside of our small chalk circle. The training hall we are in has a dozen or so spread out across it. Knox and Harlan are wrestling in one behind me. Atticus is standing over a shifter girl to my left.

Proxima is somewhere on the other side of the hall.

Ryle grunts and steps over to his own mentor, who just so happens to be Celeste. I can't help but think that this pairing wasn't an accident. I glare at him as he smugly takes a tiny sip from his water bottle. He is far stronger than he looks. He isn't exactly skin and bones, but each of his punches feels like a sledgehammer, and a glance down at his fingers shows they are thin and nimble.

"Deep breaths," Channing whispers as he takes a sidestep to block my view of my opponent. "How's your rib?"

"Fine." I lie and quickly drop my arm from where it is cradling my left side.

"It's your first fight on your first day. I didn't expect you to win straight away." Channing starts to gently examine my wrists, hands, shoulder, and everything he has seen me land on.

I grunt instead of an actual response. My mother would have chastised me for that, but she isn't here. Not physically, anyway. The memory and legacy that she has left behind seem to suffocate me with every move I make in this room. Violet Acker would not have lost. Violet Acker would have lasted longer on her feet.

"You fight with honour." Channing continues. "You fight as if everyone will be following those rules. We don't. Not during training and not after graduation."

"This is the only way I know how to fight." I bristle. "This is the only way I've been taught. Isn't it your job to teach me the others?"

"You are missing my point, Ivy." Channing prods at my wrist. He keeps his eyes on my face to check for a wince or grimace of pain. I do not give him one even though it stings. "Your technique works. You know *how* to hit him. You are just holding yourself back to be polite."

I open my mouth to argue that there is nothing polite about this but stop at the look in his eye. Those dark orbs are silently begging me to figure out what he means. I glance over his shoulder at Celeste, who is smiling as she whispers instructions to Ryle. The angel snaps his head to look at me and smirks. His wings twitch as he rolls his shoulders to prepare for the next round.

"You said that you had claws, little cub. Use them." Channing drops my hand and steps out of the circle. He shoots Celeste a nod that we are ready to continue. Celeste slaps her hand against Ryle's back to send him back into the circle. I snort. Ryle scowls at me.

"You first." His voice is deep and rumbly, a contrast to his delicate face. He would be quite attractive if he hadn't made a habit of attacking my ribs.

"Aren't you kind?" I ask sarcastically, flexing my fingers. He looks down at them. The last two times, I had gone in with a punch. It makes sense he thinks I'm going to do it again. I'm not.

I didn't like how Channing described my fighting as *polite*. I was fighting Ryle the same way I would fight Mav or Don or Corvus back home. They had come away from those fights with bruises but no serious damage. I didn't want to cause them serious damage. I had no such connection to Ryle. He wasn't my family or my friend. He was someone that wanted to knock me down.

I keep my eyes on Ryle's face as I fake a lunge forward. I throw my arm up only halfway to block the punch I know is already coming. It's been his first move in the last two rounds. Those times, I would then aim my other hand toward his neck or eyes. This time, I spin myself around so we are side by side and smash my foot down on his ankle.

An angel's balance comes mostly from its wings. They have to learn to counter their extra weight. It's why younger angels sometimes hold themselves at a slant. Their bodies are still growing and shifting, so the wings are sometimes a little too big for their tiny humanoid bodies. In a fight, balance is everything. So, it stands to reason that in a fight like this, balance will be his downfall.

Ryle roars in pain as something pops. He shifts his leg and half stumbles. I don't give him a chance to recover. I slide under his wing and grab the bone that curves just before the wings join into his back. Ryle was shocked, still in my grip. I won't break it. I'm not a monster. I'm a winner.

"Sorry." I breathe just as I use his wingbone to throw him from the circle. As soon as I tug him to the side, his whole body follows. It can't help it. It's either 'follow the wing' or 'lose it completely'.

Ryle collapses in a heap just outside of the boundary. I stare down at him, breathing hard. It took a lot of strength to move him so quickly. He stares back up at me, splayed on the ground with his teeth pulled back in a sneer.

I offer him my hand so that I can help him up. He ignores it as his face turns red. There goes the idea of making friends.

"Channing!" Celeste belts from behind us.

"Yes?" Channing replies innocently. His arms are crossed across his chest with a look of fake bewilderment on his face.

"You know you are not allowed to interfere today." Celeste grinds the words out as if it pains her not to say more.

"I have no idea what you are talking about, Celeste. I checked, and she was okay to carry on." Channing turns his attention back to me and grins. "She was."

"You expect me to believe that it was her idea to go straight for his wings?" Celeste places her hands on her hips. I realise the hall is nearly silent. There are no grunts or groans as blows land. I glance over and find the entire hall staring at the miniature showdown happening between Celeste and Channing. Harlan is engrossed in it, playing with the edges of his now torn shirt as he stares at Channing.

"It was." Channing's grin turns wicked. "She is her mother's daughter, after all."

"Apparently so." Celeste's face contorts into disgust for the briefest second before she puts on the mask of a calm and concerned mentor. She makes her way over to Ryle and kneels down to examine his wing. Ryle somehow looks even more uncomfortable than before. I smile apologetically at him, and this time, I get a smile in response.

Chapter Fourteen

"She was amazing," Harlan tells Dean as I sip curiously at the bright yellow froth he had placed in front of me. He said it was some kind of cocktail, but it barely looked edible. It fizzed deliciously across my tongue. Knox smiles at me before sucking down his own. I notice that Harlan has gotten all of us the exact same. If I had to guess, I would say it was due to a suggestion from the psychic in front of me. Harlan was a sucker when he caught feelings for someone.

"I know." Dean laughs, wrapping his arm across my shoulders. "The story spread even to us lowly servants. *Violet Acker's daughter* this and *Violet Acker's daughter* that. It's a good thing your father is so secure. It sounds like, in Althania, men are the ones who take the backseat."

"Don't say things like that." I tut at him. I'm referring to both the servant comment and my parent's marriage. My mother may be happy taking a step back into a more traditional women's role, but I wouldn't be. Ever. Dean said it almost disdainfully, as if the people that knew my mother over a century ago should only refer to her by her husband's name. It makes my skin prickle uncomfortably where our bodies meet.

"Violet was the first female fae to ever be allowed in the most prestigious academy in the world. It's quite a legacy Ivy has to uphold." Harlen plays the middleman between us. A role he has played effortlessly since the first bumbling embraces Dean and I had shared.

Knox lets out a chortle. Another flash of discomfort runs through me, but this time, it is at how quickly I find it endearing. Knox's random spasms of laughter do not scare me like they clearly scare Dean. If Knox knew anything truly bad was going to happen, then he would not be laughing. It was probably the only concrete thing I knew about him after meeting him yesterday.

"See me fall on my ass again?" I ask.

"Something like that." Knox nods.

"Can't wait to experience it."

Dean and Harlan watched us like a tennis match, heads snapping to whoever was speaking.

"You don't even know what it is." Knox points out.

"Neither do you really," I smirk.

"Touché."

"It is reassuring that I have a future, though. I was painfully worried this drink would kill me." I stirred the drink and finally saw some liquid through the thick fuzz spilling down the sides of the glass.

"Not that one." Knox jokes as he wiggles his eyebrows. Dean is the only one not to laugh at him.

My boyfriend's eyes are focused somewhere else entirely. We all slowly turn our attention to whatever has caught his. I think for a brief second that maybe Knox was right with his unspoken assumptions about me because as soon as I see the human girl that Dean is looking at, my thoughts become cruel, horrid thoughts spilling into focus as quickly as a snake striking.

She's clearly not looked in a mirror in a few hours. Her hands and wrists are dirty, nails ripped down to the nib. She sees us all looking and shoots Dean a sarcastic little wave. He shuffles back into his seat and faces Harlan once again.

"Friend of yours?" Harlan asks bluntly.

"She works at the academy. Maid." Dean grunts out his answer.

"Maid? But her hands are filthy." I frown.

"Or gardener. I wasn't really paying attention. I was a little focused on getting back to you." Dean runs his hand over the back of my own, and like a cliché little girl, I melt into his touch. I nuzzle further into his side and smile.

"Aren't you two just adorable?" Knox drawls before taking a noisy slurp from his own glass. "I thought Proxima was going to have a fit when you danced at the mixer."

"Not as much as the fit she was having at the dance with Prince Hal." Harlan laughs. "She looked like she was going to die right there when he asked her to dance."

"It was sweet." I chastise him. "She was nervous. He *is* a prince, and it is very daunting to suddenly have his attention when you aren't expecting it."

"You dealt with it fine." Dean points out.

"She is the daughter of Violet Acker." Knox rolls his eyes. The boy must have an intense need to see what the back of his skull looks like. "She is lucky the entire Althanian royal family didn't swoop down to take a look at her."

"Prince Hal is the head of the Althanian Royal family." I bristle before adding a muttered, "Technically."

"Only because his parents passed it down early, once the prince had stepped down from participating in the Vilerian games." Knox said in a singsong voice, smirking at me as he did so. "Once your mother and Sir Channing convinced him to step down and sacrifice their own victories."

"That's not what happened." I almost snarl. "My father had to leave the academy to take over our lands, and my mother went with him. It had nothing to do with Hal."

"Your mother stepped down from what would have been a spectacular victory that could provide her with any position she wanted in the entirety of Vileria for the opportunity to be a housewife?" Knox raised his eyebrows.

"She became Lady Violet Whitlock of the fae." Harlan's voice is ice cold. "She is not *just* a housewife, and even if she was, she deserves your respect."

If Knox is shocked at Harlan's change in demeanour, it doesn't show on his face. Instead, he looks my friend up and down slowly, decides he isn't worth a comment, and then turns his attention back to me. I push myself out of Dean's arms.

"You don't have a lot of friends back home. Do you?" I ask him. His eyes flare quickly before his face sets in his usual disinterest. He hadn't been expecting that response. I press on.

"You like to push people's buttons, and you realised very quickly that my mother is one of mine. You want to see how much people will put up with you because you're you, and you have the unfortunate luck of having a guaranteed future in the public eye. You're an oracle. People are always going to need you, but I don't think that you want anyone to want you when it comes down to graduation. I don't need to know why, but you need to back off. I don't care if you're an oracle. I care that you're funny and you're nice to Dean. You keep being a dick, and we will not be friends anymore. Understood?"

"That didn't take you long." Knox responds after a long pause.

"What didn't?" I ask.

"Deciding we were friends." Knox's voice hitches on that last word. None of us comment on it. Instead, I make a big show of picking up my half-empty glass, clinking it against his, and taking a slow sip. Knox grins, causing crinkles to form around his unusual eyes.

"To friends." Harlan taps his glass against Dean's. The two boys smile cheekily at each other before tapping their glasses against Knox's at the same time.

"You're going to love the Whitlock solstice balls," Dean tells the oracle. "Although maybe you shouldn't be allowed to play poker with us. Not for real money. Maybe just the candy coins."

Knox's responding laugh echoes across the bar, loud enough that the human girl turns to look at us once again.

Chapter Fifteen

My first mentor session was in an hour, and yet the room number was still missing from my timetable. My dorm master, Miss Pope, had assured me that it would appear once a room was decided. She had also very unsubtly implied that the reason behind the delay was the high-profile nature of my mentor. I briefly wondered on the short walk back to my room if choosing Channing may have been the truly convenient route. Hal had not been to a training session all week.

Someone knocks on my door three times, sharp and straight-to-the-point knocks. I scramble from the bed, throwing my open books and highlighters to the side. I was dressed in smart casual clothes, all black but comfortable. I had no idea what mentoring meant or if it would involve sitting down or extra training. Knowing Hal, it could just be an informal chat where he checks if I like everything so far.

When I open the door, it is a familiar face staring back at me, but this is the first time we have met. Ryder Terrance is the Althanian royal council-appointed oracle and has been for as long as I have been alive. His eyes are the same unnatural yellow as Knox's.

When I was younger, I wondered why yellow was the wolf's recognised colour when it came to official species identification and not the oracles. My father had told me that oracles had no recognised colour as their services belonged to all. It sounded so heartbreakingly similar to what some people said about humans that I never asked about it again.

Where Knox's hair was deep purple, Ryder had none. The bald man did, however, have the same bored expression that Knox always wore, even as he looked me over. He was wearing a dark, expensive-looking suit with the Althanian royal symbol displayed proudly on his chest.

The cross-stitched mountains with a blood-red sky draw the eye more than the gentle blue waves of the Parlitan crest. Our lands are known for their large lakes and closeness to the oceans. Only a thin strand of mermaid land stopped us from claiming the shores as our own.

"Our prince was right. You bear an extraordinary resemblance to your mother." Ryder greets me. His voice is as smooth as it was when he was on a screen when he was involved in the press conferences from the palace.

"Thank you," I say softly, my hand still holding onto my door handle.

"You took that as a compliment. Good. It was meant as one." Ryder glances behind me, trying to see inside my room. I block his view out of instinct. He smiles slightly.

"I'm afraid I am unsure of why a royal oracle would stop by my rooms without a meeting scheduled." I saw slowly. "Or what they would be after."

"I have come for Knox Dalloway. His Royal Highness requested that I pick you up at the same time. Your mentoring session will be at the palace today." Ryder looks me over once more, taking in what I am wearing and adding, "In the prince's private library."

"I'll be ready in five minutes?" The statement comes out as more of a question.

"The main entrance in ten." Ryder tells me, tilting his head down slightly before leaving. I look down at my feet, where his eyes had last been looking, and decide to shine my boots in those extra five minutes.

Once my shoes are shining, an extra notebook is shoved into my mini backpack, and my hair is rebrushed. I move quickly down the corridors to the main entrance. For some reason, it had never occurred to me that Hal would need me to meet him in the palace at any point.

The mixer had been at the palace, but we had been surrounded by people, official people with high-security access and guards to remind everyone that this was the powerhouse of the country. That had been the first night of a whole new class, a show of glitz and glamour before the hard work began.

I had only been to the Parlitan palace a handful of times, and even then, it was to the grounds and conservatories rather than inside. Never had the fae monarchs been home or available for an audience. I had certainly never been in its prince's private library. I didn't even know if Prince Atlas had one.

Knox and Ryder are waiting for me by the large entrance doors. They are three minutes early. Maybe they knew I would be early as well. Maybe they had been standing there for the entire time, and I should have come down in the five minutes I had initially suggested.

"Miss Whitlock," Ryder greets me again as he pushes open those doors and reveals a weak sunlight shining down onto the academy's front courtyard. Parked right at the bottom of the stone steps is a gleaming black limousine flying two small Althanian flags. The windows are tinted so no one can see inside.

Ryder leads us to the car and opens the back doors for us. I am surprised at the disappointment that fills me when I see no one is waiting inside. Knox gestures for me to go first, and I clamber in, huddling against the furthest window to give him plenty of room. He presses his lips together to stop from smiling as he follows me.

Ryder gets into the front passenger seat. There is a clear barrier between the front and back, but he does not raise it. Instead, he instructs the driver to go and tunes the radio to the local news station.

There is no major incident that he would need an update on, but the annual discussion between Siconia and Calent to ensure that the witches would have access to the sacred lake for their winter rituals was always interesting. The Succubus royals usually used it as an excuse to further themselves, as any of the royals would if their land had such a vital landmark for another country's stability.

Last year, they had offered the witches access to the lake in exchange for cheaper lumber from Calent's dense woodland. Their trees made the nicest furniture in the whole of Vileria, as well as items with the greatest magical impact. The very soil of Calent was brimming with magic due to all the witches that had lived and died in its forests. Their covens lived in elaborate houses built into the trunks. Their royals lived in a castle made of that wood. I had never heard of that castle ever being breached, even back during the first demon wars.

"Did you see Harlan last night?" Knox's question is a blunt whisper. Ryder doesn't even twitch in our direction, but Knox's eyes remain on the older psychic.

"No." I frown. I hadn't seen Harlan outside of class since the bar two days ago when

Dean and I had left Knox and Harlan there and headed to his apartment for the night instead. Harlan had been his usual chatty self during class yesterday, the only slightly odd behaviour being how quickly he ran back to his room after our final class. I assumed he had something pressing to finish.

"Oh. I thought he mentioned he was coming to see you." Knox mutters before turning to look out the darkened window. If Harlan ever needed me as a cover story, then he told me. He hadn't even given me a tiny vague hint of a warning that he would need me to lie for him, and yet guilt flooded me.

"I wasn't in my rooms last night." I lie quickly. "He might have tried and couldn't find me."

Knox doesn't respond at all, not verbally or with a grunt. He continues to stare out the window until the limousine pulls up to our destination. Ryder opens the door for me once again. I smile politely as I climb out and stare up at the looming towers of the Althanian Palace. As I take that sight in, I decide it is more of a castle than a palace, too tall and too ancient of a style to be called anything else.

The stone is a light grey that is almost a perfect match for the sky. It looks as if it were carved out of the mountain rock that Althania was so famous for. The most peculiar part of the design was that only half of the windows had any glass in them, stained red and black designs. From down here, I could not figure out what any of them are. It is a stark contrast from the warm inside interior I know is there after the mixer.

The outside makes the castle look menacing and terrifying as if Hal would crawl out of one of those empty windows and down the spires to come and feast on young children.

Ryder leads us inside, and I am right. The second we step through those large, dark-stained oak doors and into the castle, the candelabras and torches on the wall all spark to life. Their flames flood the space with an instant warmth and welcoming yellow light. I look at the art proudly displayed along the walls as Ryder walks straight ahead through a doorway.

This castle didn't like windows or doors, just like the Tulinth palace, if their press conferences were to be believed. For them, it made sense. Their royals had large wings and a penchant for flying.

This castle also loved a heavy red, gold and grey colour scheme. The frames of the portraits are dark gold, worn down over the centuries, for they have been hanging there. The chairs are upholstered in a plush maroon fabric, and the entire place has been decorated to emphasise the stone the castle has been carved from. It is rustic and dark and beautiful in a raw way.

"You will both be studying in the prince's private library today," Ryder calls back to us. Knox baulks, stumbling over his own feet as he stares at the back of his mentor's head. Whatever the psychic was thinking would happen here, it wasn't this.

"That's very generous of his highness," My new friend says slowly.

"You're with an Acker." Ryder drawls as he gives a careless shrug. The hallway walls become increasingly full of portraits of various sizes. The smallest is the size of my palm and too high up for me to see what it is on the canvas encased in a thick gold frame.

"Whitlock," I correct. "My last name is Whitlock."

"Acker blood runs through your veins, does it not?" Ryder turns around to show me a cocked eyebrow and a confused frown.

"Yes," I grumble. "But so does Whitlock's blood. That is my family name. It's the name my mother chose to take and pass along."

Ryder grunts softly but does not continue to argue. It feels like a hollow victory. Ryder pushes open a set of dark oak double doors. Knox follows quickly after him as if scared that this opportunity would be taken away from him in the blink of an eye. I, however, stop to look at the carvings on the door.

The wood it is made of is so dark it is almost black. The top half of both doors show the Althanian mountains and the night sky above. The mountains are drawn to be steep and fierce, a powerful shadow that outshines the small towns and buildings depicted on the bottom half of the doors. That's inaccurate.

Very few people have settled on the base of those mountains, mostly due to a large chunk of it being decreed as royal land and a river cutting through the rest. There was only a tiny settlement more towards the north, towards the shoreline. I stare down at those tiny village etchings and blink.

There is no palace depicted on it at all, only the academy and those wrongly placed settlements. It was as if this was designed before Althania was truly Althania, back before the lands were divided and the demon war had been won.

"Ivy," Knox calls back to me. He sounds like he is holding back a laugh. "Ivy, come look at this."

I shake off the shudder that floods me as I push the door open further and pad into the room.

It's gorgeous, which I should have expected. This is one of Hal's safe havens. The walls are made of bookcases, hardbacks, paperbacks and ornaments, all piled and compacted into shelves that reach up to the literal glass ceiling. My lips twitch as I imagine Hal putting in that ironic request. My mouth then drops open when I see the true masterpiece of the room - the large oil painting of Sir Channing, Prince Hal and my mother.

The painting takes centre stage on the furthest wall and lines up perfectly with the large mahogany desk and comfortable leather chair underneath it. I imagine Hal spending his

172

time here, glancing up at the painting with a soft smile in between signing important decrees and trade route approval or whatever it was a crown prince signs at a big desk like this one.

The woman in the painting is my mother. I know it is, but there is something foreign in her face. I had never seen that half smirk, those 'I dare you' eyes, and she had never, ever worn something so provocative at home.

Her dress was sleeveless, and the top of it had two thin strips of fabric that gave her a plunging neckline all the way down to her belly button. She looked skin-tight. It was a gorgeous bright blue that matched her eyes and stood out against the two boys' dark fighting gear.

The other fact that stood out was that my mother was lounging on what was a mock throne, with Hal and Channing standing behind her. They had hands clasped behind their back in a military pose as if she were not a lowborn fae girl but a royal. A leader. A *Queen*. Their smiles were soft and genuine.

The third and final realisation does not hit me until I am standing underneath it, my feet moving me to stare at it up close without me telling them to move.

I stare at the brushstrokes, the swirls of colour, and I crane my neck to stare at the bottom right corner. Hidden in the swirls of darkness, in the same way it is hidden in the swirls of colour in my portraits back home, is Filman's signature star. My mother had taken him with her when she had moved to Parlitan to marry my father.

"I feel that it is obvious, but I will say it anyway. Nothing you see or are told in this room is to ever leave this room." Ryder drawls from his chosen spot back near the door. "Don't touch anything unless you are told you can touch it. Do not speak unless he speaks to you first. Do not assume that because you are invited here, you belong here."

"Are you leaving?" Knox's voice falters ever so slightly.

"If the Crown Prince wishes it," Ryder responds. His mouth tightens around the title. Another realisation pings inside my brain as if, in this room, my intelligence has increased tenfold.

Hal never took the title of King because his parents are still alive. They gave him the throne early, something that had never been heard of before. Anyone given the throne always takes that title. Ryder would have thought he would be serving a King, and even though Hal had all that power, Ryder's title was now Prince's Advisory Physic instead of King's. That would have to sting.

"But you are my mentor," Knox frowns.

"First lesson. What your royal tells you to do, you do." Ryder finds that comment particularly funny. I turn my head away from the pair of them. This was their mentoring moment, and Ryder had said nothing about looking.

I scan over the bookcase walls, but they are too wide and too tall to read it properly. There is a ladder attached to each wall so the top shelf could be reached, but that would involve touching, so I settled for the ones in sight on the section closest to me. These are all leather hardbacks and the lettering on them is in beautiful gold paint.

A familiar title catches my eye, and I crouch down to look at the titles. My hand hovers in front of them, but I do not touch. I have these books, these exact editions, in my room at home. They were gifts from my parents throughout my childhood. I suppose I shouldn't be too shocked. They were considered the staples of childhood reading.

Hal would have had to learn to read once upon a time. He would have read all about the little lost princess who was saved by the mermaids, the little fae boy who grew as big as a giant when he laughed and the werewolf who had trouble with his howl.

He may even have had to write a paper on the story of the star-crossed lovers or on the poetic justice of the repetitive history of the slaughtered king and his sons. That had been my least favourite one. A Vampire king that had sired multiple bastards and slaughtered them all to keep himself on the throne, only to have missed one and be slaughtered by him in turn. That bastard turned king went on to sire and slaughter multiple children of his own, although more subtly if the legend was to be believed.

"The books won't bite, you know," an amused voice calls to me. I turn my head, hand still hovering over the spines, and see Prince Hal lounging against the doorway with a grin on his face. "Ryder, you are welcome to stay, but I fear you may quickly grow bored. We will only be talking today.”

Ryder eyes up Knox for a long few seconds before nodding his head once and slowly making his way to one of the armchairs tucked into a corner of the room. Knox frowns slightly before shaking his shoulders and heading towards the opposite armchair.

“Actually, Knox, with me and Ivy at the desk. If you don’t mind.” Hal turns his warm smile over to Knox and gestures to the two chairs placed in front of the mahogany monstrosity.

The desk’s sides have the Althanian mountains carved into them, a fact I didn’t notice before.

“You really love the mountains,” I comment awkwardly as Knox bows his head to Hal and slowly does as he is told. Hal glances over at me, but as he has always said, I do not bow to him.

“I’ll show you them one day if you like.” Hal’s offer is off the cuff, casual as he strolls across the room and shrugs off his jacket. It’s thick and fancy and princely. He was probably in a meeting before this. “Channing could come too. We used to sneak up there with your mother all the time. There's a spot that's perfect for a picnic."

The freely given insight into my mother's teenage years sends a small shock wave through me. My mother had a reputation for being a great water wielder, and she had always instilled in us the need to behave and train, to observe and listen rather than cause the scene, to only cause that scene if and when we had all the information we needed. She had never hinted at a wild time sneaking into forbidden border areas for picnics with a prince.

"My mother snuck into the Althanian mountains?" I blurt out, my feet once again moving me across the room. I sit in the chair next to Knox and stare at Hal as he settles in the chair on the other side of the desk.

"Violet snuck into a lot of places she wasn't supposed to," Hal's smile turns into a grin. "She used to say that if people were going to mutter she was in a place she didn't belong, she was going to make that true."

"Lady Violet wasn't accepted here," Knox joins the conversation tentatively, his statement sounding more like a question. Hal goes to answer, but his eyes flicker over to Ryder.

"You can speak freely here, Ryder. You know that." Hal's voice is low.

"Yes, sir." Ryder grounds out. "But I would much rather see how much my trainee can do without interference."

"Violet didn't have the easiest time here," Hal admits to us as he slowly drags his eyes from Ryder to Knox. "She was the first female fae to be allowed here. She tried to keep her head down at first, but that didn't work."

Hal pauses and turns his head slightly to the side as if he is fighting not to look at the painting. He turns back and stares at me instead. "Channing quickly became her friend. The only other werewolves in our class were sons of lords and dukes. In their eyes, Channing was beneath them, just like Violet was in the eyes of the fae students. Like, as they say, calls to like. There were never two people closer than Channing and Violet."

"How…" Knox frowns slightly and examines the painting as he finishes his question. "How did you get involved with them?"

"I could show you," Hal is still looking at me as he reaches over and taps twice on a small metal contraption on the corner of his desk. "But I don't think Ryder would appreciate me giving you too many hints."

I gasp slightly and lean forward in my chair to get a closer look at the device. The entire device is the size of my hand, the centre metal disc about the size of my palm and covered in small symbols. Around the edge of the disc are small, netted sections that each hold one memory crystal. Hal's sections are all full, a rainbow of colours.

"You have a memory reader?" I gape at him.

"I'm the leader of a country," Hal reminds me. "I have multiple."

I feel my cheeks turn red. Of course, he did. All royals probably had stacks and stacks of them hidden around their multiple homes. They could afford it and all the crystals they could ever want. The crystals alone cost one thousand gold coins for the smallest size. That was pocket change for someone with access to the royal vaults. They could even put it down as an expense.

"Do you not already have one?" Knox asks me slowly.

"I wanted one. My parents always said no. They thought I would spend too much time dwelling on my past or focussing on which ones to keep. Even Lord Whitlock couldn't justify spending that kind of money for his daughter to have a copy of her first dance performance forever." I shoot Knox a grin. He is still frowning, his eyes back on that painting. I latch onto his words. "Already? You see me having one?"

"It's blurry. Everything is really, really blurry." Knox grunts out.

"But you can see something? Something about her future?" Ryder's voice is suddenly encouraging, soft and low. Knox nods in response and then winces. The visions hurt him.

"Enough," I snap at him. "He's uncomfortable. He's hurting. Stop."

"Ivy," Hal sighs. "Knox needs to be trained, and this is how it happens."

"You aren't going to use me to train him. Not if this is going to be the outcome."

"My first mentoring session, and I threw up from my headache." Ryder tells me. "I was curled up in a ball for hours and hours, just trying to see more than a shadow. If Knox can see objects and you, a creature with an undetermined and always changing future, and only have you as blurry, then that tells us what we need to know. But we cannot stop. The country Knox will be assigned to cannot have a psychic that cannot see clearly. This is a good outcome."

"Knox. Would you like to continue?" Hal leans forward on the desk. Knox, once again, only nods. I scowl but settle back against my seat and stay silent.

"Violet beat me during combat training." Hal continues his story as if it had never been interrupted. "We were paired together by our professor, and everyone expected me to win. I was a prince who had been trained from birth, and she was a lowborn fae girl who had somehow tricked her way into a place among us. I was arrogant, but if I'm honest, even if I hadn't been, she would have beaten me. It was brutal and quick, and suddenly she was pinning me down and telling me in no uncertain terms that if my friends didn't leave Channing alone, she would rip my fangs from my mouth and wear them as earrings."

Hal laughs then, and I can't help but chuckle along. It sounded like something Don would have said if someone was picking on Corvus. My mother's wild youth had snuck into her firstborn in some ways, at least.

"I can't imagine Channing being picked on," I admit. "Or my mother being quite so openly treasonous. It is treason to threaten you, even if she is from Parlitan."

"Violet has certainly changed." Hal agrees with a small nod. "She has taken her tsunami heart and used it for more subtle, passive-aggressive wins. I heard she is quite a contender at auctions."

"She is good at foreign policy, too," I argue. "She isn't all pretty dresses and balls. She still has substance."

The words come out more fiercely than I had intended, fuelled by my own confusion. How had my mother gone from the woman who threatened princes and won duels to the happy housewife who tutted over dance cards? There was too big of a gap in my own knowledge of her, and I had lived with her my entire life. Something had happened to her during her Vilerian games to cause that flicked switch.

"Violet is good at everything she sets her mind to." Hal agrees. "I am surprised she hadn't told you any of this already."

"She didn't talk about her time here or her games. She thought it would glamourise it so that me and Don would want to enrol. Don is going to be lord, eventually. He can't become a member of the Vilerian guard anyway, but she wanted to be subtle about it, I suppose. I would have been even more insufferable if I had thought it was just me who wasn't allowed." I shrugged as if the years, believing my mother thought I was too weak, still didn't sting.

"All she told you was that she met your father and moved to Parlitan." Hal guessed. Ryder clears his throat.

"I heard from others that she competed in the games and that people thought she would win. We knew that she had a reputation for being powerful. People stopped talking to us about it when they realised it irritated my parents." I shrug again.

Hal looks over to Knox to see if anything we have said has worked as a trigger. Knox's eyes are scrunched up in pain, and his breathing has deepened. After one sharp intake of breath, his eyes flash open, and he stares at me. His mouth opens and shuts a few times.

"Knox?" I reach for his arm, a sisterly instinct, but he moves away from me, looking me up and down in horror. Hal nods once, and in a flash, Ryder is there, grabbing Knox's arm and muttering in his ear. Knox shakes him off and then glares at him. He turns that glare to Hal. A moment later, he lets out an agitated breath through his nose, his jaw clenched.

"Knox, I would suggest going with Ryder." Hal insists gently.

"I want to stay here. With her." Knox responds bluntly. I blink twice.

"She'll be fine. You need to be debriefed." Hal's tone changes. His voice is now hard and blunt. Knox has no choice but to leave. The psychic's yellow eyes narrow before he unceremoniously shoves himself to his feet and storms out of the door. Ryder is quick on his heels.

"What in the name of the goddess was that?"
I demand as the door closes.

"Psychics know royal secrets." The crown
prince sighs. "When they find them out, they
need to be sworn to secrecy. So, you can't
ask him what he saw because he will not be
able to tell you."

I open my mouth to argue with him, although
I do not know what I would say. Knox has
not yet been chosen for Althania. Knox has
no right to their secrets, just as Althania has
no right to his silence. Instead, Hal stands
from his seat and smiles down at me.

"Now. Time for *your* mentoring."

Chapter Sixteen

My mentoring session consists of standing on the opposite side of the library to him and using my elemental control to move things around the room to showcase my competence with them. I use air to move the furniture around, rearranging the chairs and making the books float. I use water to mimic the vague shape of a person sitting in those chairs.

Hal has me create small firebirds and fly them around my head. Since we are inside, there is little I could safely do with earth, and he promises that next time, we will conduct our training outside. None of it was particularly draining, the tasks not unique, but when the limo pulled up outside of the academy, I could barely keep my eyes open.

Knox was not in the limo with me, and when I asked if we could wait for him, the driver only told me Knox would be returning home later.

I stop by Harlan's room on the way back to my own but get no response. It doesn't even sound as if he is in there. A moment later, when I opened my bedroom door and found him lounging on my floor with Don, Corvus, and Maverick, I realised that I was right.

"What is going on?" I demand playfully as a grin takes over my face.

"We were told to tell you that we are gift number three," Don grins back at me, unceremoniously shoving himself to his feet to come and give me a hug. I wrap my arms around my brother tightly, closing my eyes as a feeling of calm settles over me. He had been answering my letters, but they were shorter than I would have liked. I had been sending at least one a day, and thanks to the portal postal system, I knew he was getting them instantly. Maybe I had been annoying. Maybe he was busy planning to come see me and wanted to have something left to say.

"I would apologise for not coming dressed in only a ribbon, but Don threatened to strangle me with it if I tried," Maverick says cheekily as he pushes my brother out of the way to hug me next. I giggle and sway with him for a second.

When Mav pulls away, I stare at Corvus and open up my arms for a hug from him, too. The werewolf pretends to debate on it for a second before pulling me into the tightest hug of them all and spinning me in circles as I laugh.

"How long are you here for?" I ask once I am back firmly on the ground.

"Until you graduate," Don says proudly.

"Or flunk out," Corvus teases.

"Or accept a dramatic marriage proposal." Maverick wiggles his eyebrows at me.

"You can't do that. Any of you. You all have lives back home…" I start to argue, but Don puts up a hand, and I immediately silence myself.

"You're my little sister. Who else is gonna look out for you better than me? And them." Don adds that last part quickly as Corvus and Maverick glare at him.

"I've been doing an okay job," Harlan grumbles playfully as he continues to watch the reality fake dating show that my brother and his friends all pretend to hate.

"You never wanted to be a student here," I remind my brother in a soft whisper.

"Oh no," Don snorts. "I won't be a student. Channing has organised a flat for us in the city. We will be here as your private tutors."

"That basically means we kick your ass at training like we always do," Corvus smirks at me.

"You don't always beat me." I snort back. "Don does. You don't."

"Ouch." Corvus puts a hand over his heart and stumbles back dramatically as if I had stabbed him in it. "Those long hours teaching you how to hold a dagger, all for nothing!"

"Channing seems to be getting everyone a place in the city centre. You think we could get a flat there for the second year?" Harlan jokes. Don frowns slightly. He knows. He knows and is not happy about it at all. That fills me with an uneasy feeling, but it's not as deep or suffocating as I thought it would be.

"I wonder how close we are to the human?" Maverick starts the teasing gently.

"He has a name. You know it. You're all his friends." I remind them bluntly.

"That is true," Maverick tuts. "However, now the lack of details about his sex life makes sense."

"Shut up," Don snaps at his friend, whacking him around the shoulder. He turns those ice-blue eyes that we share back to me and says slowly. "We have come up with a rule. We will all be completely fine with the lying and the secret relationship, and I'll be a bad big brother who won't remind you of his short life span. If you are happy, then we are happy. Okay?"

"That's not really a rule," My lips twitch as I fight back a relieved smile.

"It's a rule because if I break it, I have to let Corvus and Maverick both hit me." Don sighs. "Vice versa for them, but they were traitorously unsurprised when Dean was following after you like a love-sick puppy."

I look at him and then look over at Corvus. "You gonna hit him over that one?"

Corvus pretends to debate it for a second before shaking his head. "He can have that one. It's true. It's exactly what Dean acted like. I will say it makes me kind of sad, though. You could have cleaned up here, had lords and ladies and dukes and duchesses all crawling to you on their knees and begging to hold your hand. Guess I'll have to wait a century or two to watch Don's breakdown at that."

Maverick laughs the loudest at Don's suddenly pale face. I pat his shoulder twice sympathetically and avoid the sharp feeling in my gut as I realise Corvus's words are true. In a century, I would be here, looking very similar to what I look like now, and Dean would be gone.

Don scowls at me from the corner of his eye before rolling them and then dragging me over to sit down next to Harlan. My best friend makes room for me instantly, and I rest my head against his shoulder with a contented smile.

"How did you guys get into my room?" I ask them hours later when we are nearing the end of the latest season of the reality show. The question is sparked when Maverick wrinkles his nose at the fact that the witch, who was currently the favourite to win, came home to find the vampire love interest had sprinkled rose petals throughout her private quarters.

"You left the door open. Don was gonna lecture you about that later." Harlan says around a mouthful of popcorn, his chewing drowned out by the witch's elated scream.

"No, I didn't." I blurt out. I had checked, but I hadn't. Hadn't I?

The three boys are up in a flash, Don taking the en suite, Maverick checking the windows and doorframes, and Corvus the closet. They move so fast that Harlan and I can do nothing but stare at them with open mouths.

"Window is fine," Maverick calls.

"Bathroom's secure," Don yells back.

"What are they looking for?" Harlan whispers to me with his eyes glued on Corvus as the werewolf rips his way through my hung-up gowns and jackets.

"Got something!" Corvus growls, ripping something from the tiny ledge of a top shelf. I wince as my brother slams the bathroom door on his way to his friend's side. I scramble to my feet as the two pass something between them. Whatever it is, it's small. I can barely see it in their cupped hands.

"That could be mine!" I snap at them, going to snatch whatever it is from their palms and look at it myself. "You are all overreacting."

"You put a camera in your own wardrobe?" Corvus raises his eyebrows at me. "Kinky."

My stomach drops the same way it does when I try to use air to fly, but I fail. I obviously had not put a camera in my own room, and I somehow hadn't noticed it yet either, which filled me with shame.

"Check Harlan's." Don demands of Maverick, and the mermaid is through the main doorway in a flash. Harlan bolts after him, almost falling over as he tries to catch him.

"This could be an Academy thing," I try to say it casually, but even I do not believe it. The Academy wouldn't need to hide a camera in my things. They could implant spying devices into the walls and have us all none the wiser. This was clumsy, easy, and obvious. Amateur.

"Nothing in Harlan's." Maverick declares a moment later as he returns, shutting the door and locking it the second Harlan is back inside.

"Not an Academy thing," Don turns to give me a fake smug smile. It doesn't hide the emotion in his eyes, the flash of panic that I see before he puts on his calm façade. "Corvus. Go." Don commands. Corvus makes it one step before my brother changes his mind. "Wait."

Don digs his phone from his pocket and presses the screen three times. Once to unlock it, the second time to open a communication app I don't recognise and the third time to press the singular name on the contacts list.

Channing.

Chapter Seventeen

Channing gets to my room in 47 seconds, which, according to him, is unacceptably late.

He apologises for making us wait as he gives the room another check. Corvus and Maverick have flocked Harlan and me, standing so close to us that I could feel the heat coming from their skin. Channing finds nothing else suspicious in the room, and he checks it thoroughly. Even my underwear drawer isn't safe, a fact that makes my cheeks flush as he opens it. He makes no comment about anything, and he keeps his look brief and to the point.

When he finds nothing, he takes the camera that Corvus found and examines it in his palm. His eyes narrow, and he hisses something under his breath, but not low enough for my fae ears not to just about catch it.

"Idelons?" I repeat. The Idelons organisation was one I had heard of, but only from my snooping and snippets of gossip. They were pro-human, which I didn't consider a bad thing, but they were aggressive in their approach to everything.

Instead of working to put laws into place in the countries and homelands full of non-human creatures, they wanted to abolish the monarchies that ran them. They didn't care if the human royals paid the price for that as well. They wanted to keep a database of all hybrid children, even those mixed in with human blood, and they were, therefore, less powerful and less of a threat.

They wanted to stop all 'breeding arrangements', which was just another dig at the nobility and royalty. All these things made their stance on ending slavery in countries like Tulinth, an issue that should have been fixed centuries ago, a non-starter.

The Idelons do not compromise on their issues, and the royal councils would never agree to all of them. At least not according to the official correspondence from the Parlitan king that I snuck a look at this summer while in my father's study.

Channing's eyes avoid mine as he stalls on answering my question.

"It makes sense," Harlan says slowly, as if he is unsure he should even be speaking. "You're a fae noble who is publicly dating a human. Why wouldn't they be interested in you?"

"How did they even get in my room? I locked it. I'm the only one who…" I trail off as I mentally answer my own question. The staff. All the staff have keys to every single room.

"This is going to be taken care of," Channing promises me fiercely. "The locks will be changed immediately. The access to your room is going to be cut down. Have you given Dean a key?"

Heat flushes into my cheeks once again. I avoid my brother's eyes as I nod slowly.

"You'll have to get him a new one." Channing says dismissively, once again staring down at the tiny camera. It looked no bigger than his thumb. Whatever he is squinting at must be obnoxiously small. "I'll make sure he is still on the list after another deep dive. His background check came back clear the first time, and your parents vouched for him."

"You think Dean would have bugged my room? That he would be a member of Idelon?" I laugh harshly. "My Dean?"

"Ivy," Don says lowly. "This is serious."

"He wouldn't," I snarled at all of them. "He wouldn't do that."

"I believe you believe that," Channing's response is more political than I have ever heard him sound. I hate it. "But this is your safety, Ivy. I won't be taking any risks with that."

"Neither would Dean." I hiss through my clenched jaw.

"You think I wasn't put through every kind of check, every kind of test, spied on and questioned when I joined Prince Hal's household?" Channing asks me, his voice calm but with a hidden sharp edge. "This is not personal. This is protocol. This won't be the last time your boyfriends are looked into if you want to be a part of the Vilerian guard when you graduate."

The words sting, but they ring true. If I was going to be close to a member of a royal family, be trusted to protect them, to go on missions and to act in their name as I slaughter the demons that managed to hide away and breed themselves back into existence, then I would have to accept the fact my life would no longer be totally private.

My partners would have to be looked into, and my living situation inspected thoroughly and randomly, all to ensure I was keeping the secrets given to me.

But I do not like how Channing refers to them as boyfriends as if there would be a long line of them, as if I couldn't keep a hold of one or that I would move along from Dean mere seconds after his funeral. It rubs me the wrong way and leads me towards that gut-wrenching internal clock I had. If Dean lived an average human lifespan, I would only have forty-seven more years with him.

"Fine," I mutter in agreement.

"You'll stay in our apartment tonight as well," Don decides without asking his flatmates. "While Channing checks it out thoroughly." My brother gives the knight a long, hard stare.

Channing grunts in agreement as he meets my brother's gaze. Don is letting his barely leashed anger run the show, but Channing allows it. I don't imagine that would be happening again.

"You can have my bed," Corvus offers, looping his arm around my shoulders to lead me from the room. We make it to the door before he turns to look over our shoulders and grins. "You and I are sharing the sofa, Rose boy."

Harlan jolts as if he didn't expect to be invited, which confuses me because it's Harlan. Harlan is someone I would always want with me as my world crumbles around me. The walls around my brain or heart or both, the walls around the part of me that is keeping me calm, start to crumble as the realisation hits me.

Someone was in my room. Someone had wanted to video me without me knowing. Someone probably *had* videoed me that evening, recorded me giggling and mimicking the reality stars with Maverick, recorded me hugging my brother and sticking my tongue out at Harlan. They weren't large moments. My friendships with them were not a secret, but they were *private,* and they were *mine,* and the Idelons had no right to them.

My breathing turns ragged as Corvus escorts me into the corridor. He makes a sympathetic noise and rubs his hand up and down my arm. He thinks I am near tears, that my body is shaking from fear, but he is wrong. It's anger.

I will no longer, if ever, feel completely safe in that room. I will no longer feel completely safe at the Academy even if Channing does as he says and fixes this security issue. I will be on guard always, checking all my rooms and furniture before I dare to change clothes. I am strangely not angry at the intrusion itself.

I am angry at the fact I was ever complacent here. I should have been better. I should have known better. There is a reason my mother ran from this place without a backward glance. I cannot continue dragging my heels. I need to find out what that reason was, and Prince Hal's third gift is exactly the resource I need.

Chapter Eighteen

The boy's flat is grand and obnoxiously clean. When we cross the threshold, everything smells new and fresh. The main room is an open space, with a kitchen set up to the left of the front door, a living room set up to the right, and a large open area with a dining table tucked into the side. On the opposite walls, spaced out enough so it's clear the rooms are large as well, are four doors.

The ceiling has a large skylight in the centre of it, creating a spotlight on the light grey nine-seater sofa and glass coffee table. The whole room is painted white, and the accessories and furniture are made of glass or painted grey. There are strategically placed paintings on the walls, themed around the boy's homelands. Mav looks at the beachfront canvas with a soft smile as he chucks his keys carelessly onto the kitchen island. Corvus does not so much as glance at the rolling hills of an Alcarlian farm.

"The fridge and cupboards were filled for us. Help yourself to anything." Don tells us as he shrugs off his jacket and hangs it on the back of a dining chair.

Harlan makes a beeline for the fridge, pulling out two flavoured waters and throwing one at me. He had downed half the bottle before I even opened mine. Maverick watches him from the corner of his eye.

"Thank you for letting us stay," I smile at him. "I know it's probably not the way you wanted to break into your new place."

"You mean you don't want to let us do shots off of your various body parts? How disappointing." Corvus shoots me a grin as he comes out of what I assume is his room, juggling multiple blankets and pillows. He dumps them unceremoniously on the sofa.

"I'll sleep there. I'm not going to take your bed." I tell him bluntly. The werewolf ignores me and starts to make two separate little beds on the sofa. It was big enough that there was enough space, theoretically, but it wouldn't be comfortable.

"You are taking Corvus's, and Harlan is taking mine," Don declares in the classic older brother tone, which tells me that should have been obvious. It was the same tone he used when he chastised my footwork during training, when he finally told me his hiding spot for hide and seek and when he told me I had done a good job at my first horse-riding lesson. *You're shuffling rather than stepping. Where else would I have been hiding? Of course, you did a good job. Of course, Harlan won't be sleeping on the sofa.*

"Thanks," Harlan says around a mouthful of apple. He is standing behind the kitchen island and has helped himself to the large fruit bowl in the centre. It was already half empty. I turn to look at my brother and place my hands on my hips.

"How long have you been living here?" I demand. My brother opens his mouth to answer, but nothing comes out. Maverick chuckles as he moves to sit down on the makeshift bed that Corvus is still adjusting. The werewolf lets out a small, harmless growl at him. Maverick winks at him before shuffling into the middle of the sofa.

"This would only be our second night," My brother finally sighs.

"You've been in Althania a whole day?" I pout dramatically at him. Don scowls in response.

"I told dad that I wouldn't interrupt your studies. If I had come to see you yesterday, you wouldn't have been focussing on your mentoring session today. Which, by the way, I need to have words with you about," Don gets the unamused brother look on his face, the one he uses when I mess around during training, or I ask him the same question seven times in a row.

"Do you, though?" I retort childishly. "My mentoring sessions are my business."

"You were supposed to be mentored by Channing," Don is still scowling, but it takes the bite out of his words. "Mum told you…"

"Mum is a subject we need to discuss." I cut him off with a scowl of my own. A look flashes across his face, too quick for me to decide if it was horror or surprise. Both, probably. I usually wait a little more than two sentences before I snap back at him, and it's usually with something sarcastic.

"What's happening with Violet?" Maverick demands. He has dropped his playful demeanour and looks ready to leap over the back of the sofa and bolt to the nearest portal to get back to my mother. Corvus has become still, but his eyes are on me, those amber eyes that always light up brighter when he laughs, but now they are dark and unflinching.

For not the first time, it hits me that my mother is the closest thing all the boys have to one. Harlan's mother left when he was still knee height, and the other two had been with us since before they hit double digits. Their bio mothers sent presents on major holidays, maybe a few letters, but if there was any other contact, I had no idea of it. They didn't even travel to come to our family balls, and they were always invited.

"Nothing. She's safe and fine and sending letters constantly, so you should all be prepared for that," I put on a reassuring smile.

"But?" Don raises his eyebrows at me.

"But there's a reason she ran away to Parlitan, mid-Vilerian games when she was adored here. She has a stained glass window in the Academy. She would have been offered any position she wanted. You are all going to sit there and tell me she left all of that to run off and be a housewife?"

"Enough," Don growls at me, harsh enough that my blood runs cold and my mouth wobbles as it struggles to find more words. He has never looked so disappointed and angry at me, not ever. Not even when I nearly cut his toe off in training during my first week of holding a blade. "Just because you would not have made the same choices as her does not make those choices any less valid. She moved to Parlitan because that is what she wanted. She became a lady, she fell in love, she had us, and she is happy. Why is that not enough for you? Why do you have to assume there are always secrets, conspiracy theories and lies hidden around every corner? Why is it not enough for you? Why is *she* not enough for you?"

"Donaugh!" Maverick gapes, quickly moving to stand next to me. "She didn't mean it like that, and you know it. Apologise. Now."

Don doesn't apologise. Don stares at me, his jaw clenching and unclenching as he waits for an answer to a question I thought was rhetorical. I certainly do not know how to answer it. I scowl back at my big brother.

"It makes no sense," I whisper through my teeth. "I refuse to believe that there is nothing more to it. She could have been the right hand of a King or Queen. She is too ambitious, too competitive to let that go all for a fae lord's heir."

"That is our father you are talking about," Don looks at me as if he has never seen me before, and maybe he hasn't, not this side of me anyway. Our squabbles were always petty, and I would be the first to admit that he had spoilt me. He let me win at chess, and he always played with me for longer than he promised. In exchange, I had only ever argued with him in playful or small, simply petty ways. We had never disagreed so seriously.

But his words still sting and writhe around in my head, even as Corvus and Maverick slide in between us, stopping the physical escalation I am no longer sure would ever happen. I am no longer sure that if it did, he would let me win.

Corvus takes my arm and slowly leads me to his room, walking backwards with his eyes on Don, shutting the door behind us and giving me a soft, understanding smile. My responding smile is awkward.

"He's just stressed," Corvus begins the excuses. "Tired. Worried about you after someone was in your room. You can't take any of it to heart. You shouldn't."

"He doesn't get it. Maybe I was useless at explaining it," I shrug helpfully, looking down at my hands as I step across the room to settle on the edge of his bed. A double bed, I notice although my brain doesn't tell me why that's important. There are some band tour posters on the wall to my left, and the wall to my right holds large windows with a window ledge big enough for someone to lounge on.

"You aren't useless," Corvus tells me quickly, which is nice but wasn't exactly what I had said. "You are incredible. You are only getting more so, and if you think there is something else behind Violet's departure to Parlitan, then maybe you are right. But you also might be wrong. You have never been away from your homeland before this Ivy, not for more than a day or two, and so you do not know what it is like to be torn between returning to it or staying in a place like this. You do not know the inner turmoil of relinquishing your life in a place specifically made to tailor to your every need for a place you only *may* be truly happy in."

I slowly look up at him as he speaks. He never made it seem like there was any inner turmoil at all. He had always looked happy and at home in Parlitan, in the Whitlock estate, sitting in our gardens and at our dinner table. There is a hollow feeling in my own chest as I realise Corvus was a better actor than I had ever given him credit for.

"You think she left so suddenly, in that much of a rush, because she was homesick and saw a chance to go home with her head high and a ring on her finger?" I frown at him. It sounds cruel, heartless, too calculated for either of us to be saying. My mother loves my father, and I know that. I just wish that I knew that she loves him so much that I would never question their marriage at all.

"I think that if I was fighting for acceptance every single moment of every single day for months on end, an offer of luxury and kindness from someone as accepting as your father would be a hard thing not to think about," Corvus shrugs carelessly as if we were discussing the weather and not permanently changing my point of view.

"Do you wish to go to your homeland? To Alcarlian? Find a wife from there and drop everything that quickly?" I blurt out, and for some reason, my voice shakes. When Corvus looks at me, those eyes of liquid amber are more curious than annoyed.

"Once or twice," Corvus admits with another shrug. He moves his eyes off me and around his new room. "For a brief few moments. Your family has always been kind to me, Ivy. I do not say it, so you think me ungrateful. But I was a feral werewolf growing up in a nice fae estate full of rose gardens and finger sandwiches. It wasn't always easy. Just as it already isn't easy for you here, as a fae girl who grew up in rose gardens now living in a city that constantly smells of steel."

"I like it here," I whisper quickly to him.

"I like it in Parlitan," Corvus grins at me wickedly as if we now share a secret. Seven years ago, I would have melted into a puddle if he looked at me like that. I would have absolutely died when he turned to tell me to sleep well, and it hit me that I was sleeping in his bed.

But I am an adult now, and my thoughts are not full of playful yellow eyes and a husky voice or about drinking in the way his pillow already smells like him. They are full of my boyfriend's green eyes and whispered gossip of the Idelons, and I lay awake for hours trying desperately to convince myself that my mother was simply homesick all these years ago.

I try to convince myself I imagined the longing in Prince Hal's face as he stared at her portrait. I try to convince myself that there is no secret reason that Channing allowed Don to interrupt and order him around.

I fail.

Chapter Nineteen

Crown Prince Hal arrives at the flat at 6:13 in the morning. I am the only one awake, having slept in small fretful bursts and then tiptoed into the main room to eat fruit from the bowl for breakfast.

I hadn't wanted to wake the two boys on the sofa, their legs all entangled and arms thrown off their faces to block out the light from the skylight above. The three loud knocks and four guards that storm in the second I open the door ruin that.

The boys are up in a flash, Maverick brandishing a fork as if it were a dagger as Corvus leaps from the back of the sofa to land in front of me, claws out and snarling.

A door behind us crashes open, and Don slides across the wooden floor to stand in the gap, creating a line between the three of them.

Hal looks more amused than I have ever seen him, and he often smiles when near me. The guards have formed a square around him, and the front two, the ones within range of Corvus's claws, glance back at him as they wait for an order.

"Well," The Crown Prince of Vampires grins at us all with absolute delight in his voice. "I suppose I had no reason to be worried after all. Quite a protective unit you've found yourself, Ivy. No Ideleon is getting past them in a hurry."

"If you have come here to mock us, you might at least have had the decency to come at a later time," My brother says sullenly, his hair messier than a bird's nest.

The guard in the front left position takes a step forward as if to punish my brother for the insolence, but Hal's booming laugh stops him.

These guards have not yet received the memo, but I'm sure the message will slowly trickle through his entire details. The Whitlock children need not perform the basic niceties. My realisation from hours before twists my stomach, and I no longer want my apple.

"If you wouldn't mind inviting me inside?" Hal looks at Don, Corvus and Maverick in turn. Vampires do not need to be invited in; he could just take one step forward and be over the threshold, but Hal is too polite for that small notion of arrogance.

"Come in, your majesty," Maverick says the words slowly, with a long look at Don as if he was waiting to be interrupted. My brother's scowl deepens, but he says nothing.

Hal takes one large step into the room and beams at me as if he has just performed a great trick that I was somehow involved in. He rubs his hands together as he then takes the main room.

"No Harlan?" Hal questions.

"Still sleeping," I answer. "He can sleep through nearly everything."

Hal nods his understanding, frowning slightly as he sees the bookshelf in the corner is mostly empty. "Did the decorators not finish in time?" He turns to Don. "Is anything else missing?"

"I prefer to buy my own books," Don says tensely as he throws himself down on one of the kitchen stools.

"Well, just remember to charge them to the royal account," Hal told him gently. He clearly hadn't picked up on Don's specific wording of 'buy' rather than 'choose'. He turns to look at me again, and a genuine grin grows. "I brought you something. To cheer you up. I have also excused you and Harlan from the academy for the day, so I'm glad he is, in fact, still here."

"You didn't need to get me anything," I frown at him. "And can you…" My question trails off. He is the ruler of Althania. He can do whatever he likes.

"Nonsense. It's more like homework, anyway. I was going to give you them at our next mentoring session, but I thought you might like the distraction of watching these today. Channing says you'll be free to go back to your rooms this evening if you wish." Hal hesitates for a second, mouth opening and shutting a few times before adding, "Although you also have the option of rooms at the palace, or I can organise for you to have a flat. Right here near the boys, of course."

"She doesn't need rooms at the palace." Don cuts in. "And she will be much safer at the academy. We can keep an eye on there, and I

217

discussed new security measures with Channing."

Hal nods in confirmation and then gestures behind him. The guard at the back right reaches into his satchel and pulls out an elegant box, the Althanian family crest burned into the top. I take it with a softly whispered thank you. It's surprisingly heavy. I quickly glance up at Hal, who gives me an encouraging smile and nods. My responding smile is awkward as I place the box on the kitchen island next to Don's elbow and flip the silver catch.

Inside are small discs, titled with small handwritten labels. The handwriting is gorgeous, with large looping swirls and tiny dots. I tilt my head and mouth the titles to myself, eyebrows shooting up into my hairline as I realise what he has given me. A few of the titles are more intriguing than others.

Devil's Trio Interview number 1. Hal's twentieth birthday ball. Channing's full moon party first year. Vilerian Games round one. Violet's Valentine's Day extravaganza. Spring Solstice Camping. Violet Acker Training Montage. Devil's Trio Interview number 2.

Hal has given me my mother's years at the academy, ready to view at my pleasure and store in a pretty box.

"Devil's trio?" I frown slightly.

"It's what they called us," Hal tells me, hands clasped behind his back in a princely pose. He averts his gaze as he admits, "because of the devilish grins we shared before we got into trouble."

"Sounds like a nickname you gave yourself," Don scowls at him. Hal flinches as if my brother's harsh tone had physically cut him.

"Your mother loved it." Hal shrugs. "Our trainer used it first. He tried to warn me away from Violet and Channing, said I should know better than to get involved with people like them, and if I truly couldn't stay away, then I should know to run when they shared one of their devilish grins."

"But you didn't," Maverick spoke for the first time this morning, staring at the crown prince with a slight smile.

"You've met them. Have you ever been able to tell them no?" Hal shrugs as if such an admission was commonplace. As if he wasn't in charge of armies and peace treaties and should be above such things. As if the fact he would never tell two lowborn foreigners no was not a political nightmare if anyone with true power ever realised it.

"Never," Corvus laughs, a booming sound that soothes us all.

"Thank you, Hal," I shut the lid with a soft thud. "This was very thoughtful."

"You are most welcome," Hal moves as if to hug me and then changes his mind, giving my shoulder a gentle squeeze. "If you need anything, you just let me know. Anything at all."

"I will," I lie through my smile as I stare him in the eyes. Their deep black colour makes it hard to see the iris in the centre. There was no resemblance to...

Hal nods once before backing away and wishing us all a good day. The boys respond with various degrees of enthusiasm. Don grunts in response. Harlan strolls out of Maverick's room two minutes later, only in his boxers, running his hand through his hair as he yawns.

"What did I miss?" My best friend frowns as he catches sight of Don's frown.

"Putting on clothes, apparently." Don drawls before pushing himself to his feet. He grabs the box and heads towards the sofa. "So hurry up and do that. We are having a movie day."

Chapter Twenty

Dean arrived an hour later, just as we had all finally gotten settled with fresh clothes and snacks. He is in his academy staff uniform, a maroon polo shirt with the academy crest embroidered on the chest. Corvus moves to make room for him, shuffling further down the sofa so Dean can sit next to me. As Dean wraps his arm over my shoulder, Don huffs but says nothing.

"We should have invited Knox," I realise as I catch Harlan checking his phone from the corner of my eye. "Harlan, you should invite him."

"Knox?" Maverick frowns at us all.

"The psychic," Don provides the answer before I can. I shoot him a small frown but keep quiet. It wouldn't be the first time Don had weaselled information out of people, and

I doubt Hal or Channing would have skipped over the fact that I am now friends with a boy who could potentially see my future.

"I already tried. He says he's busy with Channing and Ryder all day," Harlan says miserably. Don, Corvus and Maverick all quickly look at each other but say nothing. My stomach twists.

"You could see if he wants to come over for dinner later. If Ivy doesn't mind making it a group thing?" Dean suggests, looking over at me. My stomach suddenly dropped as I realised that I had forgotten about our plans. I was going to go over to Dean's flat after class, and we were going to cook dinner together.

"If it's more than just us, I will just order us all takeouts," I joke, playfully nudging his side with my shoulder as I pretend I am not a terrible girlfriend. "But it would at least give these boys their flat back."

"We aren't invited to dinner?" Maverick pouts dramatically over at me, hand hovering over the remote as we have yet to start the first disc. Their machine had multiple slots so that we could load up a bunch of discs, and it would automatically shuffle them out so we wouldn't need to get up. It was hardly a memory reader, but it was a cool bit of tech.

"Do you want to come to dinner? I thought you would want to go out on the town and…score some babes or whatever," I stutter out. Maverick shoots me an amused look as Corvus straight up laughs. Don does not find any of it funny.

"Score some babes," Corvus repeats with a snort. "If you ever go clubbing Ivy Whitlock, I want to be there to see it."

"Maybe afterwards we can head to the love shack and boogie down," Maverick cackles.

"I hate you all," I declare as I reach forward and snatch the remote from the mermaid's hand. "You don't deserve this. I'm in charge now."

"Nothing new there then," Harlan quips. I use air manipulation to ruin his hair in retaliation. Harlan makes a disgruntled noise and smoothes it back into position. I nestle back into the cushions and click the button on the remote to start the first disc.

I know that I look too much like my mother and that over the last century or so, she has only physically aged a handful of years, and

yet when the first thing I see is young Violet
Acker laughing wildly into the camera, I am
unnerved at how similar we are.

Violet sets the camera down and then backs
away. I recognise the training hall from the
Academy. My mother is in training gear, tight
shorts and a cropped sports corset. She has
always been thin, but here, she looks small
enough to be whisked away in a breeze. If
anyone were to swat at her, then she would
break in half.

She poses for the camera, flexing her arms
and twisting her hips to show off her figure.
Her hair is up in a high ponytail, fringe
tucked behind her ears. She never wears her
hair in a ponytail now, not even during her
daily exercise. It's always down or in a plait.

The digital version of my mother lets out a
squeal of delight and gestures for someone to
come into the shot. There is a soft, low
chuckle, and then Channing is in the frame,
rushing to her side and lifting her in the air.
He holds her above his head, spinning around
and around, only going faster as her laugh
gets louder.

Finally, she calls out a word, although I can't
make out what, and Channing puts her down

gently on the floor with a triumphant grin on his face.

Young Channing's face was different, and I'm not sure whether I liked it. He has no scar on his eyebrow, and his ears hold piercings. A lot of piercings. His entire stretch of ear looks to be made of metal. He has so many in.

I briefly wonder why he took them out when the fight that permanently changed his face happened, but my thoughts are halted as my mother stares straight into the camera with the remains of a grin.

"To my future child who is watching this. This is your Uncle Channing. When he spins you up in the air, puke on him for me," Violet Acker demands playfully and then squeals again as Channing pinches her side.

"And watch these tapes very closely," Channing looks at the camera as well. "So you can catch your mother lying to you when she tells you that she hated it here."

"I do hate it here," Violet interjects, but she is clearly fighting another smile. Channing gives the camera a knowing look. Violet gets into a fight stance, shooting the camera a wink before telling Channing, "Okay, seriously now. Training time."

The next ten minutes of the disc are of Channing and my mother sparring, occasionally throwing a comment to the camera. This isn't an official interview or Vilerian game footage. These are two friends who had never expected to be at the Academy, taking their own version of a souvenir, putting their memories into something permanent and cheaper than a memory stone.

My mother wins each time, and the shock that fills me is quickly followed by shame. She is my mother. I should have faith in her, especially since I know her reputation. But hearing about it and seeing her in action are two different things.

My mother dodged almost every jab from the werewolf, bending in nearly impossible directions with her footwork as fluid as the water she conjured out of the air. She is graceful and impressive but clearly toying with him, a fact that is made even more clear when she sends a water ball to splash against Channing's face and then giggles before spinning away.

The disc changes to a new training session, one that involves Hal. He also looks too young, his face seemingly unable to stop smiling even as my mother twists him onto his back and presses a wooden dagger to his throat.

"You plan to rule a country, and you can't even beat one little peasant Fae girl!" Violet chastises him, her own face set into a disappointed scowl as she stares down at him.

"Don't call yourself that," Hal orders, remaining on the floor even as my mother stands to her feet and brushes herself off.

"Why?" Violet cocks her head to the side and blinks down at him. "You didn't have a problem with your friends calling me that last week. Or the week before that or the week before that, or the…"

"Okay. Okay. I get it." Hal cuts her off with a wince as he pushes himself up into a sitting position. "But I've stopped them, haven't I? Stopped them from doing it to Channing as well."

"You want a medal for not being a total prick?" Violet moves closer to the camera, although it's to grab a glass of water that is nearby. Young Prince Hal gives an uneasy glance to the camera. Violet rolls her eyes as she takes a delicate sip.

"We have a deal. You uphold your end. I'll uphold mine. Unlike Celeste, I don't want to train with you to rub against you and shudder at your touch." Violet continues. "You wanted to train with me. I said you could as long as Channing gets left alone. You never said I had to be nice *to you* during training."

"True." Hal sighed, and then that cheeky grin came back on his face. "Maybe it was just wishful thinking. Didn't agree to let you film these sessions though."

Violet fights a smile as she reaches over and turns off the camera.

"As touching as this is," Dean grunts from beside me and jolts me back to the modern day, "Why are we all watching this? It seems a bit…private for a whole house showing."

"Hal gave them to her a reason," Harlan frowns at him. "And watching Violet kick a Prince's ass is entertaining enough for me."

"Maybe Dean is right," Maverick says quickly. "Maybe we should pause it and leave the world's most annoying siblings to watch it together."

Maverick is cut off as the disc changes itself, and my mother's laugh once again floods the room. Violet is spinning in a bright red dress, the camera unsteady in someone's hand as they try and follow her route around Hal's private library. She spins herself right into Channing's waiting arms. The werewolf is in a tuxedo.

"Ladies and Gentlemen, the future victors of the Vilerian Games!" Prince Hal cackles from the screen, and I realise he is behind the camera.

"Including-" Violet rushes back towards the camera, and there is a shuffle as the camera changes hands. Prince Hal is now on screen, wearing a matching tuxedo to Channing. He is wearing a golden circle engraved with his family's crest around his brow. "Vileria's most eligible bachelor, future king and bane of my existence, Prince Hal of Althania, first of his name and lord of losing at hand-to-hand combat!"

Hal gives her a mock scowl before bursting into laughter. Channing and Violet join him, and the sound is full of pure joy. My mother laughed at home, laughed a plenty, but it had never been the same loud wheeze that was captured here. It had never been as youthful.

The camera spins again, and this new angle shows us all three of the devil's trio. My mother's eyes sparkle as she declares, "And to *my* future heirs, I hope you see this and remember that your dear mother, the *greatest* of Althania's Vilerian guards, had King Hal and his bravest knight, Channing of Alcarlian, at her beck and call. So, eat your vegetables, or I'll have a royal decree declared that you have to anyway."

Don and I both glance at each other, the same icy blue eyes as on the screen locking onto each other, and we smile sadly. I wish I could stroll through the screen, take my young mother's shoulders and give her a hard shake.

She doesn't get sworn into the Althanian section of the Vilerian guard. She doesn't continue to go to Althanian balls, and she never wins the Vilerian games. At some point after this, she meets my father and runs off to Parlitan to become a lady. I wonder if Don is thinking the same, but then his words from last night echo around in my head.

Why is she not enough for you?

She is enough. But the story she has spun
isn't. It makes no sense for the woman on the
screen before me, and it makes no sense that
a random fae boy got into the friendship
between them, either. There is a lie, a
betrayal, a secret, I know it, and maybe it is
in these tapes.

The screen changes yet again, but this is an
official interview. There are three chairs in
front of the camera, and the camera quality is
significantly better. My mother sits in the
middle chair with the boys on either side of
her. A pleasant voice off-screen introduces
the trio as candidates for the Vilerian games.
Hal's full title is given, and most of the
questions are directed at him. He bats them
over to my mother and Channing to answer.
The interviewer eventually got the message
and started to address my mother.

"Violet, you are the only female fae to ever
be accepted into the Academy-"

"First," Violet corrects her.

"I'm sorry?"

"First female fae." Violet puts on a polite
smile. "Not only. I plan for my daughter to
follow in my footsteps one day. If I have one.

For a whole bunch of girls to follow after me if I don't."

"You want to be an icon," The interviewer says as a subtle accusation. Violet realises it as well because her smile widens into a wicked grin. No. A *devilish* grin.

"I want all the little girls, everywhere and of every race, to know that they belong anywhere that they want to be." Violet stands after her answer. "Now, if you excuse me, we have a game to win."

"Go, Violet," Corvus whispers softly as Channing and Hal scramble to follow her.

The scene changes yet again, but this time, the entire room leans forward in anticipation. The screen shows a large sunken arena, with sides made up of thick glass panes that keep the water back as if the competitors were simply fish in a bowl. There is a large trench spanning all the rectangular sides of the arena. The ground is compacted dirt and already full of at least thirty competitors.

The camera is placed in the stands high above and surrounded by cheering spectators. The crowd roars loudest as the devil's trio is announced. They roar loudly for the prince, who bows lowly as he catches sight of his people. They adore him. My mother takes Channing's hand and follows Hal's lead, bowing to the crowd as well. The applause continues.

The competitors all arrange themselves into a loose circle. I see my mother gesture to a woman across from her that she is coming for her. The blonde waves back, and with a jolt, I realise that woman is Celeste. An announcer starts to talk, but I am too focused on my mother and Celeste, focused on how my mother tenses when the witch blows Channing a kiss and how Hal grabs my mother's arm to get her to focus.

A horn blows, and the Vilerian game's first round begins.

Chapter Twenty-One

My mother bolts across the circle, making good on her promise to go straight for Celeste. Other competitors get in the way, but she doesn't bother to dispose of them properly. She debilitates them with kicks to the knees and stomach or hits to the neck. She waits for others to grab them and wrestle them down to the trenches where already a few competitors lay, wallowing in their failure.

The two men that stood next to Celeste flock away from her, bashing their way through the competition. If they were clever, then they would loop around and try to take out Hal and Channing and then my mother from behind.

Hal and Channing are playing the game as they are meant to, fighting competitors to completion and finishing them off by throwing them into the trench to ensure they were disqualified. They split away from each other, and I am filled with dread.

My mother is stuck fighting an angel, and Celeste takes the opportunity to make some space between them. She gets caught up in her own fight with a fae boy. His face also looked familiar, and I gasped when I recognised him as my Uncle Ballard.

Ballard introduced my parents back when he was also a student at the Academy, the youngest son being visited by his older brother on a night when all the fae students went out to a local bar. I had never thought he might have also competed in the games. He had never mentioned it.

I hear Dean swear softly under his breath, and I follow his gaze to the top left of the screen. Celeste's friends had been smart. They had looped around to catch someone from behind, but that someone was Channing and Channing only. One of them is a fae, which I only realise as he summons the moisture from the air and holds the giant water ball over Channing's mouth.

"He's drowning him," Harlan says in horror, his eyes glued onto the thrashing Channing. The other person holds him in place, probably using magic since Channing's feet were glued to the floor, so he couldn't kick them away.

Even knowing what I know, even knowing that Channing lives and that he is now friends with Celeste, I cannot breathe through my panic at seeing him in that state. Channing was not supposed to be beaten so easily, not in a serious fight, not in a life-or-death situation. He was not supposed to have nearly drowned on dry land.

A scream echoes around the room, yet another sound I had never heard come from my mother's mouth in real life. My mother had never sounded so fierce, so angry, so passionate. But then, as the glass holding back the torrent of water in the arena cracks and as my mother runs across the arena to get to him, I realise that my mother had never had a reason to. Maybe this is what scared her straight into my father's arms.

The water breaks through the glass in the shape of a stampede of galloping horses. Competitors scream as they are washed away, but the focus is on Celeste's two sidekicks.

The horses kick them off Channing and then into the trenches with a neigh that sounds like a crashing wave. As my mother falls to her knees at Channing's side and checks that he is breathing, the water sluggishly retreats to its now broken cage.

The Devil's trio are the only three competitors left standing as the disc cuts off. There are more getting ready to play, but Don snatches the remote from me and turns the television off.

"I think that's the important one watched," He declares in a shaky voice. "Why don't we go out to lunch? My treat."

My brother stands and heads to put his shoes on, clearly expecting us all to follow. Maverick does so immediately, Corvus more slowly. Dean follows their lead without a glance at me. I remain staring at the black screen for a whole extra minute with something in my brain whispering at me too quietly for me to hear what it is saying.

Chapter Twenty-Two

Proxima immediately takes a shine on Maverick, which is more annoying than I anticipated. She feints being bad at blocking with a sword so that he will wrap his arms around her to get her in the right stance. Corvus notices it quicker than I do, but being the friend that he is, he just makes sure that Maverick goes to fix all her mistakes, and he stays with Harlan. Atticus is paired up with Don and is getting angrier every second he isn't winning.

The group training session was Channing's idea, and as he helps me up from the floor, I have to remind myself he didn't do it to embarrass me. My eyes keep catching on his half-pointed ears, trying to find scars from the old piercings. They are faint, and I have to squint in decent lighting to catch sight of them.

I think of the earring my mother wears, the hoop that is too big, and so she wears it near the middle of her ear when it's clearly supposed to be in the lobe. Was it Channing's? Was that why she never took it out? Was it a permanent reminder of who she almost lost and the fear she would always have if she stayed in the Academy? A permanent what-if that she could gently run her fingers over whenever she wanted.

I look over at Don as I get into a fighting stance once more. I want to tell him my theory, my suspicion and my fear, but I bite my tongue once again as I had been for the last two weeks since we had watched those discs. He would not take the conversation well, and he certainly wouldn't listen to me until I finished.

As far as he was concerned, our mother and those discs were now a taboo subject between us. As far as I was concerned, I didn't want to yell at him again.

Would it truly be so bad anyway? Would he ever have to know? It wouldn't change anything. I had already decided that. Yet whenever I looked at my brother, I looked for similarities between him and the werewolf in front of me.

Don and I looked too much like my mother, but there had to be a hint of our father inside of us. Don did not look like a hybrid, and he had never shown the power surges of one, but I could not let the idea of my mother's affair go. I adore my mother, but there are too many unanswered questions that lead me in that direction. I can't ignore it, but I certainly can't talk to…

"Ivy?" Channing frowns at me, waiting for me to make the first move.

"Harlan. Did you invite Knox to this?" I shout across the open space. Harlan and Corvus paused in their grappling, arms around each other's waists as they tried to wrestle the other to the floor.

"I tried," Harlan calls back. "He said he was waiting for you."

Waiting for me. Waiting for me to invite him because he felt awkward or waiting for me to piece together what he had seen that day in Hal's library?

Once more glance at Channing, and I know the answer. The werewolf was quick to hide his shock, but not quick enough. I start to move slowly backwards before turning and jogging back to the Academy's main building and forcing myself not to fully sprint.

Knox and I hadn't spoken more than two sentences to each other since that day when Ryder made him have a vision in front of me. I would wave, and he would only nod in response. He would leave the table pretty soon after I joined with the excuse of mentoring. Harlan said that Ryder was pretty hard on him.

I hadn't focussed on it, not really, not when I was juggling Dean, the Academy and my brother all at once.

My own mentoring was still basic elemental work, but I thought Hal was just being nice because of everything going on with the Idelons. There were no updates on that front, but Channing is still searching for the spies. My parents hadn't been told about it and wouldn't be, not until there were some concrete answers. Maybe Knox would have some of those.

By the time I had jogged for ten minutes to Knox's bedroom door, my breath had barely changed. Training is keeping me fit even if it hasn't yet made me a winner. I smash my palm against the door three times. I hear rustling around in the room and some mutters of conversation. He isn't alone.

The door opens, and Knox does not look happy to see me. Ryder, however, grins. It's unnerving.

"You shouldn't be here. Go back to training," Knox begs me softly.

"Nonsense." Ryder puts his hand on Knox's shoulder and looks me up and down. "Miss Whitlock clearly has something very important to ask us."

"Ivy. Don't." Knox begs me. "Go back to your brother."

I am clearly behind in the conversation, but considering it's a conversation between me and two psychics, I don't feel too badly about that.

"I need to speak to you. Alone. When's your mentoring over?" I insist.

"I'll come to you," Knox says quickly. "Alright, just…go back to your brother."

"What, is something bad going to happen if I'm not glued to Don's side?" I ask him playfully to try and break the obvious tension. When Knox only stares at me, that joke becomes significantly less funny.

"Knox. Is something bad going to happen to Don?" I ask in a hiss.

"Something big…Some…fixed point is coming. I don't know what it is, but it's not happy. No one is happy when it happens." Knox finally relents. "So please, go back to training and Channing and Don. Please. I'll come to you when I know more. Please, Ivy."

I turn my head to look at Ryder. The older Psychic only stares back at me with his face completely neutral. He knows. He knows something, something that will be linked to this fixed point. He can help.

"Is this something to do with Channing?" I ask in a pathetically low voice. A fixed point, something unchangeable. Was that my suspicion being confirmed? Was that Don finding out?

"Not fully," Ryder tells me. Not the answer I wanted. Not a helpful answer either. All it does is make the ball of worry in my chest twist and grow.

"Ivy," Channing calls. I turn on my heel and find him standing at the other end of the hall, glancing between Ryder and me with a small frown. Ryder ducks his head at him but says nothing. "I think Knox is already doing some training of his own. Why don't you go back and start sparring with Don?"

I look at Knox once again, but this time, he does not look me in the eye. His eyes are closed and lips pressed together as if he is fighting back words. I gnaw at the inside of my cheek and nod once before making my way back to Channing.

Once I pass him and he stays in the same position, I look back. Ryder catches my eye and ducks his head in the same way he had to Channing. That ball of worry grows so big it feels like it's suffocating me.

Chapter Twenty-Three

Seventy-three hours later, Knox knocks on the door of Dean's apartment. Dean lets him in, and I make him coffee using Dean's special Siconian coffee grounds. It feels almost like a bribe, giving him the best cup of coffee, but I know that if he has come here, then it is solely to give me the information I want, and he doesn't need that extra push.

"Sugar?" I ask him softly as I give it a stir. He holds up two fingers, and I heap two generous spoonfuls into the chipped ceramic mug. I hand it to him wordlessly, and he takes a gulp even though it's still scolding.

"I'll go for a walk," Dean offers after an awkward moment. I open my mouth to tell him that isn't necessary, but he adds, "We need milk anyway."

Knox watches him go, eyes never leaving my boyfriend, even as Dean slides on a pair of shoes and searches for his keys. Knox only blinks when Dean presses a soft kiss to my forehead. As soon as Dean shuts the door behind himself, Knox turns those florescent eyes to me.

"You need to go back to Parlitan," Knox demands. I bulk at the tone and the request. I had not been expecting that.

"No," I tell him bluntly. "But let's pretend that's not a ridiculous request and that I'll entertain it so you can explain why,"

"Most people would kill for free life advice from a psychic, you know," Knox scowls at me.

"I'm not most people."

Knox finds something amusing in that, his face twisting into a small crooked smile as he shakes his head. He looks down at his hands and rubs them together.

"Ivy, please don't make me beg you," Knox's voice shakes.

"Knox, please don't make me beg you to find out why I should do that," I keep my voice soft.

"Something happens. Something…triggers, and I can't figure out what it is or what happens. I just know I need more time to try and get around it. If you go to Parlitan, then I will have that time. I just…I don't like what I see when you stay here."

"What do you see?" I press, reaching forward to place a hand on his wrist like Don does to me.

"People get hurt." Knox chokes out. "Harlan…Harlan gets hurt. I don't know how or why…I just see him in pain with blood all over his face."

My heart drops into my stomach, and it feels as if it is starting to dissolve in my stomach acid. Would that be Harlan's future? Pain and blood? It had to be my fault if it could get delayed by me leaving the Academy. I hold my breath in my lungs, relishing in that physical pain rather than the emotional one.

"Your mother is crying." Knox continues, his voice now soothing and low, almost hypnotic. "Channing is throwing things. But…none of them are the same. They don't look like they are from the same…the pain lasts a while, Ivy. I may not be able to stop everything from happening, but I need time so I can stop some of it."

"Don…Don and Hal. Can you see their future?" I ask in a panic, my unspoken accusation flashing through my mind. *Secret love child, illegitimate heir, half-sibling.*

Knox finally looks up at me again, but now his eyes are wide, and he is gnawing at his lip so hard he starts to bleed. He says nothing, and my half-dissolved heart slowly moves back up in my chest and expands, the pressure of it causing sharp pin-prick pains with every sliver of breath.

"Knox," I hiss. "Knox, tell me."

"It's not my place," Knox whispers back thickly. "Please, Ivy. Just go back to your parents and their balls and… Ivy, where are you going?!"

I shrug on my jacket, throw on my shoes and turn to glare at him. "You aren't the only psychic in Althania."

Knox yells after me, but he does not follow as I leave the apartment. Maybe he thinks he will have a better shot at convincing Dean.

Chapter Twenty-Four

The Althanian Palace was far too easy for me to get into. I have no idea what Hal must have said to his staff, but I am greeted warmly at the underground station, escorted by the staff and let in through the front door with a soft smile. I added it to my list of evidence that Hal was in love with my mother.

"Lady Whitlock," Ryder's voice echoes around the entrance hall. "I thought you might be on your way. Come with me."

I stay silent as I follow him down the halls, my footsteps echoing around the stone. It's warm in here, a nice heat compared to the bitter air outside.

I am becoming used to the sharp, cold smell of this country, although I doubt it would ever be as welcoming as the spring scent of Parlitan. The lakes here would never be as warm, and the grass would never be as green, but Althania had its own kind of grey metropolis beauty. I would miss it.

Ryder has walked me directly to the crown prince's private library. The doors are closed and, I would presume, locked, but Ryder throws them open like they are as light as air. He gestures me inside but does not follow.

"Make yourself at home. He'll be along shortly," Ryder winks at me before shutting the door with a soft thunk. I am completely alone in what might be the most exclusive room in Althania. The level of trust feels undeserved.

I walk slowly towards the desk, running my fingers close to the shelves but still not daring to touch them. Each one is likely more valuable than all of my parent's lands and accounts. My eyes travel over to the desk, and let out a low whistle.

The memory reader is in the centre, with a small organised pile of multicoloured crystals next to it. A small pink crystal was in the centre of the metal disc, and the runes around the side were gently glowing. It's been left on, which means Hal was in here only moments ago.

I come to a stop behind the desk, legs pressing against the side of the chair as I stare at the symbols. They glow brighter as if

begging me to reach out and touch the stone,
to take a deep dive into Hal's precious
memories. It's probably something boring,
something work-related. Treason to look at,
but the temptation is overwhelming.

My fingertip gently brushes against the rose
quartz just as I hear a yell of "NO" from the
doorway.

Chapter Twenty-Five

This memory stone has more than one memory locked away in it. Once my stomach has settled and I am comfortable in my skin again, I look around. The mental travel was quick and jarring, but I am fine. My body would be back in the office but my mind is here, reeling in thick, condensed air.

I am surrounded by a deep darkness, the only light coming from two large projected images in front of me. I know enough about these things to know that in order to pick which memory, I had to walk through the image, and I would be transported inside.

My options right now are not what I expected. The first screen, the one to my left, shows my mother holding a baby in her arms, the face hidden inside the thick green blanket it is swaddled in. My heart twists. Don.

The other screen, the one on my right, shows Don holding me in a similar green blanket.

His cheeks are chubby, and his hair is all over the place. I dimly remember my mother complaining about how much he hated having it brushed when he was younger.

I looked between the two a few times, torn between which should be the priority. The one with my mother in the frame is more likely to give me the answers I want. But Don's toddler face, his tiny little fists tangled up in my baby blanket. I would like to have that memory for myself.

I hear shuffling, and my name echoes around the room. I have no idea if more than one person can be in a stone at the same time, but even if they can't, I need to start moving. I may only have time for one memory before the royal guards drag me out of here.

I force myself to make the clever choice, and I move quickly toward the picture of my mother. I take a deep breath and hold it as I step through the image. It's uncomfortably hot to step through, a wave of intense heat that leaves me feeling cold as the memory starts.

I am in one of the guest rooms back home. I recognise the wallpaper, but everything else is different. There are trays upon trays of medical equipment, and the bed has been stripped of its fancy bedding. The bin in the corner is overflowing with bloody rags.

My mother is lying in the bed, her hair plastered to her face with sweat. In her arms is a baby, bundled up in a green blanket embroidered with gold. She looks exhausted and far too pale. Her every breath causes her to wince in pain, and she looks near tears, even as she puts on a smile and gently strokes the baby's face with one of her fingers.

My father is at her side, arms wrapped around her shoulders as he stares down at the baby with a soft smile.

"You did amazing," A voice calls from the corner of the room. I snap my head to the side and see Prince Hal. He is dressed in casual clothes, dark jeans, and a dark button-up with the sleeves rolled up. There are traces of blood on his hands.

My mother's lip wobbles. She squeezes the baby tighter to her chest and swallows something down.

"Ivy," My father's voice is firm. I jump, spinning on my heel to look behind me, just in case this is the impossible scenario where my father is in Althania and has followed me into the stone. "We…we want to call her Ivy."

"The plant that will thrive anywhere," My mother's voice breaks as her tears finally start to fall. She brings the baby closer to her face and presses a kiss to its nose. *My* nose. My tiny little baby nose. The room turns blurry. I can hear my own heartbreak, loud and erratic. I was wrong. I was so terribly, terribly wrong.

"Of course," Hal agrees with a frantic nod. He takes one step towards my mother and the baby version of me but seems to think better of it as my father's - my adopted father, I suppose - gaze latches onto him.

"Every year," Dalerian Whitlock insists. "We get to see her every year."

"Every year. More than just once. If you want. If you would like." Hal keeps his eyes on my mother as he answers the question. She sniffs and nods her head, but I don't think she has really heard him. She is too busy adjusting the blanket, making sure I am comfortable. Once she decides I am, she gestures for Hal to come closer.

The Ruler of Vampires, as by now he would
have been given control of his nation and
denied the title of King, blinks before nearly
throwing himself across the room. He takes
me from my mother's arms and holds me
awkwardly but not incorrectly. He stares
down at me, and his face breaks into a grin,
fangs poking into his lips.

A child's giggle echoes around the room, but
the baby version of myself doesn't open her
mouth. I realise that this must be my first
telepathic conversation with Hal. I couldn't
remember when I officially gave him
permission to enter my mind because I had
done it within my first few hours of life.

A tiny baby hand reaches up and starts to pat
Hal's mouth. Hal quickly moves his head
back so that I do not hurt myself with the
sharp points of his fangs. Baby me starts to
whine and slaps harder at his face until he
shows his fangs again.

"I can't," Hal tells the room in a broken
whisper, much like my mother's a moment
ago. "I can't take her."

"You don't want her," Dalerian snarls,
pushing himself to his feet and moving

towards the prince as if he intends to rip me from his arms.

"Of course I want her," Hal growls back, his teeth bared at the fae lord. "But she does not belong in Althania. She does not deserve a life like your fae prince, poked and prodded and watched. She deserves a childhood where she isn't pressured to move mountains. She deserves to simply live and be loved. I cannot give her that. Not now."

"You mean it?" My mother's eyes catch on Hal's. "You'll let me keep her?"

"I want the same deal," Hal says quickly. "Once a year, at least. You don't have to tell her. In fact, you probably shouldn't. Not for a few years, and then when she is old enough… When she is grown up. That's when she should know all of this. Not one second before,"

"Same deal," My mother nods desperately. Hal doesn't look at her. He looks over at the man who would raise me, who would smile and teach me to ride horses and sneak me ice cream at midnight.

"Same deal," Lord Whitlock promises the Crown Prince of Vampires.

Hal nods once, presses a kiss to my tiny forehead, and hands me back to my mother. He leaves the room slowly but without a backward glance.

The memory ends, and I am back in the private library. I gulp down, breathe and blink at the sudden change of light. I look up towards the doorway, where someone had yelled just before I left, and find myself staring at both of my fathers.

Chapter Twenty-Six

Beside Dalerian stands Don and my mother. Next to her is Hal, who is flanked by Channing. Corvus, Maverick, Harlan and Knox create an awkward group in the corner. It's quite a formidable lineup, or it would be if I wasn't furious at the most powerful of them.

"Ivy-" My mother begins, taking a small step forward.

"Who else knows?" I ask, and the calmness of my voice surprises me. None of them answer, so I repeat myself. "Who. Else. Knows?"

"It never mattered to me," Don blurts out. "I want you to know that it never, *ever* mattered to me."

Something inside of me breaks. A small, gentle crack that echoes around my ears. I let out a small breath, my finger twitches, and my brother flies through the air. He crashes into the door with a soft grunt and then a moan as he curls in on himself.

"Ivy!" My mother gapes at me as she rushes to my brother's side. "If you want to be angry at someone, you be angry at me! Don has done nothing wrong."

"It's okay. It's okay," Don tells her through his teeth as he pushes himself into a sitting position. He keeps his eyes on me, those icy eyes that we share, that have always bonded us, that have always made me feel safe and loved and a part of this family. "She didn't mean it."

"Ivy, I am going to need you to calm down," Channing moves in front of Hal. "You are upset. That is natural. But you weren't supposed to see that yet."

"You knew," I accuse him. "It's why you always call me Violet's daughter. I never realised before, but that…that makes perfect sense. It's not a lie, after all. I am her daughter. I'm just also *his.*" I point a finger at Hal.

"You're my daughter, Ivy." The man who raised me interrupts. "Blood or not. You are my daughter. There is nothing anybody will ever say or ever do that is going to change that fact."

"You didn't want me," My calm voice finally breaks, and my father's face swims as tears fill my eyes. "You were going to just hand me over and only see me once a year."

"We always wanted you. Always. But we didn't think it was fair to keep you from Hal and this life. To take away your birthright just so we could be selfish with you," My mother says calmly, helping my brother to his feet.

"But then you snatched me right back. What, did you realise that you had the power if you kept me? You thought that your *precious Prince Hal* would care enough about me to let you walk all over him? Because, newsflash, *Violet,* he doesn't! He couldn't even stick to once a year!" I snarl.

"Ivy, that is enough." Channing growls, the sound ripping through the room. Everyone else recoils from him or jumps. Everyone except Violet and Hal.

"You know, for a split second, I thought it might have been you," I admit in a hoarse whisper as my tears start to fall. "When I heard them name me in that memory. You call me little cub. You smiled at me, and you checked in, and you looked so angry and worried about me when we found that camera in my room. So, when I realised, I thought maybe, just maybe, it would be you."

"What camera?" My mother demands, spinning to look at her two old friends. They both ignore her, their eyes still on me as it gets harder to breathe.

"The way she reacted in that video of your Vilerian games. That big show of force to save you. It seemed to all click into place. Then, less than two seconds later, I remembered that it was not you in that room. It was him. Do you know the survival rates of hybrid babies? It changes with the species, but I took a particular interest in it when I was younger. I still know the fae one's."

I rest myself against the desk, hands gripping the sides of it, and take a deep, calming breath.

"Fae and human babies have a 93% survival rate. Fae and Shapeshifter babies 78%, Fae and Angels 32%, but the mothers pretty much all die cause their bodies aren't made for the wingspan. That also kills a good chunk of the babies. They get stuck, or their wings get

broken and then infected, and they die."
They all stay silent. I force myself to look
into my mother's eyes as I continue.

"Fae and Mermaid babies, 56%. Fae and
werewolf babies, it's 9%. Werewolf babies
rip and tear at the uterus, and fae bodies just
aren't made for that. *That* is also the reason
that Fae and vampire babies have a 3%
survival rate. The babies suck all the life right
out of their mother during the pregnancy.
They don't get enough nutrients, so they die
in the womb, or they take too much, and the
mother dies. Three... Percent... Chance."

"You were always special," My father tells
me in a weak attempt at a joke. My laugh
catches in my throat and nearly chokes me.

"This isn't how I wanted you to find out,"
Hal interrupts our moment. "I had a plan. I
had an order I wanted to show you those
memories in, and I had six different versions
of the same speech trying to tell you that."

"I don't care about any of that," I interrupt
him. "I care about why you had a deal. A deal
that meant you could see me at least once a
year, and you just stopped coming around. I
want to know why you abandoned me."

"It hurt," Hal admits, his voice a low rasp. "More than I ever realised it would. For a few years, I could convince myself that the pain was worth it because you needed me. You needed to see me once a year, and if I got hurt from that, it would be fine because you got what you needed. Then I couldn't convince myself of that anymore."

"Without a word. You stopped coming by without a word." I snap at him. "No goodbye. No good luck. No check-ins or postcards. Just silence. You think that was best for me? You think I deserved that?"

"Ivy, I never want to say goodbye to you," Hal tells me desperately. "I don't even know how I would. From the second you were born, you were my entire life. My entire soul. You deserve better than me. But I can't give you that. I can't change the fact that you are mine, and I wouldn't want to. All I could give you was the distance from me."

"I am not yours," I tell him. No. I tell the whole room. "I am not interested in being a lost princess. I am not interested in wearing a crown and calling you father. I am not interested in you or your life in any capacity. You do not get to claim me in any capacity. I. Am. Not. Yours."

Hal flinches but does not argue. My father takes slow steps towards me as if I am a rabid animal that will bite at whoever dares come close. He wraps his arms around me and pulls me into his chest as my tears turn to sobs.

Another pair of arms wrap around me, soft and smelling of lavender. My mother. My brother's arms join a second later. I sob harder.

The group hug gets even bigger as everyone except Channing and Hal comes to join it. It gets harder to breathe, but I relish in that pain, the suffocation that smells like home. Like Parlitan. I open my eyes and stare straight at Knox as the door to the library softly clicks shut.

Chapter Twenty-Seven

I have to fight my way out of the hug moments later, jabbing with my elbows as my mother refuses to fully let go. I wipe my face self-consciously.

"Boys," Lord Whitlock's voice is scratchy. "Could you give us a moment?"

"Course, Lord D." Maverick gives my shoulder a gentle squeeze before dragging an unhappy-looking Corvus from the room. Harlan and Knox look at each other before slowly slouching after them. Harlan kept looking back at me, specifically at my pointed ears and then my mouth, as if he was looking for fangs.

I reach up automatically and gently run my fingers over my incisors. They don't feel any different. They are slightly more pointed than humans, but not as long as wolves or vampires. Fae teeth. I have fae teeth and fae ears, and I don't even like my steaks cooked bloody, so how in the name of the goddess could I be a hybrid?

The door shuts softly once again, and I am alone with my parents and brother. Don looks at my mother, waits for her to say something, and then shakes his head at her as she fails to.

"It didn't mean anything to me. It never did," Don repeats his sentiment from earlier.

"How long have you known?" I ask him, settling myself against the desk again. I don't trust my legs to keep me upright if any more family secrets come to light.

"Always," Don admits in an ashamed whisper. I nod once, but the lack of verbal response causes him to panic and continue to explain.

"You bit me while you were teething. I got…well." Don laughs a little too much.

I know what vampire bites do. They make you high. They make you high so you won't fight back while you are drained of your blood. What had my bite done to him? I had never bitten someone hard enough to draw blood, not that I can remember. I had always been told not to, that it was unladylike and a dirty fighting tactic.

"I was out of it for days. I had a fever, but I was frantic about getting back to you and checking on you. Mum told me that I would scream and cry until she showed me you were okay. Hal's visit was the next week, and when he arrived, I wouldn't let him hold you. Dad went to hand you to him, and I lunged for him. I dislocated the Crown Prince of Vampires kneecap at six years old." Don tries to catch my eye. I remain silent.

"We had to tell him, and then we made him promise to never, ever tell you," My mother's voice was thick with tears. "Don't blame him. Blame me."

"Oh, don't worry. I do," I scoff. "All those jokes about how Don was dad's heir and I was yours. All those comments about how I was lucky enough to look like you. I can hear them echoing in my head and reminding me how stupid I've been."

"You are not stupid," My father tells me fiercely. "We went to great lengths to make sure you never knew. You are not stupid for not seeing a cover-up. You couldn't have realised. You couldn't have known."

"You have all been lying to me my entire life," I run my hands through my hair, giving it a rough tug. "Corvus. Maverick. Did they know? Harlan didn't. Knox's visions told him. Exactly how many people were in on this secret?"

All of them hesitate, glancing at each other with small frowns. It is just physical proof that I have always been on the outskirts, that my entire life has been a lie.

"Corvus and Maverick found out the first year that Channing and Hal didn't visit. I was drunk and angry and ranting. I'm sorry. I should…I should never have told them," Don looks ashamed and finally stops trying to catch my eye.

"No one else knows," My father promises me. "Only the people that were in this room just now and…"

"And Alice," I glare at my mother, yet another puzzle piece clicking into place. She flinches as if hearing that name causes her pain. "I met her. She got me confused with you and then, right at the end, called me little cub. She knows you had an affair. Doesn't she?"

"She knows more than that," My mother admits.

"Violet," My father murmurs and reaches for her hand. My mother moves it away. I stare into her eyes and find them hard and unflinching.

"She knows that you weren't the first hybrid baby I was pregnant with." Her voice is neutral. "I was pregnant during the first challenge of the Vilerian games. I miscarried."

"The water horses," I let out a slow breath. My eyes close. I had never seen my mother do anything remarkable with her power because she could no longer do it. Her power that day had come from the fetus inside of her.

"I didn't know until after. Until I was bleeding and in agony. I would never have gone into those games if I had, and I never used any of my magic while I was pregnant with you or Don. Not for anything, no matter how small." My mother moves towards me, takes my face in her hands and makes me look at her again.

"You and your brother were always my priority. Keeping you safe. That is my job, and I may have lied to do it, but I did it, and I will continue to do it. I will lie and fight and damn myself over and over again until I am dust in the air if it keeps you safe. You can hate me. You can never want to speak to me or see me again. But I love you, and you *are* mine."

"Safe?" I repeat the word.

"You grew up without being pressed and prodded for a trigger, without being a political pawn or target. Prince Atlas is a royal hybrid. He was sold off within days of his birth. He has had countless assassination attempts that have been covered up, but they happened. I made sure I knew if they happened. He is cold and rude and miserable. You were kept safe from all of that because of Hal's sacrifice. You can hate me. But please don't hate him too." My mother's voice cracks at the end, the strong façade broken.

"You love him," I accuse softly. I don't know why the idea fills me with sadness rather than disgust or rage. There is something broken deep in my mother's eyes, shining with her second round of tears.

"Family secret number three," Don whispers under his breath. I try to meet his eyes this time, but he looks towards the ground. Maybe

272

this is something we could bond over, bridge the gap between us that would undoubtedly be there after this.

"Hal is your mother's mate," My father tells me, eyes focused on the painting behind us.

Mate.

Mate.

"No," I shake my head out of my mother's grip, recoiling away from her touch. "No. No, she can't… You can't…"

"Ivy, please." My mother begs as she reaches for me again. "Please, you must understand. If you just listen to me-"

"NO," I scream. My mother flies through the room, colliding with my father and sending them both tumbling to the floor. I hear a crack echo throughout the room.

"In the space of an hour, I have found out that my father isn't my father. I have found out that my brother knew and did not tell me. I have found out that I am secretly a princess, I am not fully fae, and now…now, I have to sit here and understand the fact that I am also the product of a mating bond and that my mother is the mate of the ruling monarch of Althania.

Excuse me if I am a bit lacking in sympathy for *you,* " I snarl at the couple on the floor.

"Ivy," Don grabs at my arm, but I shake him off. There is the sound of another crack. My father shifts his position so he is blocking my mother from view from my next attack if one should come. I haven't exactly been giving them much notice with them. His eyes flick upwards towards that glass ceiling.

"Ivy." My father warns lowly. "Move to the left."

"Why? Why would you do that to yourself?" I demand as Don tugs at me again. I do not move. "Why would you marry her, knowing she has a mate? Knowing she would never pick you?"

"She did pick me, Ivy," My father looks back at me. "She picked me to save herself. How could I ever be angry at her for that? Now move. MOVE."

A third cracking sound, and then suddenly I am on the floor, Don on top of me, and glass is falling all around us. No. *NO.*

Chapter Twenty-Eight

"Ivy?" Dean's voice drifts around my brain. My eyes flicker open to find that I am in an unfamiliar room. I am in a comfy bed in a large room, the windows set into the stone walls devoid of glass.

Last I remember, I was pinned safely under my brother's body as glass crashed around us. How had I gotten here?

"She's awake," Dean calls to someone behind him. By the time I went to look, the door had closed again, and we were alone.

"How are you feeling?" My boyfriend asks as he gently soothes my hair. "You've been out for hours, and you were so drained."

"Drained?" I repeat, my voice raw and gravelly. My tongue feels like sandpaper rubbing against the roof of my mouth. Dean rushes to bring a glass of water to my lips.

"You don't remember?" Dean frowns.

I remember a lot. I remember my voyage into the memory stone, the confrontation, and my father's heart-breaking answer to my question. I do not remember anything after that.

"The glass ceiling was coming down," Dean started to explain. He gives me a look as I let out an amused snort. "Don was covering you, trying to make sure you didn't get hurt. He says you pushed him off, screamed 'no', and the glass just stopped falling. Right then and there."

"Don says that I stopped gravity?" I raise my eyebrows at him.

"Ivy, when Channing opened that door to the library to take me to see you, you stood there glaring at the hole the glass had made. You didn't let it fall until everyone was out of the way, and then you just collapsed. We were terrified." Dean's fingers flex around mine.

"I don't remember any of that," I admit in a horrified whisper.

"That's normal in hybrids after their full powers are triggered. According to research." A voice says hesitantly from the doorway. I tilt my head. My biological father stands awkwardly, half in and half out of the room.

"Normal?" I repeat. "So I'm normal and not some royal hybrid freak?"

Hal flinches as if I had hit him. Dean runs his thumb over the back of my hand and says nothing, but I can feel the disappointment radiating off him.

"What research?" I ask lowly, less of an olive branch and more because I need to know. I am proficient in the air but nowhere near enough to stop a room full of glass shards falling without a single injury.

"Prince Atlas is the closest match we have for you. Closest living match." Hal amends. "His parents made it their mission to trigger his powers as early as possible. They succeeded when he was around seven years old. They never released how, but for a year or so after that, he caused incredible damage to the Parlitan palace grounds. It's rumoured that's why he was moved to reside in the Alcarlian palace instead."

"I've heard of Prince Atlas." Dean nods. It's a useless comment, but I love him for it. Everyone has heard of Prince Atlas.

"Maybe now I'm a princess, and I will run into him at all those scandalous royal balls. We can exchange tips and tricks." I keep my eyes on Hal, and my sarcasm thick.

"You have made it clear that you do not claim me as your father," Hal's face remains neutral. "I cannot make you. I won't try to make you. But if you ever change your mind, then you will be welcomed into this palace with open arms. I will not claim you as mine until you wish me to. You are free to come and go as you please, just as before. This room has been yours since your mother told me she was pregnant. You are free to use it if you do not feel safe back in your dorm."

"Have you found out anything? About the Idelons?" I ask, focussing more on that issue than everything else. That issue seems manageable. Changeable.

"Channing is still looking into it," Hal tells me with a sad smile. "But we will find the person that put the camera in your room. They will be punished."

"You can also stay with me," Dean offers. The offer is undermined by the look of confirmation he sends Hal's way as if he is looking for praise. It makes my stomach sour.

"Corvus wanted you to know that you could always have his bedroom again if you needed it," Hal smiles slightly. "Quite the family you have built yourself."

"Is Knox still here?" I ignore the compliment. I haven't built myself anything.

"They all are. Would you like me to send them in? Your mother is particularly anxious to see you." Hal offers.

"Only Knox. I want to ask him something first." I sit up in my bed. The room spins but settles after a few seconds of heavy breathing. Hal nods and makes a hasty exit. Dean looks at me and then settles back further in his chair.

"Only Knox," I repeat. "If you don't mind."

"And if I do mind?" Dean teases me. At my scowl, he forces out a chuckle and plants a kiss on my cheek. "I'll be right back as soon as you want me." He promises before leaving.

Knox enters the room a few minutes later to see me downing water straight from the giant jug. He presses his lips together to stop from laughing, shoulders shaking delicately. I drag the back of my hand against my mouth.

"Could be worse. Could be blood," I smirk at him. He stops laughing and shuts the door behind him. He settles into the seat that Dean has just left. It looks comfy and wide enough to curl up in. It would be perfect for reading, which is good because the walls are full of books.

Books for toddlers, younger children, pre-teens and a few new adult titles that are on my to-be-read pile. There were a few older gaming consoles hidden away in cupboards with glass doors, clearly unopened. The latest console is connected to a large television mounted on the wall, ready for use.

"Ryder said he redecorates it every year," Know tells me as he looks around the room. "Just in case."

"You should have told me," My voice sounds more like a whine, a child complaining they weren't told it was so close to bedtime.

"How?" Knox doesn't argue, but his question makes me falter. How would I have preferred this to go?

"Fair point," I admit after a few moments of silence. I can't think of any scenario that would have ended with me happy or even content with being told.

"I scared you. Didn't I?" Knox looks down at his hands, rubbing them together slowly. His shoulders are tense.

"You? No," I say slowly. "Where did my mind go when you said there would be pain and a trigger? Yes. This isn't anywhere near what I thought, but…does Harlan still get hurt? He didn't look hurt today, and I don't want him to be. I want to know what you saw. All of it. No matter what."

"You finding out what you are and what you're capable of is a fixed point. That's *the* fixed point. It was always going to happen. You can't beat yourself up about people getting hurt during it. That's not your fault," Knox looks up at me again. His eyes are brighter than before, more fluorescent than I had ever seen on anyone.

"Does Harlan still get hurt?" I repeat. My throat feels tight as my mind wanders. Harlan could be stabbed, shot, beaten, kidnapped-

"Not as badly as before," Knox interrupts my spiralling thoughts. "Something in how you handled it today. He isn't hurt as bad. Still hurt, still bleeding and bruised, but not as bad.”

That is not the answer I wanted, but it eases the heaviness in my chest. Harlan being hurt could be in training. If he isn’t as bad, then it means he’s more likely to survive, and if Harlan survives, then I can handle the rest. As long as they all survive, I can handle the rest.

“My trigger…” I trail off as I try to find the end to my question.

“Your trigger was finding out. Your powers were locked away and hidden for so long that they have never been part of your identity. Finding out about them set them free. It’s beautifully simplistic, really.” Knox shrugs. I suppose for him, simple things are his favourite. Less tangents and what-ifs to ponder over. Less possibility to agonise over.

“I wonder what Atlas’s one was. If he was triggered so young and knew all along,” I whisper. “I wonder if that would be better, easier in a way.”

“You wish you had grown up here?” Knox frowns.

"No. I wouldn't give up my family for the world. But I am going to spend the rest of my life thinking about that. Thinking about the differences."

"You have adjusted very quickly," Knox makes it sound like an accusation.

"I thought it was Don. I had already been doing some mental leaps when this disaster of a day happened," I mutter.

"I did try and warn you," Knox smiles to show me the 'I told you so' was meant in jest. I reach over and give his shoulder a playful shove.

"I'll listen to you more," I promise.

"And insult me more?" Knox asks.

"Oh, of course," I snort. "The best of friendships are built on insults. Have you seen Maverick and Corvus? I'm surprised both of them made it to adulthood with how horrible they were with each other during training."

"You don't hit me with wooden swords," Knox reminds me, although I notice that he looked away from me when I asked my question. Was he hiding things from me already? Or was I so paranoid that I would always assume that people were lying to me from now on?

"Not yet," I smirk. "Next training session. Me and you. See who wins."

"And take away Proxima's fun?" Knox shook his head sadly. "She likes kneeing me in the stomach. It's probably something her therapist should deal with. Seems like a weird fixation."

I start to laugh again, the sound echoing around the room as the door opens and my brother, Corvus and Maverick tumble into the door. Maverick falls onto the floor as Corvus shoves him, and Don is bent over, hands gripping the door handle.

"Were you seriously eavesdropping? You have nothing better to do?" I scowl at them.

"Something better than finding out if my little sister is going to hate me for the next five centuries? No, not really," Don's forced smile makes me more uncomfortable than the joke.

"I'm team Ivy for this, by the way," Maverick interjects with a wicked grin. "Whatever my princess wants. I'll kick both their asses and swear fealty on both my knees."

"Traitor," Corvus mutters as he gently taps his foot against his friend's ankle. He turns to look at me and smiles. "Seriously though, we three can have a fight to the death, and the winner can be your soul-bonded slave. Or slit their own throat or cut out their own tongue. Whatever makes you happy."

"I am not a princess," I hold up one finger and then continue to tick off points. "I do not want any of you to die. A silencing spell from a witch would work better than you slicing out your own tongue, and it's a wonder none of you have lost a limb yet."

"She still loves us," Maverick beams, strutting over to my bed and throwing himself down on it next to me. He wraps his arm around me, giving my temple a loud, dramatic kiss. I grin despite myself. For some reason my eyes are watering as they catch on my brother, still standing awkwardly by the door. I hold my arms open to him even as I hug Maverick back.

Don leaps over, throwing himself down so heavily that we all bounce, and cradles my

head into his chest. We both sniff back tears
as he squeezes me a little too tight.

Chapter Twenty-Nine

Two days later, I am back at The Academy, much to my parent's dismay. My mother is staying in the Althanian Palace until Channing puts the Ideleon situation to bed. Maverick and Corvus had been snitches, letting that information slip to my father, who, in turn, told my mother. Ironically, with the excuse of 'no secrets' between them.

This doesn't mean that my life is back to normal. I don't walk through the halls alone, I don't stay in my rooms alone, and I can only go to the bathroom without one of the boys following me inside.

None of my teachers say anything, but Professor Gallagher eyes up Corvus uneasily during *Lawful Ethics*. The werewolf makes a point of looking as menacing as possible when it's his turn to escort me anywhere.

Maverick is more of a charmer, mingling in with the students and shooting everyone his typical dazzling grin. He asks other students questions and soothes Proxima and Atticus's egos if they get something wrong. Harlan and I get playful tuts and handwritten notes. He is everyone's favourite.

Don always stays by the exit or my side. Proxima tries to talk to him, batting her eyelashes and hanging on to every word, but he is only polite in return. Atticus tries not to acknowledge he is even there, which is really the point of this useless guardian routine.

For private training sessions, all three of them spar with us in a separate room. Other students talk, but it's all petty grumbling.

If it was just me in these sessions, then there would be a reason to talk. But it's me, Atticus, Proxima, Harlan and Knox. Instead of looking like I have been singled out by the Prince of Vampires for a strange reason, it looks like the Prince has taken a specific interest in certain noble children. Let that rumour fester in everyone's minds for a while.

Proxima and Atticus haven't been told about my true nature, but I can see the vampire eyeing me every time my magic is a little too powerful. We have been working mostly with air and water since the fire was too dangerous for me to use inside right now. Whenever I catch her eye, I purposefully stumble over something. I don't think it is convincing.

Dean is encouraging every time he watches a training session, which is rare as the Vilerian Games preparation begins. The games themselves are still months away, but the Academy's arena had not been used in almost two centuries. There were major renovations to be done, and Academy staff were given a significant pay increase for shifts spent helping there instead. I knew it wasn't a coincidence that Dean was always picked for those shifts.

He was missing from this training session, which I was thankful for as Maverick managed to pin me yet again. At least this time, it had taken him a few minutes of wrestling around on the floor first.

"You are getting better," Mav promises me as he helps me to my feet. I scowl at him.

"I think so, too!" Proxima yells across to me quickly as she narrowly avoids a swipe from Harlan. When those two spar, it is like a dance. Proxima will bend and twist out of Harlan's way, and he will glide out of the path of her returning blows. He has always been more attuned to Earth, but his air skills are slowly getting better. I shoot her a weak smile.

Channing moves from his spot in the corner of the room and to my side. He has been at every session without fail. I have not spoken to him at a single one.

He gives me advice, and I grunt. He adjusts my posture, and I nod my understanding. Every time I think of speaking to him, my throat closes. It is too much of a betrayal, too accepting of the decades-long lie. It is the same reason I have yet to speak to Hal past blunt, pedantic answers during mentoring. I tell him, 'Yes, I understand' and 'I will try that,' but when he asks how I am feeling, I blank him. He still asks every session.

"Your mother wants to have dinner with you tonight," Channing tells me softly.

"I have plans," I answer bluntly. While I am on speaking terms with my mother, the exchanges are brief and solely for Don's sake.

"Plans more important than dinner with your parents?" Channing raises an eyebrow at me.

"It's date night," I bite back.

"I'm sure Dean wouldn't mind rearranging," Channing presses on.

"I would mind."

"Perhaps tomorrow, then?"

"Channing. When I want to eat dinner with my mother, I will tell her." I snap at him, patience already worn thin.

"Ivy, this is a conversation that cannot wait," Channing speaks slowly and with purpose. When I finally look at him, those dark amber eyes have the same look as they did at our first training session. He is begging me to figure something out. The problem is I don't care enough to figure it out.

I am still mad, and from my point of view, rightfully so. I have been lied to and hidden away. I have family that I have never met, and I'm unsure if I even wanted to.

Did I want a new set of grandparents, especially ones with such public personalities? Did I want the possibility of them rejecting me, of forever seeing me as some stranger who had been manipulated into their lives? What chance would I have to bond with them now that I was already grown? All of these were questions that wiggle around my brain when I think of the cutoff possibility of keeping Hal in my personal life.

He would almost always be in my professional one. He was an international powerhouse that would always have to be in consideration for whatever other country I pledged my undying allegiance to as a Vilerian guard. The thought of pledging it to Hal or to the future hybrid king of Parlitan makes my skin crawl.

Maybe I could live with the humans in Jarian. Maybe Dean would be happy with me there. Maybe he would want to go to Blendora and cut down on his coffee bills. We could go anywhere as long as my secret was kept.

"Ivy. Please. I know that you are upset, but…"

"Is this about the camera you found in my room?" I cut Channing off. He says nothing, his face a neutral mask. The smirk drops from my face. It is. Oh, Goddess.

"Fine," I grind out. "Let's go."

"It's not time for dinner yet," Channing tells me. I stare at him.

"So…it's no news then." I realise. "You were trying to trick me into going to dinner under the guise of Idelon information, but your information is that there is no new information. Do I look like a child to you?"

"IVY," Don's voice booms across the space. I snap my head to look at him. A strangled cry breaks free from my throat. The walls and windows were covered in frost, the floor glossy and slippery. Each person's breath was now visible, and poor Proxima was physically shuddering.

"I…I…" I start to stutter and stare down at my hands, but I know that it is useless. My magic bursts out of me randomly now, and my hands do not control it well.

The last time me and Dean had private time alone, I had burst all the lightbulbs in the apartment. The issue this time was I couldn't just buy new bulbs. I had to try to change the whole room temperature, but I didn't know how.

"Hey. Hey, look at me," A deep voice coaxes me out of my panic. His hands on my shoulders are so warm they feel like they are burning. I glance up, and Corvus's golden eyes bore into mine.

"Deep breaths," The werewolf orders before he starts to take large breaths of his own, leading by example while he continues to stare at me. I stare back, and my breathing changes to match his.

I focus on anchoring myself the same way I had when I was first learning magic as a child. I ground myself in the earth, absorbed in the magic of each breath, and reminded myself that it is constant, and so, therefore, am I.

"Jesus," Harlan says after a moment, giving a dramatic shudder as the room changes temperature. It is a few degrees hotter than before, but nothing too uncomfortable.

"Sorry," I whisper.

"What. In the Goddess. Was that?" Proxima screeches in panic, hands in fists at her side as if she were ready to fight us all.

"You two. With me. Now," Channing points at Proxima and Atticus. He starts to walk to the side door, the small room where we keep the practice weapons.

Atticus waits for Proxima to move before he does as he is told. From the look on Proxima's face, she is only doing it because

Channing outranks and could out-finesse her.
She goes willingly or forced, but either way,
she goes.

When she comes out moments later, there is
blood around her mouth. She looks at me but
not directly at my face. She moves forward,
and I tense. If she hits me, then that's fair.
Freezing must have hurt.

She doesn't hit me. She kneels before me and
bows her head.

It makes me want to scream.

Chapter Thirty

Don convinces me to dinner. Don with the help of Corvus and Maverick anyway. It also gets me away from my Academy friends for the evening, and frankly, I want to be far away from Proxima and her adoring gaze. The girl is a royalist through and through.

"Ivy. We will be late!" Don calls into Maverick's room, where I am getting ready at the mermaid's insistence. He has the best mirror. I pick a dress that is Parlitan blue and when I leave, I find that all three boys have had the same thought.

Don wears an elaborately detailed blazer, Corvus a tight button up t-shirt. Maverick, in true fashion, is wearing a one-piece with embroidered edges. It is flamboyant for a casual family dinner, but then I suppose nothing about my family will ever be casual again. Too much has passed. Too much was hidden.

All the boys offer me their arms so we can walk to the portal. They live in a nice building close by to Dean's place and a public portal. The silk of my dress swishes around my ankles as I take my brother's arm. He smiles, and he leads me outside.

The air is harsh, cold and smells like metal. It is a far cry from the fresh grass smell of home, but I find myself taking deep gulps of it to calm my nerves. Althania was alive and thriving, people bumping into others on every street. It's different to the sounds I was raised around. I wonder if the sounds of nature will be too quiet for me now.

The line to the portal is small, and most people keep their heads down as they scroll their phones and wait for their turn. A couple of people glance over at us and at our attire, but no one makes a comment.

The vampire portal operator looks surprised at Don's request for the Althanian Palace. Not surprising - most people invited there would have their own private portals. He gestures for Don to place his thumb on the scanner, and his eyebrows shoot into his hairline as it is immediately approved. He waves us forward. Don does not let me be hesitant for even a second and drags me through straight into a fancy dining room.

The table is the centrepiece of the room, made of some dark rock with silver strands like spiderweb running through it. It is overflowing with delicious-smelling dishes, steaming bowls of vegetables and thick slabs of meat. The twenty chairs around it are carved from the same stone, and not all of them are empty.

Lord Dalerian Whitlock sits in the centre of the table, dressed in a navy three-piece suit. My mother sits to his left, closer to the head of the table, in a matching dress. Hers has no embroidery or fancy pattern. It is long-sleeved, modest and plain. My mother back in action.

Opposite her is Prince Hal. He has a thin golden band around his hand, not a crown that I had seen before, but a crown nonetheless. His suit is pure black, and his tie is a bright scarlet. He makes his stone chair look like the onyx throne on which he rules.

Channing sits to his left, opposite my father. He wears an all-leather ensemble that resembles his gear enough that I feel instantly more comfortable. A lot more comfortable than how Dean looks, settled on Channing's other side in a new tuxedo.

The sixth person at the table makes me laugh, a sudden sound of joy. Opposite Dean and next to my father is Valentina in a gorgeous ruffled rouge dress. She grins at me, fangs digging into her bottom lip. She stands from her chair as I rush to her. She drags me into her arms and holds me there, as comforting as always.

"You-How-Why?" I laugh into her collarbone.

"You have been in Althania months and have not tried to see me." Valentina says in mock displeasure. "So I needed a drastic measure."

"Drastic indeed!" I giggle as I finally pull back. I had missed her, a realisation that hit me like a train as I took in her pale skin and thick dark brown hair, the crinkle under her bright blue eyes, and her smile. I hadn't seen her smile, seen her at all, for far too long.

"I thought you would still be with your father," I say as a flimsy excuse. She gives me a knowing look, and my smile turns sheepish.

"It's a lot, moving countries and being accepted at the Academy. Harlan has been keeping me up to date. You are forgiven," Valentina gives me a squeeze before letting me go.

I have no proof that she knows who I really am. Harlan would not have told her specifics, just that there were family arguments, but I am so paranoid now that everyone who looks at me for longer than three seconds sees a phantom crown on my head.

This dinner with a ruling royal was hardly a normal occurrence for Valentina and would be a massive hint. How exactly had my parents managed to keep this secret for so long if they were doing things like this?

"It is a pleasure to have you here with us, Valentina," Prince Hal grins at my friend. She smiles back politely and bows her head lowly.

"It is an honour to be invited, your grace." Valentina says softly.

"Any friend of Ivy's is a friend of the crown. You are invited to be here whenever you wish to be," Hal is still smiling as he casually hands out access to what should be the most secure building in the country. I have the sudden urge to whack him.

Valentina's eyes widen as she turns to look at me, her mouth dropping open for a second as she stumbles over her stuttered thanks. Hal's grin stays stuck on his face before he gestures for her to take her seat again.

This won't make me want to come here, I think as I find myself staring at my biological father. He jolts slightly and turns to meet my gaze. He looks proud, and one horrifying second later, I realise why.

He heard me. I had somehow sent that thought into his mind without him opening the connection first. My stomach drops.

Was that not a skill I should realise I was using? What if I did it accidentally again to other people and had no idea? What if that was what was out of my heritage? What if I was the reason this all came tumbling down, the reason I would be shackled to a crown and throne?

I can show you how to control it. Hal's voice is soft and reassuring, and it squashes down some of my panic. *If you will let me.*

Fine. I spit down that bond even as I turn away and head to my seat. My mother beams at me, but I can see straight through it. Her body language is tense, and her wine glass is nearly empty. She wants my forgiveness tonight, but I cannot bring myself to give it to her.

"How was class?" My dad- Dalerian- asks me with a real smile. I smile back.

"Class has been fine. My assignments have all been in on time and most of them I've enjoyed," I respond as I look down the table at the food.

"Good. That's good. Are you still looking at entering the Vilerian games?"

"Yes," I answer automatically. I do not look at my mother, Hal or Channing even as I lean over the werewolf to grab a small bowl of buttered peas. "Hopefully, with Harlan and Knox."

"Another fae and a psychic? Interesting choices. But good ones." My father nods approvingly. "Your uncle will be the first in line for tickets."

"Ballard could always come and sit in the royal box with us to watch her. I was going to invite you all," Hal interjects as he slices into an almost raw steak. My father tenses for the briefest second before nodding.

"That would be most kind. Thank you, Your Highness." My mother reaches over to give my father's wrist a gentle squeeze even as her eyes stay on Hal.

"I still can't believe you and Harlan are actually going to fight in those things!" Valentina says as she cuts her raw meat into delicate pieces. "I'm going to have to watch through my fingers."

"You think I would let anyone hurt Harlan?" I ask her teasingly.

"I think the amount of damage you'll do to anyone that tries will put me off my popcorn," Valentina teases back. "Sienna already has us on a waitlist for tickets."

"If you tell me how many of Ivy and Harlan's friends want to see the games, I can organise a box for you as well. Perks of the games being held in Althania this year. I get to demand as many outrageous things as I want," Hal grins over his goblet.

"Add us onto that," Maverick says as his knife makes a scrapping noise against his plate. "I already have signs planned out."

"Don't worry. We've already told him nothing about your ass," Corvus winks at me. It causes me to choke on my drink, the same magic water from our first night at the Academy, but my laugh echoes around the hall.

The dinner continues like that for the next hour. Hal interjects with kind offers, which Valentina accepts gratefully, and the boys break the tension with jokes. Channing stays silent the entire time, barely looking at my parents as he eats. When the servants come in to clear all the plates and replace the dishes with desserts, he smiles and thanks each one. We all do.

"Three more places have been set," Don points out as his gaze turns to the crown prince. "Why?"

"The dowager King and Queen have returned from their vacation to Tulinth. They asked to attend this evening if they were back in time. I suppose they have just got home," Hal says nonchalantly, although he makes a point of looking down the table at the various cakes and pastries.

"The third?" My voice comes out colder than intended.

"Alice went with them," Hal's voice softens. My eyes move over to my mother, who is staring with her mouth slightly open, unsure if she should respond.

"How has Alice been?" I ask genuinely. My biological father looks up into my eyes, and while they look nothing like mine, the emotion in them is familiar. Sad acceptance.

"She has her good days and her bad days." Hal says slowly. "She has more good days when she is back at her childhood home."

"She must be important for her to be escorted by royalty," Don frowns as he takes a gulp of his wine.

He might be imagining some tall warrior woman with flaming wings and a sword. Maybe she had been once upon a time. I hadn't asked. I was ashamed to admit the angel had slipped from my mind these past few weeks. All I knew was that she knew. She just didn't know what she knew, and that was the heart-breaking part.

"Very," My mother agrees with his statement as her hand digs hard enough into my father's for her fingers to turn white. Her clear anxiety fills me with a sick mix of satisfaction and shame.

The door opens, and I am overwhelmed with various emotions that I am not sure I truly feel any of them. I feel nervous to finally see the dowager royals in the flesh, but that is cancelled out by how happy I am to see Alice smiling. I am angry that I am meeting my third set of grandparents without warning, but that is cancelled out by the exhaustion from my long day until it is a simmering ember in my heart.

"Violet," Alice says my mother's name as if it were a prayer as she hobbles to her side. My mother moves slowly, carefully, from her chair and towards Alice with the intent to meet her halfway.

"Hello Alice," My mother's voice hitches as her hands cover the angels. Her hands are smooth, and against Alice's paper-thin skin, they look almost tan. "It's been a long time."

"My letters. You got them, didn't you?" Alice looks up at my mother with wide eyes.

With her hunched back and shedding wings, Alice is half of my mother's height.

"Everyone." My mother's smile flutters in time with her eyelashes as she blinks back tears. "I wrote back. Every time."

Alice pulls her hands from my mother's grip. She places her wrinkled hands on both sides of my mother's face. She traces her thumbs across her cheekbones before nodding once.

"You should have had so many portraits," The angel tells Lady Whitlock of the Fae sadly. "Perhaps in another life."

"Perhaps," My mother kisses the angel's palms before leading her to a spare seat next to me. I was so focused on their interaction, on watching Alice's feet so she would not trip, and on moving plates of food closer to her seat so she wouldn't have to reach so far that I jumped when someone else said my name.

The dowager Queen Rochelle is beautiful. Her raven black hair hangs in natural waves down her back and is pinned from her face with small emerald hairclips. Her mouth is painted bright red with dark outlines and is currently set into a dazzling grin. There are

faint wrinkles around her mouth and
forehead. Her eyes have weak laugh lines. It
is her eyes that cause me to stop, hands still
holding a silver platter.

Those eyes are glorious, bright green like the
jewels in her hair, but with a thick band of
gold around her iris. Unusual, rare and
stunning. The sudden wish to have inherited
them is overpowering and sickening.

Her husband, the dowager King Buchanan,
stands tall with his hands behind his back. He
stares at me with eyes of pure onyx. Hal's
eyes, although his, had never made me feel
like I was drowning in despair as I do now.
He has no laugh lines, and I have to squint to
see his wrinkles, although if memory serves,
he is fifty years older than his wife. His hair
is a thick chestnut colour like his sons. There
was no denying who Hal's father was.

"Ivy," The Dowager Queen repeats my name,
rolling it around on her tongue as if she were
testing it out. "What a beautiful name for
such a beautiful girl. You truly do look
exactly like your mother."

"Thank you, your grace," The response
comes immediately even as my eyes move up

to find that neither she nor her husband are
wearing their crowns.

Buchanan and Rochelle abdicated to their son
decades ago. If they had not done that, then
they would be the current rulers with all the
responsibilities. But then, Buchanan was only
king because his elder brother Percial had
abdicated so he could marry a werewolf for
love and not have to worry about legitimate,
unadopted heirs.

The irony was not lost on me. The Dowager
Queen winks at me as if she is in on the joke
that she thinks I made. She then turns her
gaze to the table, and her smile becomes
more polite.

"You must be Donaugh. Such a pleasure to
meet the Whitlock heir and to host him here
in Althania. Ah! And Violet's wards, Corvus
Dalloway and Maverick Kanlore. A pleasure
to meet you as well." The previous queen
takes her husband's hand.

The three boys all duck their heads in a sort
of bow and mutter their polite agreements
that it was an honour to meet her. Valentina
seems to not know what to do, so she keeps
her head down in a permanent bow.

"This is my father. Lord Dalerian Whitlock."
I say pointedly as a few seconds pass, and it
becomes clear that they do not intend to
acknowledge him at all.

"Of course!" The dowager king turns his
body to give both my parents a large,
practised grin. "It is good to see you both
again after all this time. We should catch up
once the children have left. I have some
disturbingly old whiskey in my study that I
need to share."

"Such a kind offer," My father says with a
small, polite smile. His tone is the same one I
use when I am invited to a social event. I
would rather be mauled than attend.

"Mother. Father. If you wouldn't mind sitting
so it isn't considered the height of rudeness
when I devour this Siconian cheesecake," Hal
shoots his mother a lopsided grin. For a brief
second, he looked like the young man I had
seen in those home videos.

"Save some for the younglings," The
Dowager Queen tutted, smoothing down her
son's hair as she passed as if he was not the
most powerful man in the country.

They sit in the remaining two spots, the King
on Alice's other side and the Queen next to
my father. She keeps those unusual eyes on
me for every second I stay in that dining
room. When Don loudly states that he is
tired, I am the first from my chair.

Chapter Thirty-One

I am early to my next mentoring session. I had been in the Academy's library all night, finishing off the last of my assignments before our first set of exams in two weeks. My entire body aches and my hands shake from all the coffee I have guzzled, but I am too paranoid about my new magic to think about anything else. I need to know how to keep my thoughts mine, and I need to know it now.

I stand outside Hal's library doors, pacing back and forth. Ryder told me I could go inside, but the idea of being alone in that room again sends a shudder through me. Who knows what other hidden things I would find.

Maybe I was secretly able to turn into a dragon. Maybe I was actually a tribrid if such a thing was possible. I had never heard of one. Maybe I should look into that. Would I even be able to have children of my own? Would they have to be with a fae or a vampire? If I could, would those children be tribrids?

"Gold coin for your thoughts," Hal teases me, his voice echoing slightly down the empty hall.

"You don't want them even for free," I scowl and stop pacing.

"I'd give up my entire country just for you to tell me your favourite colour," Hal tells me earnestly. A few months ago, that would have warmed my heart, the idea that I was back in a prince's favour and that my uncle Hal and Channing were back in my lives for good. Now, it all just leaves a bitter taste in my mouth.

"Althania is worth so little? Don't tell the witches." I mutter darkly.

Hal lets out an unamused sound before opening the door to his private library and gesturing me inside. I side step around him and head to the seat set in the corner, far away from the large desk and the memory reader on top of it.

Hal pauses as he closes the door behind us, looking at me and then the distance between me and his desk. He decides against sitting at it and instead props himself against the bookcase closest to me.

"How many slip-ups have you had?" He asks me bluntly.

"None. That I know of." I answer.

"You would know." Hal scratches his chin. He hasn't shaved this morning. "People are not very good at hiding their shock when someone else is speaking in their head. Not without practise."

"That's reassuring," I say honestly.

"When you were little, you would always squeal whenever I spoke to you that way," Hal continues hesitantly as if I will lash out at any small reminder of what he is.

"I didn't know that was something I would be able to do. My powers have always been that of a fae. Elemental. Nature-based, which this isn't," I say around the lump in my throat.

"What do you know about the Althanian royal line?" Hal slowly walks around the bookcases near me, searching the shelves. I can't tell if it's to avoid looking at me or if he is genuinely looking for something.

The question is somehow a nice distraction, and I rack my brain for anything from my history classes or from my research into my 'uncles' when I was younger to try and figure out why he called himself Prince when, by all rights, he was a King.

"Your father was second in line, but his elder brother abdicated so he could marry a werewolf. So that the Althanian royal line would continue with a legitimate bloodline. They've adopted two children who are in line to the throne. I think they are…third and fourth. Before your uncle Flanier and his multiple love children. Also, depending on whether your father would ever want the throne back." I say slowly. I avoid looking at him as the unspoken extra comment hangs in the air. *Hybrid fertility is too unreliable. The line would die.*

"We are an unusual line," Hal agrees with a slow nod. "We abdicate more than most. We do not let our egos get ahead of us."

"Your parents gave you the throne after your games." I look at the shelf he has paused in front of. The hardbacks look old, but the leather covers are well looked after.

"They gave me the throne after I let my mate move to a different country because that was the best thing for her. After I showed that I am willing to put the people I love about my own wants and needs." Hal's voice is suddenly hollow.

"I thought…I thought that being apart from your mate was agony. That's what all the stories say." I look down at my hands as he turns. I can't bring myself to look into his eyes.

"It…" Hal presses his lips together as he thinks over his answer. "It was. Every time I left, it hurt, leaving her and leaving you. It took me a long time to be able to leave her in Parlitan and not come back here and completely shut down. I threw myself into projects with the hope that one day, eventually, she would come back and see them. This library was her favourite place in this palace. I spent every moment I could in here, remembering and imagining her being here."

I try to swallow that lump in my throat, my mother's recorded laugh echoing in my ears as I take a long look around the room. Had she thrown herself down in that armchair, curling her legs up and flicking through the pages of some seedy romance novel? Had she scribbled her assignments on that desk, spilling ink on her fingers in her panic to finish it on time?

"Yet you still left. For years," My whisper comes out as a hoarse accusation.

"She is happy in Parlitan. She is happy with Dalerian. When she is happy, I can be happy. Even if that happiness is because I am leaving and our daughter still does not know who I truly am," Hal's voice hitches. I look at him, but he has ducked his head. This time, he does not want to look at me.

"My point about our…about *my* bloodline is that thousands of years ago, when Vileria was first named and the countries divided after the demon wars, Buchan, the first king of Althania, was married to Princess Elneyia of Calent. They had one hybrid daughter, Bufiel, who married a witch lord and moved back to Calent, where she had no children but lived happily. Their heir, Ianel, and second son, Trevial, were adopted orphans from Buchan's home village, which was destroyed in the war." Hal removed a thick black leather book from the shelf, whose title was in large golden calligraphy.

"Elneyia could not stand the idea that her children would not be able to speak every day, that she would have to send letters through portals to her daughter, and so she created a spell. Legend has it that the spell involved parts of the last demon her husband had slain in the battlefields and that Buchan had a secret chamber of demon remains under this very castle as his medals of victory." Hal finally glances over at me and smiles slightly as he hands the book over to me. "We tried to find it once, your mother and I. There is no chamber."

The book is heavier and larger. It covers my entire lap. I trace my fingers over the gold paint. *Althanian History Vol I.*

"That spell made it possible for all of her family to communicate telepathically no matter the distance." Hal tells me as I slowly open the front cover. Inside, on the front page, is a handwritten note.

Buchan, the first King of Althania.

This is the first of many history books to be written about you, and it shall be written by a woman who loves you. May you always do something to be worthy of the honour bestowed upon you.

Your Queen,

Elneyia

I let out a small laugh. On the surface, it was kind and doting. A stupid man would probably think that it was meant as a compliment. As a woman who had been scorned, I could see it for what it really was. It was a warning.

"Your mother found it funny too," Hal's voice is back to its normal warmth. "I asked what she was laughing at. I thought she was laughing at me, at my future, at the fact I would be honoured with the weight of a country. She looked up at my confusion, and she laughed even harder."

"Elneyia was a witch." I remind him. When our eyes meet, we are both smiling. "Witches are petty like the nature circles they draw power from. She was warning Buchan to remain worthy of her."

"I suppose he must have," Hal chuckled. "Since she gave him access to her and her children's minds. When Elneyia died at eight hundred and seven years old, her husband was quick to follow her. Ianel found his father with his wrists cut on his mother's grave the day after they laid her to rest."

"That spell. It must have been powerful to have lasted generations." I turn the conversation back to the reason I was here.

"It was. A side effect of the spell was the children being able to access other people's minds. That power became diluted until it is as it is now. We, with the power, must have permission from the people whose minds we are in. But we can always coax it out of someone. They simply have to say 'yes' or lower their mental wall, and we have access for as long as they live."

"You didn't give me access. You looked shocked I could do it," I frown.

"But you are my child. The purpose of the original spell was to keep a family connected. You will always have access to my mind just as I will always have access to yours." Hal's smile turns sad. I suppose I didn't disguise my split second of horror well enough.

"I just thought that I had let you in back when I was a child," I admit. It was yet another hint that I had missed.

"It takes some practise learning what the limits are, how soft to be to stop from hurting someone. I would like to show you how. I don't want you to be unaware of what you can do now that your hybrid part is unlocked." Hal tells me slowly.

"Do you think I will suddenly want to drink blood now? That I will want my steaks rare or that the vampire part of the smoothie menu will seem more inviting?" I blurt out. "I keep overthinking everything. Every time I stay up late or run a little faster than I could before, I wonder if it's because of this new part of me or because of my training. Everything just seems so different now, but I'm not sure which change to blame."

"Althania is a new world for you, Ivy." Hal starts to reach out towards me, then changes his mind and lowers his arm. "But it is your world. If you want it to be."

With that statement echoing in my mind, it's no longer a secret other meaning, causing my heart to beat anxiously in my chest. I stand to my feet and start our lesson.

Chapter Thirty-Two

When I stumble out of the portal closest to Dean's apartment, I am not sure which part of me is more tired, my mind or my body.

Hal was taking it easy on me, making it obvious when he was about to try and prod into my mind so I could practise mental shields.

When I could quite easily deflect him, he moved on to having me try and invade his mind. I was good at that, too, although from the way he winced each time, I think he was only being kind, and I was far too heavy-handed. He didn't want to push me even further away. My issue was that his mind was strong enough to take it, but when it came to Don or Dean or Maverick or when it came to my family, their minds might not be.

The private training session afterwards had me constantly falling on my ass. Even Proxima managed to pin me, and she was clearly trying to let me win. Since everyone in that room was aware of my biological situation, there was no need for her to hide her obvious adoration. She ducked her head in respect, and she got halfway through calling me 'your grace' before my glare made her stop in her tracks.

I twist my keys in the lock, shooting Dean's neighbour a polite smile as he passes by on his way to the elevator. I know that Dean is friendly with them, going to the building meetings and picking up post from the management office for them if he saw it there, but with my busy schedule of school and mental breakdowns, I hadn't been quite as nice.

"Hey, babe!" Dean grins over the back of the sofa at me. I smile but freeze in the doorway as I see that he isn't alone.

Two other humans are on his sofa, one of which is the brunette girl from the bar that night a few months ago. The other is a scrawny teenager, fourteen at most, with similar brown hair and facial features.

"Hi," I say as I shut the door behind me. "I'm Ivy."

"This is Carrie and her brother Josh. They just moved in downstairs," Dean tells me with an easy grin. It melts away any reservations I had, although a small part of my brain complains that I won't be able to go have a scalding hot bubble bath now.

"Oh, that's cool!" I say politely as I drop my keys in the tiny bowl by the door and loop my arms around Dean's shoulders from behind. I kiss his cheek quickly. "Are you guys all settled already?"

"Couple boxes left to unpack but small decorative stuff, ya know," Carrie shrugs, her hands wrapped around a ceramic mug. *My* ceramic mug with a small cartoon otter on the side.

"They haven't done a proper food shop yet, so I said they could stay for dinner tonight. I'm cooking up some burritos." Dean tells me, planting a soft kiss to the nearest part of me he could reach.

"Yeah, that sounds great. I was gonna take a nap. Training was super intense today," I half-lie. If I can't go and sulk in some bubbles, then I would sulk in my blankets. I don't have the energy for politeness.

Dean moves out of my arms, something changing in his eyes as he looks me over. I know he is looking for physical bruises, maybe some cuts, but something in my face convinces him I need that break.

"I'll bring you in a plate. Go curl up," Dean orders me, planting a kiss on my inner wrist before giving me a gentle shove towards the bedroom.

"It was nice to meet you both!" I use the last of my energy to grin at Dean's guests as I move. As soon as the bedroom door closes behind me, I collapse onto the bed, still in my training gear.

When Dean climbs into bed with me later, I don't know how long it has been. I just know he smells like spices, and he is warm. I wrap myself around him as much as possible, taking in deep breaths of him and letting out a contented humming sound.

"I love you," I mutter as he starts to run his hands through my hair.

"I love you too, princess," Dean mumbles back. I pull myself from his arms with an unamused scowl and finally open my eyes.

"That's not funny," I tell him bluntly.

"It's true though," Dean argues back. I pause and sniff the air quickly.

"Have you been drinking out in the living room? I thought you were just making them burritos," I look to the bedside table and find there is no promised plate left for me there.

"I did. Then Carrie invited me down to theirs to try some of their wine. It's from Weloris. It's made of seaweed!" Dean grins goofily at me. I tilt his alarm clock to face me.

"It's almost six in the morning! How long were you down there? Ya know what? Never mind." I sigh, scrubbing my hands over my face. "I just want to cuddle for another hour before I shower and go to class. Can we just do that, please?"

"Whatever Her Highness wants," Dean drawls, moving to wrap his arms around me again. I scowl, throw his arms away from me and storm towards the bathroom.

"Babe, I was kidding! Come on. We need to start learning to joke about it!" He calls after me.

"No. We don't!" I call back in a sing-song voice. There are towels already on the warming hanger, but the sink area is a mess.

There is toothpaste smeared in the sink, and the handwash only has dregs left in it.

I scour the cabinets for more but find only painkillers, skincare ointments and backup shampoo. I let out an agitated breath before turning on the hot water and deciding I would deal with it later.

As I stand under the water, I hear Dean moving around the bedroom. There is a stumble, a whispered swear and then a thump as I assume he throws himself back into bed. I roll my eyes as I squirt a generous pile of his apple-scented shampoo into my palm.

I make a conscious effort to leave enough hot water for him. I wrap a toasty towel around me and carefully tiptoe out into the main room.

Dean is sprawled out across the bed on top of the covers in just his boxer shorts, his clothes piled up in the corner next to the basket. I move them into it before heading to the spare drawer of my clothes.

I throw on a pair of leggings and a loose vest. The Academy has no dress code, and this way, I'll be able to roll straight into combat training. I check my old clothes for my essentials and transfer them over. I pause as my fingers wrap around our coin.

I stare down at it and then at Dean. I lean over to press a gentle kiss to his forehead and then place the coin on his side of the bed as an apology for snapping at him.

Even though he had been downstairs drinking with the neighbours for hours, the living room had been cleaned up from dinner. The dishes are piled up into the sink, and every side is cleared and wiped. It's an effort at least. I grab my keys from the bowl and lock the door behind me as quietly as I can.

The portal is unusually busy this morning, and the guard tells me there is a festival going on in Trevial Park.

The name strikes a chord in me, although I knew it was a leftover feeling from my discussion with Hal yesterday. There was a park named after an ancestor of mine. An ancestor who, according to Hal, went 'a little eccentric' after his mother cursed - I mean *spelt* - him to be telepathic. Not a legacy I want to focus on. Still, I smile and thank him before I move through the line.

The Academy's halls are surprisingly busy, considering classes didn't start for another hour at the earliest. Most of the students look like fourth-years, juggling books and gear as they sprint throughout the halls. Their exams and the Vilerian games are soon. Maybe in a few years, I will look just as determined. I wanted to end up in any country that wasn't Althania, and that meant being impressive enough for multiple offers.

Harlan and Knox are already at our first class. I spot the purple hair first and go to call out a hello, but my voice catches in my throat as I see my best friend's hand brush the psychic's hair into place. I slow my steps and make them heavy as a warning. It's not that I think they need to hide their relationship, but if they aren't ready to tell me, then I wouldn't force them to.

"Ivy!" Harlan catches sight of me seconds later, hands now at his sides. "You are here suspiciously early."

"I've decided to become a morning person. A decision I hate immediately," I grin at him.

"You just hate being awake," Harlan teases me.

"Only recently," I mutter as I reach them, and Harlan pulls me in for a one-armed hug.

"How many times am I dying painfully today?" I shoot Knox a wink.

"That's not funny," Knox frowns at me.

"It's a little funny," I argue back.

"Says the one who can't see the gruesome deaths," Knox shoots back.

"Fair point," I laugh before gesturing for him to go first into the empty classroom. The psychic smirks as he leads the way.

Chapter Thirty-Three

When Channing comes to get me after lunch, I don't need Knox to tell me it's not good news. Our combat training isn't for another two hours, and we are fifteen minutes into a lecture. It is also not reassuring that he not only asks for me to leave but Knox, Harlan, Proxima and Atticus as well. I look over at Knox, but his face is suspiciously blank.

"What's happened?" I ask as soon as the classroom doors shut behind us. Channing ignores me and takes strong strides down the halls. I scramble to follow, close enough that I almost trip over his heels, but I do not ask again. I realise a moment later that he is headed towards my room. That really can't be good.

"Inside," Channing mutters as he uses his key to enter my room. One of the very few keys that exist now, I have been told. I frown but step inside only to be greeted by a group of people standing in the centre of it.

Don and the boys are here, in muttered conversations with my parents. Don looks pale, and my mother is gnawing at her lip in an unladylike fashion.

Prince Hal stands away from him, his back towards us as he hisses instructions at Celeste. In his hands is a ripped-apart box and the memory reader.

Oh, this really can't be good.

"What's going on?" I demand as I hear the door shut behind me.

"When did you last see your human boyfriend?" Celeste snaps at me.

"Watch how you speak to my daughter," My mother growls back.

"Why?" I snap back at the same time. My eyes drop down to the box in Hal's hand, and I point at it. "What was in that?"

"Ivy. It's very important that we know when you last saw Dean," Hal speaks to me slowly, like I am a spooked animal. Maybe I am about to be.

"This morning. I stayed at his last night. Why? The Crown Prince of Althania calls a meeting because someone missed their shift?" I ask sarcastically, even as I can hear my heartbeat getting louder in my chest.

"What time did you leave?" Hal probes further.

"I don't…early, I left early." My heart now feels like it is dragging itself up into my throat and trying to choke me.

"You must have just missed them," My father whispers.

"Missed? Missed! What's happened to Dean?" My confused sentences come out as a strangled sound.

"Your brother went to his apartment. It was ruined-" Celeste begins. I turn on my heel and start to push my way through Proxima and Atticus to get to the door and then get to a portal, and then…

Multiple sets of arms and hands grab at me. One set grabs me around the middle and starts to drag me back even further.

"No! No! let me go!" I thrash against Maverick's arms.

"He's not there, Ives. He isn't there." Maverick promises me in a grunted whisper

as my elbow hits his stomach. He still does
not let go.

"Yes, he is. You're wrong, you're wrong,
you're wrong! I was just there. I was just - I
left him - he was sleeping!" I screech at them
all, even as a glint of metal catches my eye.
Hal is setting up the memory reader on my
bedside table. My mother moves to block my
vision, and she grabs my face in her hands.

"Calm down," She orders. "Now. He isn't
dead. Okay? Can you hear me? He isn't dead.
He isn't dead, so you can calm down."

I stop my thrashing but I am anything but
calm. My heart is beating in my throat,
choking off my air supply, and my eyes are
burning as I blink away tears because I left
him. I just…I just left him. We knew I was
being watched by an anti-multi-species
relationship cult, and I had just left him drunk
and vulnerable.

"They made him record a message. It's for
you." Hal calls over to me. I hear a soft
whine as the memory reader comes to life.
"But you are not watching it alone.
Understood?"

"You haven't watched it?" I snarl at them all. "What if it's a ransom? What if there was a time limit on it? How long- how long have you known about this? Why didn't you come get me earlier!"

"The crystal is encrypted. You need to be the one to watch it. But that is where your involvement ends." My mother tells me fiercely. "Depending on that message, Hal and your father will organise a rescue plan if that is a viable option. You stay in this room with your friends who know your secret, and you do not leave until this threat is neutralised."

My mother's voice is calm and collected. She sounds in her element, like a general commanding her soldier. If only I planned to obey.

"Dean's survival is not an option," I warn her lowly. "If anything happens to him, then not even you and your mate will be able to stop me."

"You stay. In. This. Room," My mother repeats. We keep our eye contact in an intense mockery of the staring contests we would have when I was younger.

"Ivy. Come here." Hal orders me softly.
"Let's see what this says."

Maverick loosens his hold around me to march me over to Hal's side. He takes a singular step back only when the prince takes a gentle grip on my arm. They don't want me diving into that memory stone and using whatever it holds to my own advantage. I find some dark amusement in their belief that Hal, as a chaperone, is enough to stop me.

I shoot the prince a quick nod before reaching for the small slice of ruby that was on the memory reader.

Chapter Thirty-Four

Unlike the last time I used a memory reader, I did not have to choose a memory. There is no large black room with frozen screens. No. Now, we are straight into the memory.

We are in Dean's living room, and he is strapped down into an armchair, the rope already irritating his skin. His face is bruised and bleeding, as are his knuckles. He fought back.

Dean is surrounded by people all wearing a distortion spell. Their faces are blurred to the point they are unrecognisable, and their voices will likely be altered as well. All I can tell is that four of them are male, and one of them is a woman. I can't even tell if they have wings or not, as if I were taking a closer look, and the world around them blurred and made me look away.

"Go on," A gruff voice tells Dean. "Say goodbye to your princess. Tell her what we told you to say."

Dean shoots the one that spoke a glare and spits a mouthful of blood in his direction. My heart swells with pride. Dean turns his gaze to the person in front of him, his bright green eyes blazing.

"Heya gorgeous," Dean's voice is rough, but he tries to fake a smile. I close my eyes for a brief second, but I can't bear to look away from him, even in this state.

"These guys came bursting in looking for you. Bet you can't guess how disappointed they were when it was only me. They are gonna take me to some super secret base somewhere and torture me," Dean swallows thickly.

"They want me to tell you to come rescue me. They want you to show the world that hybrids are too powerful to be allowed to exist. To take your birthright of the throne of Althania and to start a war to get me back. But we both know you would be miserable like that. We both know you were only ever going to get a few decades with me at most. You are going to live for a thousand years, Ivy Whitlock. Don't you dare spend them miserably because of me. Don't you dare come get me." Dean's eyes start to water, but he blinks until only a single tear runs down his face.

"I love you. I can wait a thousand years on the other side for you. I can wait longer. Stay safe. Be happy." Dean whispers and then goes silent. That is apparently not enough or maybe too much. The person that ordered him to speak takes the butt of a gun I didn't notice he was holding and slams it into my boyfriend's face repeatedly.

I scream, moving to defend him as if this was happening in real-time, as if I could protect him at all here. Hal drags me out of the memory, kicking and screaming for them to stop.

Chapter Thirty-Five

Don

"This is my fault," I whisper for the hundredth time as my eyes refuse to move from my sister's blank face. The memory is a long one, and it's unnerving to see her and Hal so empty.

"No. It's mine. We should have put a protective detail on the apartment. We thought the sigils would have been enough," Channing runs a hand over his face.

"If Ivy had been there…" My father says hoarsely.

"The whole building would be rubble," Corvus cuts him off confidently. "There is no way Ivy would have let anyone take Dean."

"I can't believe you kept this from me," Celeste snarls at Channing. "A *hybrid* at the academy. The entire student body was in danger! There is a reason Prince Atlas of Parlitan was…"

"Don't finish that sentence," Knox warns her darkly. We all jump, forgetting that Ivy had not come in alone, and when I look at the psychic, he is glaring at the witch tutor with a ferocity I didn't think he possessed. Celeste opens her mouth to reprimand him and then decides against it. Even at her age, a warning to stop from a psychic was to be heard.

"We need to save Dean," Maverick is still mere inches from my sister's side, ready to catch or grab her the second she returns to her body. A ghost of a smile threatens to take over my face. To think I had once been convinced they would be a couple. Watching Ivy as she got the news that we had failed her and seeing her focus only on Dean…I cannot believe I was ever so stupid.

"They are sending a location. That's what the note says," My mother begins to pace around the room, rubbing her hands together as she thinks. "We send members of the Vilerian guard. Swear them to secrecy. Quick, brutal, efficient."

"Ivy has not claimed her title, and according to you all, she never will. She has no right to the Althanian sector of the Vilerian guard," Celeste scoffs.

"You think that will stop Hal from sending them?" Channing raises an eyebrow at her. He seems almost disappointed.

"He would be crucified for using them for direct personal agendas that are not for the good of his realm. One human life is not going to change the fate of Althania!" Celeste gapes at him.

"Oh, how terribly wrong you are," Knox whispers. Celeste's nostrils flare, but she still does not argue with him.

"I'll go and save Dean," I volunteer. "I was late to answer the sigils. This is my fault."

"You will not," My mother shakes her head. "You are skilled, but you are not trained to the scale of a Vilerian guardian."

"We will go with him," Corvus continues, acting as if my mother had never spoken. The shock of that is clear on her face. Maverick grunts his agreement.

"I'll lead them," Channing promises my mother.

"I will come too!" Proxima is quick to throw her name in the ring. "For Ivy."

"For Ivy," Harlan nods and steps forward.

"Absolutely not!" Celeste laughs. "I cannot stop Violet from sending her son and wards into slaughter, but there is no reality where I allow students to join them."

"We need to go." Knox overrides her. In other circumstances, I would find the conflicting emotions on the witch's face amusing. But with Ivy on the line, nothing is. "If we don't go, something worse happens."

"Worse. Not something in general," My father latches onto that word. Knox avoids his gaze as he nods once.

"I want Ryder's opinion on that," Celeste speaks only to Channing.

"Ryder will agree," Knox scoffs. "There is a reason that each royal family has one official psychic, Celeste. Conflicting visions cause tragedy. My gut tells me that every single person in this room needs to go after Dean. If we don't, then an *avoidable* larger tragedy becomes unavoidable. Would you like to further argue with me or the Crown Prince you are sworn to obey?"

Celeste bites her tongue, and her breaths are audibly angry. My parents share a solemn look, but not a single one of us argues to stay.

I look towards my little sister. Knox said,
"Everyone."

"Does she really have to be there?" I ask
lowly.

"More than any of us," Knox answers
solemnly a mere second before my sister and
the prince burst back to life.

Chapter Thirty-Six

"I'm going," I snarl at Hal the second I have control over my mouth. "I don't care what he said. I..Am..Getting..Him..Back."

"Ivy, you heard him…" Hal starts to argue, trying to look me in the eye to make his argument more sincere. I do not look him in the eye. I look at his mouth, at his fangs, as I make my play.

"Claim me," I tell him bluntly. "Claim me as your heir. If I am heir, then he is the heir to Althania's consort. I declare him my consort right here and right now, with all these witnesses. Save him. Save him and claim me as your heir."

"You don't really want that." Hal's voice cracked, but it was not a no. I do not falter, and I do not turn to look at the rest of the room even as I hear my mother's breath shaking.

"I want Dean safe. I want him alive. I want him by my side for those decades that I can have him. I do not care if I must have them shackled to a throne. I do not care if I spend the rest of my life in this country, in this place, if I get those moments with him first. My happiness for his life is not a price I have to debate over. I will pay it willingly, forever. Just…Save him." I beg with my breath hiccupping as I replay how his body slumped when they hit him over and over again in my mind.

"You will one day rule Althania. Your mother's affair will be outed to the entirety of Vileria. You will be watched and criticised every moment until your soul passes over. You will never be appointed as a member of the Vilerian guard. Parlitan will never be your home again." Hal finally catches my eye. His warning is falling on deaf ears. I do not care about any of that. I care about Dean.

"I understand that," I tell him. Hal searches my face in the overwhelming silence. I see my friends from the corner of my eye, see them all looking at Knox. He has his eyes on me. He nods slightly. I let out a relieved breath. This is the right path.

"Then I claim you, Ivy Whitlock. I claim you as the heir to the Althanian throne. I claim you as my daughter. As they follow me, the people of Althania shall follow you. As they protect me, those sworn to Althania shall protect you. All that has been handed down to me shall one day be handed down to you. You are now, and shall always be, Princess Ivy Alenium, daughter of Crown Prince Hal of the vampires and Althania."

I wait for a feeling to wash over me, some sudden sense of responsibility. I feel nothing, no extra weight on my shoulders. In fact, when I turn on my heel and find the room on its knees with their heads bowed, I feel only dread.

Chapter Thirty-Seven

Knox convinced the room that we all needed to be on the rescue mission, but that does not mean they are happy about it. My mother does not look me in the eye at all, even hours later when we convene in the library after changing into gear and loading ourselves with weapons.

I move to my father, to Dalerian Whitlock of the fae. I open my mouth, but no explanation comes out, even after I had spent time in my room trying to think of how to apologise to him. He pulls me into a bone-crushing hug. He rubs my back and holds me close. No explanation is necessary.

"We will be escorted by eight Vilerian guards," Channing announces to the room as he pours over a map placed on Hal's desk. The Ideleons had sent coordinates shortly after I had been claimed. We assumed it was based on when I left my lecture. The spy that let them know was a problem for someone else.

"One for each of us," Atticus points to our group and the three boys in the corner. He isn't wrong. We will each be getting a babysitter if they let us fight at all. Knox got the gut feeling that we all needed to be there but nothing else.

"They will stay with you." Channing doesn't bother to lie to us. "Protect you if you have to get off of the ship at all. Celeste and I will lead the charge into the base. Violet and Dalerian will be extracting Dean, and once they are on the ship, we leave. Victory or no victory."

"Dean is the victory," I remind him bluntly.

"You've forgotten one key component," Maverick points over at Prince Hal. "We are taking the leader of a country with us. He stays on the ship as well, I'm guessing, which means you have the brunt of your force on the ship. That makes no sense, and they will never believe it is only the four of you. They want Ivy there. They will know she is there. They will come after the ship."

"That is why the guard is there. That is why *you* are there. You, Corvus and Don have been protecting her in more ways than one for years. Are you going to let her get hurt now?" Channing raises that scarred eyebrow at him.

"I would rather die," Maverick answers immediately.

"You just might," Celeste tells him coldly.

"Leave your attitude in this palace, Celeste," My mother steps into the witch's line of vision.

"You don't have the power to order me to do anything," The witch taunts.

"I do," I purr over at her. "You swore your services to Althania. Do not make my first royal command be for you to bite your own tongue off."

Celeste glances over at me, mockingly bows her head, and then returns her gaze to my mother. "You truly have raised a miniature you. How terrifying."

My mother grins at her in response, and I finally see a tiny part of the young girl from those videos who is still alive inside of her. I see why that grin gave them their nickname.

"If I need to fight, then I'm going to fight," I warn Channing. "I won't just sit there in the jet while Dean is being tortured."

"Stay with your guard," Channing begs me. Begs me because he cannot order me. Not anymore.

"They are here," Harlan interrupts us, the first he has spoken since I came out of the memory stone. He is right. Seconds later, the doors to the library open and in walks Prince Hal, flocked by eight Vilerian guards all dressed in their uniforms.

The jet-black fabric looks soft and flexible, but I know it was spelt to the highest standard. Defensive runes are etched into the inside of the fabric, too tiny to see with the naked eye. Their boots are thick, black, shining leather, and I know the toecaps have hidden steel inside them to protect their toes. There are too many hidden weapon slots for me to count, and until I am one of them, I will never know exactly where and how many there are.

The realisation that I would never be one of them stops my thinking, dead in its tracks. My lungs feel heavy, and it's hard to take my next breath until I remind myself that my sacrifice keeps Dean safe. Keeps him alive. I had meant what I had told Hal. It was a price I was willing to pay.

The Vilerian guards, most of whom are vampires, turn on their heels to look at me and bow deeply. My breath threatens to choke me. I tilt my head quickly in their direction in recognition.

"The jet will be landing in the next few minutes," Hal informs us all as he moves to his desk, opens a drawer, and pulls out two daggers the length of my hand. He hands them over to my mother silently, but she stares at them as if they are a gift from the goddess herself. "We should head out."

As if that was the secret phrase, the eight Vilerian guards spread out to each flank one of us. The one that moves to my side has a thin strip of maroon around his neckline. A commander. He nods his head at me, calls me princess in a voice as smooth as butter, and then gestures for me to lead the way. As soon as I was two steps in front of him, he started to follow.

All guards stay exactly two paces behind their designated person. Don is a girl barely five feet tall and thin as a grapevine. She must be fast, which is why she was given to Don. She had to be fast enough to stop him if he tried to break orders.

Hal leads the group through the halls of the palace, twisting around the walls and through narrow passages with ease. The fact my mother matches his familiarity with this route unnerves me.

After we pass through an underground passage so shallow that I have to duck my head to avoid hitting it, we enter a large underground hangar with one of the most impressive jets I have ever seen.

It is as black as the night sky, its windows tinted to the point that I can't make out where they start until I am close enough to touch it. The door opens fluidly, sliding out into steps as soon as Hal places his hand on the metal.

The inside is deceptively large. Everything is black and red, clearly expensive and made to be comfortable. The seats are spacious, with snack holders built into the walls next to them. I have no doubt that there are hidden compartments full of the prince's favourite drinks.

"We would have had to wait for a military jet," Hal explains as he gestures for us all to take a seat. "This seemed quicker and easier."

My mother is the first to sit in one of the seats clearly meant for four. My father slides into place next to her, and Don is quick to take the space opposite her. He looks at me expectantly. I almost smile as I sit next to him. Almost.

The Vilerian guards do not sit. My commander moves to the cockpit at the front of the jet, still within my vision. I blink in surprise as he sits in the pilot's seat and starts to initiate take-off.

Corvus, Maverick, Knox and Harlan take the four tops directly across the aisle from us. Channing, Celeste, Proxima and Atticus sit behind them. Each of them can see me, but it is only Proxima who outright stares. The rest of the guards get into position at various points around the plane. They can also all see me. I bite back the comment about charging admission to the freak show. Everyone, everywhere in the world, would be looking at me soon.

"I am going to get him back for you," My mother promises me in a low whisper. I reluctantly move my eyes to look at her. Her jaw is set, and her gaze hard, as if she is already prepared for the fight. Or as if she was already in one.

Maybe she was. Maybe this coldness I have been displaying to her wasn't so I could have some space to process the betrayal but was, in fact, that first level of defence to keep them all away from me.

"I don't want you both to run in there thinking that…" I trail off and place my hands on the cool tabletop. I try to think over my next words and how to best explain the tumbling and squirming of contradicting emotions in my stomach.

"We know," My father reaches across the table to place his hand over mine. "We also know that this is a lot for you to have thrown at you all at once. After Hal agreed to let us keep you…We did our best. We truly did think it would be best for you not to come to The Academy and test fate. It was never that we had no faith in you."

My breath caught in my throat, and I held it for a second, telling myself that if I was going to cry, then it was going to have to be later. Once Dean was safe, I would have something to really cry about. This was a time to focus.

"You would have been an amazing Vilerian Guard," My mother takes my other hand. "But you will also make an amazing ruler. No matter what happens, what you must do after this mission, know that is what we think."

"And know that I am never leaving you," Don interjects thickly. "You won't be alone in Althania."

"You are heir to the Whitlock lands and estate in Parlitan. You cannot live the rest of your life in Althania. I won't be alone anyway. I will have Dean and Channing and Hal," I shoot my brother a soft smile.

"And me," Corvus pipes up. "I am heir to nothing. I have nowhere else I have to live."

"I always planned on pledging for Althania when I become a guard. If you will have me, then I will stay with you too," Proxima vows.

"You know I really didn't like you at first," The comment comes out with a laugh as her vow fills me with a comfort I could never have imagined weeks ago. "But now the idea of you constantly by my side is incredibly reassuring.”

Proxima starts to laugh with me as she hesitantly tells me, “I thought you were a rude bitch,” which only makes me laugh harder. It feels bittersweet to laugh right now when we are all on our way to fight for my boyfriend’s life, but I cannot help but revel in the small joy.

When our laughter dies down, I look over at Harlan and Knox. They don’t know that I know, and I don’t want to force them to tell me, but I wish they would just hold hands on the table rather than try to hide them between their laps. There was no reason for them to hide it. If anyone made a comment, then I would create my legacy early by ripping out their throat with my clearly fae fangs.

“We should be landing soon,” Celeste announces to the cabin half an hour later. It does not go unnoticed that Hal has remained silent the entire ride so far. He has been looking out of the tinted windows or tapping gently on the thin tablet in front of him.

Celeste’s words are like an order to the Vilerian guard. They quickly change their positions and flank their specified person once again. My guard remains at the wheel.

"Dalerian, Violet. You two will wait on the ship until Hal tells you to go. Celeste and I will be the main distraction at the gates," Channing shoots the witch a look. She stands tall and heads to the door as the plane starts to descend.

"What should we do, sir?" Proxima asks.

"Stay here with your guards. When and if we need you, then we will call for you. Prince Hal will remain on the ship and will communicate to you what is happening," Channing glances over at me then. I nod my understanding of the unsubtle message. Hal will remain here to keep me in line and reassure me. I am the ticking time bomb. If anything will massively affect Knox's predictions, then the odds point to it being me.

The plane lands with a soft thud, and we all shift in our seats as we get used to being on solid ground again. I peer around Don to the window. All I can see is a jagged, rocky shoreline as it is hounded by a dark, frothing ocean. A look at the set of windows on the other side of the jet shows a scattering of large trees across a rocky landscape.

"Where are we?" I frown and keep my voice low.

"On the border of Blendora, Calent *and* Tulinth," My mother frowns. "Smart. No country will care about a tiny Ideleon faction in such an ignored area."

She was right. There was no tourism here due to the dense witch woodland that was prohibited from being touched, the cold Tulinth forest that was full of frost and snow and a Blendorian noble that owned a large chunk of the land on the borders. Those clashing factors mean that it is a largely untouched area with the three tiniest docks in Vileria. Each country had their own. My tutor once commented that if each country set up a small inn or lodgings, then there would be more traffic for that gimmick alone. Instead, it was empty, avoided by all three countries due to its proximity to the others.

"You should have warned them that we would be coming here. If we get caught fighting rebels on Blendorian soil…" My mother looks at Hal with a frown.

"It is being handled," Hal cuts her off bluntly. My mother blinks quickly. I would guess that happens very rarely. "As Ivy pointed out, they have taken the heir to Althania's consort. Politically, we can spin that if they complain."

"They do not know that Althania even has an heir," My mother speaks more hesitantly now.

"Of course they do," Hal checks over his weapons and avoids her gaze. "What do you think I was doing while you were convening in the library? As soon as the jet left Althanian air space, the rulers of Vileria all received important correspondence through immediate portals that I have claimed my daughter and that invitations to her crowning ceremony will be following shortly."

Crowning ceremony. Oh, goddess. I had not thought of the specific ceremonies and responsibilities I would have to endure when I offered up the rest of my life to the Althanian throne in exchange for Dean. For Dean. ForDeanforDeanforDean.

"We can discuss that later," Don says after a quick glance at my face. "But now we are just sitting ducks. Let's get moving."

"Easy, little lord," Celeste smirks. "This jet has shields. The enemy cannot see we are here. The ship is invisible to their eyes."

"Us being invisible does not give Dean immortality," Maverick glares at her. "Our friend is still in there every second we stay here."

"Such impatience," Celeste mutters under her breath, but she is fighting back a smile as she gets into position by the door.

"Wait," Violet demands, turning her head to press a gentle kiss on her husband's cheek. She kisses Don's brow and then looks at me. I pull her into a tight, quick hug. She kisses the top of my head as she moves to the side so our father can have his turn.

As Dalerian Whitlock pulls me and Don into a group hug and whispers for us to stay safe, my eyes follow my mother. She comes to a stop in front of Hal.

"You made me a promise once," She reminds him softly. "Break it."

"Are you sure?" The Crown Prince raises his eyebrows slightly. My mother nods once and closes her eyes. The mates take a deep breath and open their eyes in complete unison. They both nod, and then my mother turns her back on him to go and stand by the doors.

Channing gives his old friends a pained look before he catches me staring. He ducks his head in a bow. I bow mine back.

"Stay safe," Don orders our father. "I'm not ready to be lord yet."

Dalerian lets out a small chuckle and gives his heir's shoulder a squeeze before responding, "We will be back with Dean soon. I promise."

With those final words, my parents, Uncle Channing and Celeste, all slip out of the jet and into the dark night.

Chapter Thirty-Eight

The seconds feel like hours, which in turn feels like a cliché, but with each breath I take, I can feel a weight being added to my chest.

Back with Dean soon. Back with Dean soon. Back with Dean soon. Back with Dean soon.

It was rare that my father broke a promise to me, but when he did, he made up for it tenfold. A whole new jewellery box instead of just the bracelet I wanted after he promised to buy me one on a work trip. A new stallion rather than a new pony when he missed half of my showcase. But I do not think there is anything in this realm that is worth more than Dean.

"They are fine," Hal whispers out loud. I know that it is for Don's benefit rather than mine. If it was only for me, then he would use our telepathic link.

"Violet and Dalerian have made it inside," He continues. I notice his eyes flitting back and forth as if he is looking…as if he is looking through my mother's eyes.

You made me a promise once. Break it. Of course, my mother would have allowed her mate unfiltered access to her mind. Of course, he would promise her not to use it without permission once she was no longer his.

Hal is looking for Dean just like she is, a backup pair of eyes that might see something she missed. It is annoyingly brilliant, but if it works, I will never judge them for it.

The silence of the outside world ends with a guttural scream, followed by yells that are quickly cut off.

"Go," Hal snaps at the two guards closest to the door. "Go to Sir Channing." The guards are out of the ship within seconds, weapons of choice drawn. I notice one of them has picked a shortsword.

"Are they…" Proxima looks even paler than usual but kept a steady stance and hands curled into fists.

"They are fine. They've been spotted, but they got most of the sentries before that happened." Hal's eyes zoomed all over the place again. "Celeste was stabbed in the leg, but it's a flesh wound. She's carrying on."

"Our parents?" Don presses. Hal closes his eyes for two seconds as if he is switching channels before he shoots my brother a gentle smile. "They haven't been found."

I take deep breaths and hide my hands in my jacket pockets to hide the fact that they are shaking. The sound of the fighting outside is twisting my stomach. Celeste had been stabbed, but what about Channing? Was he okay? Had he been hurt?

For the first time tonight, it hits me that someone might die all because of my love. Maybe I was only okay with that in theory. Maybe I was only okay with that if it was me dying.

"They've found him," Hal's voice cuts through the grotesque background noise. My heart soars in my chest and then immediately falls at the quick flash of horror on his face.

"How bad is it?" My voice comes in a grated whisper. I hadn't truly allowed myself to think of the state Dean would be in after all these hours, and yet his capture was all I could think about. I had been thinking of his torture through rose-tinted goggles, his wounds only as bad as when I last saw him in that memory stone.

"He'll be fine," Hal's answer is not reassuring as it is not a true answer. He could be fine and have had all of his limbs cut off. He could be fine but has been cursed by a witch to never open his eyes again. Fine was not an answer you wanted to hear when your question was about something being *bad*.

But I do not get to chastise my biological father over his poor choice of words. His face changes, and he takes a sharp breath inward. Suddenly, I want him to say the word 'fine' again.

"What? What is it? What's happened?" Corvus demands of the vampire prince as my brother and Maverick move to the windows to watch the fight unfold.

"There's a child," Hal whispers, eyes fixed on one particular spot on the floor. My mother must be staring at something. I pray that something isn't Dean before the realisation of that statement hits me. "Dean wants them to get her out first."

"No!" The word is out of my mouth before I can stop it. I don't know if I even mean it. My mind is just running through all the risks that increase the longer the people I love stay in that place. We don't even know what that place is. The building wasn't recorded anywhere. They had gone in blind. I ignore my brother's disappointed look.

"Channing is going to head into the building after your mother. He is going to get the child while they get Dean," Hal tells me in a hurry. I assume he is telling Channing to do the same thing, quickly forming a whole new plan.

"Go," I snap my head to look at my guard, the commander on this mission, and order him. "Go now. Take the rest of them. Replace Channing, and if you get the chance, storm in and get the hostages. Cover for the Lord and Lady Whitlock."

"Ivy-" Don warns me but cuts himself off as the commander does not hesitate. He gestures to his team, a quick sequence of sign language, and then the Vilerian guards are bounding out into the fight, following my orders.

My orders. Oh, Goddess.

"How many do we think are in the building right now?" Don looks straight at Hal.

"Most will be in the fight. Celeste has been drawing them out. But if they are smart, and they clearly are, they will have people in the building. Your mother would be able to handle them while Dalerian got Dean to cover, but with two hostages…" Hal pauses, looks over at the door to the jet, and then looks over at the psychic.

Knox slowly stands, avoiding the Prince's gaze as he takes Harlan's face in his hands and places a firm kiss on the other boy's lips.

"We need to fight," Knox mutters softly, lovingly, although the tone is almost mournful. My own breath catches in my throat. *Harlan gets hurt.* "For Violet."

"For Violet," Harlan says back.

"For Violet," Maverick checks over his weapon, his feet a mere inch from the doorway.

"For Violet," Corvus moves to his side.

"For Mum," Don agrees.

"For *Ivy,*" Proxima changes the chant. She smooths her clothes as if the Idelons will

368

have a battle photographer waiting for her. Atticus mimics her, and when he is done, his hand hangs awkwardly a mere centimetre from hers.

"For Ivy," Atticus grunts. Proxima blinks twice as if she didn't expect anyone to copy her. I certainly hadn't. She looks at Atticus with soft confusion as if seeing him for the first time.

"For Violet and Ivy," Hal completes the vows, adjusting his weapons.

"You are the Crown Prince of Althania," I remind him lowly. "You should stay on the jet."

"You are the heir to Althania. They have your consort. I will not let that stand." Hal tells me in the same tone. Our eyes lock. Neither of us will be staying in this jet. Neither of us could stop the other from leaving.

"For our consorts," I whisper, as close to an acceptance of their affair as I will allow myself for now.

"For our consorts," Hal's lip twitched into an almost smile.

Chapter Thirty-Nine

The fight turns quiet as soon as I step into it, but I do not think that it is from a spell. Everything has slowed down as well, the grappling fighters moving as if through sludge. I see the Vilerian guards focused on their targets, half of them with a clear aim at the building while the other half focused on the enemies in front of them.

The enemy has no uniform to speak of. Their weapons look dented and badly maintained, as if they had stolen them from the rubbish. One of them is half of my height, scrawny and…

And familiar.

Rage fills me, and suddenly everything around me is too loud, the fighting too fast as I try and push my way through it to the human teenage boy who has also caught sight of me. Josh.

Josh, who had sat in Dean's house that night, had given him booze and chatted with him on the sofa. How had I not pieced it together? How could I have forgotten? Of course, they had been involved.

Harlan and Knox do not leave my side, Knox shouting out random commands at our friends without any pattern that I could see. But then all I can see, all I can focus on, is that messy brown hair as it retreats to the building with a yell that sounds like my name.

"JOSH," The name leaves my mouth like a curse, and I am running, twisting out of the way of things thrown in my direction, slipping and sliding over the bloodied stones under my feet. I hear a strangled yelp from the left of me, from Harlan, but I do not stop. I do not falter, even as a seven-foot man slides in the gap between me and Josh and blocks me from grabbing him.

His skin was smooth and a gorgeous brown, the colour of polished oak, and his eyes were as bright as a setting sun- Succubus. The recognition hits me, but again, I do not stop. I do not stop reaching for my weapon, do not stop the swing towards his neck as I see his mouth move, as I feel his persuasion magic caress my skin.

I do not stop moving forward even when I pull my dagger from his jugular and his blood sprays my face and neck. I do not stop moving to jump over his legs as he collapses to the floor. I only stop when I make it six more steps, almost halfway to the base, and I realise that Josh has already slipped into the building.

I scan the building, looking for an open door or window or something that means I can climb onto the roof. There are archers there, but I could take them. I could use air to swipe them from their perches. The building is a decrepit mansion made from broken stone. It is no fortress.

I only turn when I hear my brother scream my name, and then suddenly I am on the floor, a body pining me down with more wet, hot blood pouring down onto my face. I gag as some make their way into my mouth, fighting the person out of instinct until I realise his hair is auburn, his body thin, and he smells like roses.

Harlan.

Harlan, whose breath is coming in pained rattles. Harlan, who has an arrow embedded in his shoulder, an arrow shot with such power and precision that over half the shaft was pointing down into me, the arrowhead snagging at my armoured jacket.

It would have been a kill shot. Should have been a kill shot. It would have gone right through my heart, should by all rights have gone through Harlan's if he hadn't tackled me at an angle.

Harlan would have died. The scream that rips itself from my throat is angry, terrified, as inhuman as I have ever sounded. I cradle Harlan to me, shift us so now it is me covering his body even as the Vilerian guard flock to make a barricade around us, even as my brother and my friends scream to get me back to the jet, as my biological father tries to get into my head.

Calm down. The voice in my head that is not mine begs. *Ivy, you have to calm down.*

I look up at the roof and find that it has collapsed as if it were the sole target of an earthquake or a bomb. Where the archers had been standing, there were only piles of bones and parts, as if they had been exploded from the inside out. As if their destruction was what destroyed the building.

"KNOX," I screech as Harlan makes another gagging sound. "KNOX."

The psychic falls to his knees beside me and shoves me off his boyfriend to look at him. He doesn't look at the wound. He doesn't look at how much blood Harlan is coated in. He just looks at his face, the smears of dirt and blood on it and nods once.

I let out a relieved breath. Harlan will live. This is the not-as-hurt option, even though it doesn't feel like it. This is a good ending, even though it feels like the end of everything.

"Take him back to the ship," I order him, pushing myself to my feet. Knox wraps his arms around Harlan, but when he goes to lift him, the fae boy screams.

"You," I snap at the nearest Vilerian guard. They all have basic medical training. They have to pass that course with certain scores, or they cannot be sworn in. It was the part of the training I had been least looking forward to. "Take Knox and Harlan back to the ship. Stay with them. You, cover her." I order the guard next to her, even though the fighting is nearly done.

The Ideleon fighters lay in broken, crooked positions all around us, scattered as if thrown down by a displeased god. The ground has completely changed colour, with rocks in various states of red and brown and the spots of packed dirt and grass looking more like a swamp than the edges of a forest.

"Where is the Prince?" Celeste screams at us from across the way as she gestures with one hand, and her already-beaten opponent goes flying into a tree. His spine makes a sickening cracking sound, but not as sickening as the realisation that she is right. Hal is not here.

Hal ran in. Hal ran into the building after I made it collapse, potentially onto my parents and my love.

Everything moves in slow motion again. Don and I look at each other, and the same horror I feel in my gut is reflected in his eyes.

We turn to look at the entrance, the door now a large gap with the metal twisted on the floor as if someone had ripped it apart. We move as one, Don making quicker progress from his place outside of the Vilerian guards, but after I shove them aside, I am quick to meet him.

Then there is a loud explosion, a flash of searing heat against my back, and I faceplant the floor. I struggle to push myself back up. I don't dare look at what was just destroyed, but I am too slow. Celeste yells my title and an order to go along with it, but I do not hear exactly what as my ears ring. All I can feel is too many arms around me, too many hands scooping me up, and the backward pull as they drag me kicking and screaming towards the jet.

Chapter Forty

Don is dragged with me, but it only takes one of the guards to move him. My guard, the commander. Don shrugs him off, catches sight of me, and then moves with the rest of us. Traitor. They could need him. They could need me. They could be dying in there, beaten by the rubble I sent hurling towards them, but I was not allowed to go to them.

The explosion was from the forest, more of a distraction technique than an actual target. This political nightmare just got worse. The Calent trees are on fire, still blazing, even though Celeste is rushing to them, waving her arms and screaming in Latin to try and put out the blaze.

I fight against my guards once again, even as we are back near the jet. I go to wave my hand, finding the water particles that are always in the air, but I am beaten to it.

A wave of water conjured from thin air smashes against the forest, dousing the flaming with an obnoxious sizzling sound that echoes. Celeste spins on her heel, face slack with shock, to find Lady Violet Whitlock of the fae by the ruined building. She was alive.

Alive and almost unscathed. There are marks on her face. She's limping as she tries to move quickly towards us, but that could be from the extra weight of the little girl in her arms.

The girl could be no more than seven, her thin white hair a tangled mess full of sticks and leaves as if they had dragged her backwards through that forest before shackling her under that building and shackled she most certainly was. Her wrists and ankles are rubbed raw and bleeding. She was wearing what looked like a poorly sewed-together pillowcase with the arms cut out, and she clung to my mother tightly even though I could see her joints and bones through her skin all the way from across the battlefield.

Hal comes through the doorway next, and a gasp leaves my lips. The Vilerian guards stop moving, half of them melting from my side to rush to his. Hal himself looks fine. The only blood on him was clearly someone else's. Clearly, my fathers, as Hal holds him upright with his palm pressing against a wound on my father's shirt. A wound that stained his entire shirt, a wound that had cost him so much blood he was as pale as the moon, and his eyelids were drooping.

"Papa!" I screech. I can't remember the last time I called him that. I start to fight against the guards again.

"All clear!" The Crown Prince of Vampires yells to them when it is clear they will not let me go. The hands holding me drop instantly. Don and I rush forward again just as we head towards the doorway, but this time, terror has made my limbs unresponsive.

Two more people leave the building before I can get even close. My heart soars, and the terror melts away. Channing and Dean.

Channing and Dean were with all of their limbs, and they were breathing, and Dean, Dean even looked as if he had been healed recently. His face was completely unblemished. He catches sight of me, and his face drops open in shock. It is not the wild grin I wanted, the relief I was hoping for, but it pushes me forward even more. I want to wipe that look away with a kiss, smother his pain with my love and hear his heartbeat beat against my own.

I did not get the chance because, not for the first time, Prince Hal was wrong. It was not all clear.

As I am three steps away, as Don breaks away from me to help Hal move my father to the jet, and like the traitorous daughter I am, I move past them. Another arrow flies through the air.

This time, it is a kill shot.

Chapter Forty-One

Channing is too slow. Hal is too slow. My mother, child in her arms, is too slow. My father, goddess bless him, screams and reaches backwards even with his wound, but he is also too slow. Don, Don doesn't even register what is happening until I am screaming.

I am also too slow.

Dean drops to his knees in front of me, blood blooming across his chest. It is not the perfect shot, and that is clearly on purpose.

Dean does not die instantly, but he will die before a single one of us can help him and before we are able to get him to the ship. I know, somehow, that his heart has been nicked by the arrowhead, that he is bleeding out internally quicker than even magic could stop it, but not quick enough that he won't die in my arms.

"Nononononononononono," I say as I grab
his shoulders, dropping to my knees so our
faces are level. "No, you can't. You can't,
you hear me? You can't."

"I said don't come," Dean forces out, blood
and saliva dribbling from the side of his
mouth, even as he traces his hand over my
face.

"I love you," I sob. "I couldn't leave you
here. I couldn't. I couldn't lose you. I *can't*
lose you."

"I love you," Dean's hand drops from my
face to my hand, my hands that are keeping
him upright as he starts to lean back. His
body is already failing even as I hear people
rushing to us.

"Don't leave. Don't leave," I beg.

"P…pocket," Dean wheezes as he fights to
keep his eyes open. His beautiful green eyes
remind me of summertime apples, of the
sunlight piercing through the trees as we lay
in the gardens and wish we could be together
forever.

"Pocket?" I echo. His head moves in a nod, I
think, but I sob as I realise that could just be
his final heartbeat wracking through him.

Dean slumps fully backwards, and I move with him, collapsing half on top of him as I start to scream for him to wake up.

I hear the whoosh of wings and look up, looking towards the remainder of the roof that I thought was empty. An angel holding a bow, his wings as dark as the night that surrounds us, his hair curling around his shoulders, and his mouth set into a cruel smirk. He shoots me a mocking bow before shooting into the sky faster than my fireball can hit him.

The magic doesn't stop after that fireball. It should. I am not thinking of doing anything else except shooting him from the sky, of bringing him crashing down to the floor next to Dean's body, of making him broken and unrecognisable, just like my heart would now be.

I scream, fingers curling into Dean's shoulders as if the tighter I hold onto him, the more likely he is to start breathing again. I keep screaming even as the angel is no longer in sight, as the people behind me fall silent, as the building starts to shake.

The stones rumble, the trees groan, the air whips my hair around my face so fiercely that

it almost hurts, but it doesn't really because
nothing can ever hurt again. Nothing could
ever measure up to this pain inside me, the
pain inside of Dean in his final moment in
this goddess-forsaken realm. Nothing could
hurt this much. Nothing could be worth as
much as he had been, so what was the point
of it all?

Oh, Ivy, the voice inside my head tells me in
a broken whisper as it makes everything go
dark.

Chapter Forty-Two
Don

"I had to do it," Hal tells us all for the seventh time as the jet's engine springs to life.

We had all been silent other than him, even Corvus, who had moved to pick up Dean and bring him onto the jet with us. No one had objected. No one had objected when Channing picked up Ivy, knocked unconscious by the prince to stop her from killing us all in her fury, and placed her body next to Dean's on the floor of the jet.

"We know," My mother tells him in a gentle sigh. "She would have…she could have…"

"We failed her," Channing tells us bluntly. "*I* failed her."

"We all failed her," Corvus's voice is empty. He blinks slowly, but he keeps his gaze on Ivy as if he is afraid she will disappear if he looks away, that she will crumble away as that power and anger rips at her insides.

"She'll be okay," Proxima says with such forced positivity that her entire body shakes. "Won't she, Knox?"

"No," The psychic's answer is instant and causes Harlan to let out another sniff. He had been crying ever since he was hurt, but I think now it is not from the pain. Not the physical one, anyway. My eyes prick, and I am tempted to join him.

"Yes, she will," Proxima's entire tone shifts as she looks at the psychic with bared fangs. "She will."

"Okay is not the word to describe what she will be, Proxima." Knox sounds tired. "The future around her is uncertain. But she will not be okay. Dean's death has changed her. It has changed her future and Vileria's. I just cannot tell you how. I do not know how."

"The Althanian heir's consort has been murdered by an angel on the Calent and Tulinth border," Celeste is calmer than all of us, but she is also the only one of us not to look at the bodies on the floor. "That is how. It is not your fault you cannot see her future.

It is not just her we need to be watching now."

"You think we need to look at Tulinth's royals?" My mother frowns in her old foe's direction.

"I think it is highly convenient that the Calent woods were damaged while the Idelons have a secret base on the border with a tunnel leading them to safety in one of the other lands," Celeste shrugs. "But we can look into that later, once this political nightmare has been appeased and our heir crowned."

"Our heir?" I repeat numbly, eyes focusing on my sister's forehead as I try and imagine a crown upon it. It isn't the first time I have done so, but now the image is stained with blood and bruises, gentle tendrils dripping down her face as the metal pricks into her skin like a bear trap.

"I have sworn myself to Althania," Celeste looks over at me. I feel like I am seven steps behind, the kid who gets stuck in the corner during school investigations and gets told not to cause any trouble or try to answer any questions. "Althania's future is my future. Its ruler is my ruler. Its heir is my heir to protect."

"So if Calent comes for her…" Maverick looks at Celeste, his tone and gaze cold. We clearly both remember that Celeste cared more about those trees than my little sister. "You will stand between them and her?"

"Side by side with you," Celeste promises. "So I would suggest starting to trust me. Even Violet does that, and we've tried to kill each other on more than one occasion."

I look at my mother in alarm, but she is staring down at Dean and Ivy with a sad look in her eye. She tilts her head as if she can catch either of their eyes, but that is useless. Dean and Ivy are facing each other, hands splayed out on the floor mere millimetres from each other. When Ivy opens her eyes, it will be to Dean's dead face.

The thought makes me move, crouch down next to my baby sister, and gently tilt her head the other way. I would rather she wake to Hal, to a familiar and living face, if not the preferred one, than to a reminder that the life she wanted is forever gone.

"She has to be okay," I whisper, voice breaking as the tears finally begin to fall.

Chapter Forty-Three

I wake up in Parlitan. I recognise my old bedroom, the view from the window and the way the light shines through them. I do not sit up, do not relish in it. I rip the covers from my skin and kick the blankets and pillows away from me.

Dean had once laid in these sheets, held me in them, laughed with me in them, and sat on the edge of the bed with a fresh cup of coffee for me. The silk brushing against my skin feels like acid, eating away at me and the fragile mental wall I had perfected over the last week. I had spent those seven days drinking weak sedatives and thinking.

Hal had thought it best for me to stay in Parlitan as he calmed down Calent, Blendora and Tulinth. Safer, he said. Better for me, my mother had agreed.

How could they both be so old but so wrong? This was not better. This whole estate was a tomb of memories, every fresh step down the halls a new way to suffocate me.

At least in my room at the palace, I had only one memory of Dean, one horrible foundation that I could build everything else on. The only memories from that room were ones from the day I found out my true nature, a nature I had thrown myself into for Dean's safety. Let my legacy continue to build there, for me to fester in one place rather than two. Let this be the place for Don's future rather than my fruitless past.

I do not tell my parents I plan on leaving them until my father is well enough to walk and ride and laugh again, although his laughs around me are forced and hollow. His wound has healed nicely, and Celeste's herbs have helped.

My mother is always at his side, fetching his favourite meals from the kitchen herself. Maybe one day I will ask her how she does it and love him so much while having a mate halfway across Vileria. But for now, all talk of love sours my stomach to the point I do not eat.

Why should I get to eat when Dean no longer can? Why should I get the days in the sunshine when Dean is now ashes in an overly expensive container on his father's mantel? Why do I deserve the breath in my lungs more than he did? The most important question stays in my head on a constant loop, even when I am asleep, even when I am drugged up, to keep me calm.

Why did the angel not aim for me?

To her credit, when I walk into my father's study, my mother knows exactly what I am about to say. She hugs me before I can even finish the first word.

"You will be a brilliant princess," She smiles at me with teary eyes. "A brilliant ruler."

"I don't know when I will next be back," I warn her. I warn them both, really, but I am too much of a coward to look at my father.

"A piece of you will always be here," My father calls to me from behind his desk, his now useless cane leaning against the side of it. "As you will always be a Whitlock. No matter the name they declare at that crowning. No matter the name you have in the history books. You are always Ivy Whitlock, and we are always proud."

This, I think, maybe our best goodbye. I take his words, cradle them to me and find a place for them deep inside my chest, right next to my sluggishly beating heart. When I step through the portal to the Althanian Palace a day later, I play them on a loop in my head.

No matter the name they give me, I am always Ivy Whitlock. I will show them what a Whitlock can do.

Acknowledgements

The first *thank you* should go to you, the reader, for taking a chance on my books. I hope you like them.

As always, yet another thank you goes to my father. This book is dedicated to you and the life lessons you gave me. No matter what, I am always grateful to have had you as my father.

To my editor, my proofreader, my beta readers. This book would have been a mess without you. Thank you from the bottom of my heart.

Finally, Thank you to Jack. You may not have been there when I wrote it but you have been there for every headache and exciting moment since.

www.ingramcontent.com/pod-product-compliance
Lightning Source LLC
Chambersburg PA
CBHW021230190726

48289CB00005B/1249

9 781739 648961